GW01525508

中华人民共和国
外国人旅行证

The People's Republic of China
Aliens' Travel Permit

羊 字第 8264 号

No.

THE GREAT DESSERT RAID OF 1882

L'oys

The small print

First published in 2007.

Copyright © Rt Hon Quincey Riddle Esq.
The moral rights of the author have been asserted.

ISBN: 978-0-9556290-1-3

Published by L'OYS in association with Poison Pen Publishing.
Poison Pen Publishing.
1/2, 63 Finlay Drive,
Dennistoun,
Glasgow G31 2QZ.

All rights reserved. No part of this book may be reproduced in any form or by any means without permission in writing from the publisher, except by a reviewer, who may quote brief passages in a review.

Set in Times New Roman and Monotype Corsiva.
Printed in Great Britain by Gilmour Print: www.gilmourprint.co.uk
Image manipulations by Crofton Graphics: www.croftongraphics.co.uk

What follows from hereon out is the truth, the whole truth, and nothing but the truth. Not a word of it is a lie. Honest!

THE GREAT DESSERT RAID OF 1882.
(A FROG IN THE HALL OF DISTORTIONS).

Volume one.
By the Rt. Hon. Quincey Riddle Esq.

"History is a myth that we agree to believe in" – Napoléon Bonaparte.

("So, that's where all this Post-Modernist codswallop started. Always figured I'd been marching on the wrong side of the street." Ed)

Copyright © 1227 Genghis Khan. All rights expired.
Any part of this page may be reproduced, stored in a retrieval system and transmitted in any form and by any means: electronic, mechanical, photocopying, recording, scanning, robotic, telepathic or otherwise. References to any individual, location or event, actual or surreal, are entirely delusory. All illegal actions are welcomed by members of the Borjigin family.

Author's Foreword.

Just don't tell Marlowe what ever you do! One lame Uzbek was quite enough thanks!

Introduction.

ON THE STEPPE, WHEN THE SKY IS BLUE AND THE CLOUDS ARE COTTON, THE HORIZON IS ENDLESS.

De Vol-au-Vent had clearly lost his way.

"*Look! He's there!*"........Cholmondeley.
"*Who?*"........Stirrup.
"*Him!*"........Ricardo-Coutts.
"*Why?*"........De Ath.
"*Who knows?*"........Arbuthnot-Arbuthnot.
"*Shambhalah!*"........De Ath.

The diminutive figure scribed a lonely outline along the massive Dun Huang ridge in search of his nemesis. The dunes stretched for hundreds of miles along the northern limit of the Tibetan plateau as it merged with the Taklamakan before reaching Kashgar and the Pamir. Zhong Nan Hai of course knew full well how isolated the spot was: which was why its residents had designated Lop Nor as their nuke test site. After all, who would be likely to give a monkey's for a bunch of Turks who had supported the Tang and the Yuan dynasties all those centuries previously: particularly since they had inconveniently deviated by converting to Islam. Let'em glow in the dark!

"*Shambhalah?*"..........Stirrup.
"*The Great Tea Party in the Sky!*"..........Ricardo-Coutts.

"*Just don't go barefoot over ze sand; scorpions underfoot, mes amis!*" was the last anyone could remember de Vol-au-Vent uttering before he strayed from the path.

De Ath had always been a bit of a wild card. So, it was no surprise then that when the bullet brushed his pate, he went ballistic! Maintaining de Vol-au-Vent out of the corner of his eye, he charged down the dune atop his Bactrian releasing a volley of 9 mm rounds towards the source of his ire as he galloped forth.

"*You want a pot shot! I'll give you one. Pogue mahone, you bloody Chinque blackguard!*" he raged diplomatically with every inch of his descent.

The sniper had no chance. Only dust. De Vol-au-Vent trudged on across the sands in total ignorance.

("Phew! Glad we got all that expletive stuff out of the way early on." Ed)

Welcome

CORE MEMBERS OF THE GREAT DESSERT RAID OF 1882.

Back row, left to right: Dr de Ath, The Marquis Claude de Vol-au-Vent and Wing Commander Reginald Plantagenet Arbuthnot-Arbuthnot (Ex Red Arrows). **Front row, left to right:** Lady Callista Sinclair Ricardo-Coutts, Sister Ruth 'Lemony' Stirrup and Dame Emily 'Lister-Jag' Cholmondeley.

THE CAST
(in order of appearance)

Lady Callista Sinclair Ricardo-Coutts.
Dr. de Ath.
Sister Ruth 'Lemony' Stirrup.
Chinese Undergraduate.
Mongolian Maître d'.
The Marquis Claude de Vol-au-Vent.
Dame Emily 'Lister-Jag' Cholmondeley.
Wing Commander Reginald Plantagenet Arbuthnot-Arbuthnot.
Special Agent Titus Burgermeister III.
Al Capone.
Rolf 'The Austrian' Harris Tweed Schultz.
Chinese Farm Hands.
Sergeant Pe Luo De (*Renmin Wuzhuang Jingcha Budui / People's Armed Police Force*).
The Pathologist.
Commander Lionel 'Buster' Crabbe (*Royal Navy*).
Hassan 'The Assassin' Babur.
The Ghost of Amir Timur.
Lieutenant Wong Xu Zi (*Zhongguo Renmin Jiefang Jun / People's Liberation Army*).
Mullah Nazrudin.
Pony Express Rider.
Yul Khan.
Commander Duscha Duncanova (*Военно-морской флот CCCP/ Naval Military Forces of the USSR*).
X.O. (*Военно-морской флот CCCP/ Naval Military Forces of the USSR*).
Railway Ticket Salesman.
Brother Wolfred (*Glasgow Celtic*).
Aleister Crowley (*Golden Dawn*).
Stanley Kubrick.
Lord Lucan. ("Who?" Ed)

EPISODE ONE
In The Land of the One-eyed Crustaceans

The journey had begun for Ricardo-Coutts and de Ath towards the end of their stint as lecturers working in a provincial university somewhere in the north of China. 'In' is important to appreciate here since, as with almost every Chinese work unit, the font of knowledge was enclosed by its own great wall and guarded at the main gate by an immense statue of 'The Great Helmsman' himself - striking a suspiciously fascist pose. Outwith lay the fires of industrial hell. Taiyuan was precisely the kind of growth on the arsehole of the human landscape that de Ath hated to love. The poor man simply couldn't help himself; he would sit for hours at the foot of a blast furnace with bated breath awaiting that glorious, incandescent moment when it was tapped, and out flooded that spitting, searing river of molten metal. There was something elemental about it, a quite irresistible attraction, like standing atop a caldera at the instant of eruption, with of course the knowledge that one wasn't going to end up as a museum exhibit in Naples. Coal mines too came high on the list; he'd break out into a cold sweat at the mere prospect of feeling the rush as the lift plummeted down the shaft with the temperature rising as the depths approached. It was as close as he ever got to sex in a lift!

For Ricardo-Coutts (a descendent of the St Clairs/Sinclairs), magma was less of a draw. For her there was no death wish, only a simple desire for happiness and green meadows. De Ath, perversely, seemed to derive a kind of manic pleasure from dissatisfaction and the challenge of the quest, you know: the old Garden of Eden stuff. Lady Callista was unquestionably clutching the short straw in Shanxi. The province, where not under the cosh of heavy industry, had been ravaged by erosion through centuries of inappropriate agriculture. Confused telegraph poles stood like question marks on loess plinths overlooking fields of sorghum that struggled to survive beneath.

She was the daughter of an eminent banking family, and therefore, tended to the pragmatic, yet quite unaccountably also found herself strangely attracted to de Ath's 'life is a dice game' approach to existence. The first she suspected of what destiny may be holding in store was during the plane's descent to Peking as it flew over the grey of northern China. Transfixed in horror at the prospect of two years spent in suffocating industrial desolation, she turned from the window to see a smile on de Ath's face. Grinning like a Cheshire cat.

It hadn't been all bad though. They'd made some solid friendships despite the efforts of the one-eyed crustaceans who dominated the party hegemony. De Ath had even managed to get himself arrested on a couple of occasions. Initially, following a traffic incident: when he resorted to violence after a Chinese truck driver had questioned the doc's understanding of the 'right of way rule' (was there one?), and promptly punched out the nearest headlamp. *"Roll up, roll up! Come and see ten tonne Chinese flatbed versus lone 'Big Nose' and his brakeless Phoenix push bike battle it out in the city centre!"* Let's face it, in a city of two million with only six foreigners, the tickets sold like hotcakes! Once he had recovered from his hangover, and realised the potential consequences for the stunned trucker, the doc accepted full responsibility for the event, took his bow, and duly signed a self-confession at the local cop shop. On the second occasion, when he took a swipe at the Japanese Ambassador to Mongolia during a dispute over railway bookings, he categorically refused to accept any guilt whatsoever on being hauled in front of the uniforms at the Chinese-Mongolian frontier to sign yet another self-confession document. The Chinese officials eventually concluded that it simply wasn't worth the candle, and decided that they should just let the nutter pass over the border to see how much devastation he could wreak amongst the woolly-back barbarians beyond. If anybody could sort him out surely they could.

All the minders in the unit wanted was a quiet life and the chance to benefit from some central government dosh; the system permitted the unit a generous grant for every outsider that they employed, you see. The lucre, they got. The peace, they did not! Run-ins with jobsworths were par for the course. The Prof, bless him, sensibly steered well clear of it all.

The first inkling that the authorities figured they might have a hot-potato-juggling-act on their hands was when demands came to restructure classes and timetables in an attempt to reduce the hordes that arrayed themselves before our friends. After much brow-beating, it went through. Later, a number of Russian-retreads suspected a deeper malaise at the heart of Europe when de Ath, upon finding himself keyless outside his office with a class of a dozen or so of these tutors in tow, casually demonstrated how to slip a yale lock with a plastic card. Jaws, needless to say, dropped to the floor. Russian-retreads, by the way, was the local euphemism for lecturers, and peasants that had been promoted to academia during the reversals of the 'Cultural Revolution', who had found themselves having to retrain as English teachers after years spent as Russian specialists. The party bosses finally waved the white flag, however, when the loons from elsewhere very openly, and extremely publicly, marched across the main prospect (I like that word, don't you? Prospect. So visual, don't ya dink?) to the door of the university Gestapo and demanded that the penultimate episode of J. Bronowski's 'Ascent of Man' be screened for the students. The leaders, whose comprehension of English was fragmentary to say the least (despite the title of the department), were tasked with vetting all material prior to its being unleashed on their charges, and had deemed the said item as pornographic. It all proved too much. Zhang opened his door to find himself confronted by two fuming foreigners reaching for their belt buckles and suggesting that if he wished to indulge in some real pornography, they would be more than happy to oblige there and then! So, the film went ahead and the lobsters came to the boil. After all, the faculty censors had already seen the previous ten episodes in order to establish well beyond reasonable doubt that the material was far from pornographic. Meanwhile, nor did it help when one day, de Ath turned up to lecture on some of the finer points of English grammar dressed in an immaculate set of Chinese underwear! It had been a perfectly innocent mistake. The fact is that northern Chinese underwear, in the soviet mode you understand, bears an uncanny resemblance to your average western track-suit. So, naturally enough, he slipped into something more comfortable, and addressed the proletariat. The doc immediately became aware that things were not quite as they should have been when the only response that he could elicit from his class was averted eyes and blushes as red as the party flag. It was like drawing teeth! Eventually, at the end of the lesson, one brave soul approached the 'mad professor' and enquired: *"Excuse me Doctor de Ath, is it customary in Scotland to teach in your underwear?"* Oh dear! It all proved to be something of a challenge for the local diplomatic corps.

However, forgiveness and mutual understanding finally prevailed when the foreign fruitcakes demonstrated their heartfelt socialist cred. The party secretary, who, by sheer coincidence you understand, lived next door, one day found himself undergoing a Noah-like experience. Upon returning from their office, Ricardo-Coutts and de Ath immediately registered that something was amiss; they had become overwhelmed by a deep suspicion that Niagara had relocated itself from the New World to their stairwell, you see. Promptly, they kicked off their shoes, rolled up their trouser-legs, and set to in attempting to save the secretary's family from their immanent departure for Ararat. If the party could have doled out honorary memberships, they probably would have; as it was, a public accolade at the following Friday's party meeting was the next best thing. From then on, they were officially referred to as 'comrades' no less. This truly stuck in the craws of certain members of the party and academic community whose relations with the secretary, and our wayward couple, were far from even cordial.

And so it went on. When the time for departure came though, it was a rather sentimental affair. After two years, they had managed to remove at least a couple of boulders from the barricade. That is not to say that they had ever wanted to infiltrate, despite what the crustaceans had thought. Far from it, their only intention had been to understand.

Ever since his schooldays, when his Latin teacher had grassed to his parents that perhaps their offspring was being led astray by dubious political theories, de Ath had found himself drawn to communism, and wanted to experience the system at closer quarters. Whilst he despised Lenin and Mao for their heavy-handed, top down, intellectual arrogance (which ultimately produced governments indistinguishable from that found in fascist states as far as he could see), he nevertheless identified with Trotsky's politics, but however, couldn't quite reconcile himself with the man following the atrocity of Kronstadt. Despite this though, he still maintained the hots for Rosa Luxembourg, and also knew full well that there was something deeply rotten in Denmark!

Another thing that entranced both Ricardo-Coutts and de Ath was The Silk Road. Ah yes, The Silk Road. They were already well acquainted with it following their earlier sojourns in Persia and Afghanistan, when in a previous epic (yet to be written), they had journeyed parallel to the Amu Darya (Oxus) culminating high in the Pamir. Cherished in the bottom of their suitcase then had always been the dream that when in The 'Muddle' Kingdom, it may be possible to complete the link by travelling to Kashgar from Xian. Oh, the romance!

In some respects, it wasn't such a far cry from de Ath's ancestral background; some of the earlier representatives of the family liked to travel around a bit too. He'd managed to trace the genes as far back as the Hospitallers in the twelfth century, but beyond that, things had become slightly blurred. Naturally, as with most families, it was all a bit of a chequered affair. Eventually, documents emerged from The Scottish Registry Office stating that one of the clan had obviously fallen in with a bad lot at the time of King Philip IV's purge on that infamous Friday 13th 1307: resulting in the wayward knight having to skedaddle to Edinburgh with a squad of cavalry wearing entirely the wrong colour of surplice (that of the Order of the Temple). **("I certainly hope that that is the closest we are going to get**

to hearing the 'T' word." Ed) De Ath's relatives tended to gloss over this period in hushed tones - as they also did the thuggery of the Crusades. Something of a blot on the parchment really. Nevertheless, by the time of the Great Siege of Malta in 1565, the family had returned to the fold: redeeming itself with some considerable gusto during the defence of Fort St Elmo against the Ottoman Admiral Turgut Reis. All prior misdemeanours were forgiven, and so it stayed. Actually, de Ath's old man in addition to having been a colonel in The Royal Army Medical Corps also served as a United Nations observer for The Sovereign Military Order of Malta (SMOM) in his latter years.

But to resume our tale. Whilst entertained by all this historical exotica concerning the antics of his predecessors, de Ath's true interests lay, as must already be glaringly evident, entirely elsewhere. In fact, quite apart from indulging in 'inappropriate' political literature (frankly, I don't blame the Latin teacher), de Ath had developed a thoroughly unhealthy curiosity, when in his public school geography lessons, concerning those strangely extensive plains that we call the Mongolian and Central Asian Steppes, and their equally singular nomadic inhabitants. This was enhanced during his history classes, where he was introduced to: 'The Man of Steel' no less. *"How was it possible for an illiterate nomad, living off a diet of rodents, fish and berries, to establish a nation, a written script and a legal code for his people, carve out an empire greater than Alexander's, and lay the foundations for one of China's most renowned and cosmopolitan dynasties?"* he pondered. How indeed.

And thus it was then that Ricardo-Coutts and de Ath prepared to shake hands with fate.

Above: 'All hail the Great Helmsman'. Mao in his latter years became a traffic cop. Occasionally though, he would get his hand signals a bit mixed up.

Left: De Ath and his charges do battle against the university authorities. The 'Long Nosed' pornographers won the day!

Right: The loneliness of the long distant student. The undergrads frequently forewent breakfast in a desperate attempt to avoid being assigned postings to the 'autonomous' provinces. Such efforts, however, were invariably in vain since the most effective means of acquiring a juicy little sinecure normally depended on the age old method of establishing a good 'back door', or being fortunate enough to take advantage of a spot of nepotism.

Below: The prof samples the peasant lifestyle during the reversals of the Cultural Revolution when Mao got his revenge on the intellectuals by sending them out to the fields and promoting the farm hands to academia.

Above: *"Dunno who my dad's dentist is, but I'm signin up. Not so sure bout the barber though."* Despite the fact that our peasant friend, here illustrated, clearly has an excellent set of gnashers, most of the population of Shanxi Province suffered from tooth decay resulting from the excessively high doses of naturally occurring fluoride in the water supply. Many of the academics aged forty and above, however, had false teeth due to having their own kicked out during the excesses of the Cultural Revolution.

Right: *"Well, what do you think of it so far?"*
"Frankly, I could do with a new hat."

Above: Siesta time for the coal board. Delivery of essentials such as coal briquettes was tough work, particularly for those who had to hump the stuff to the tops of mountains!

Above: Bespoke blinds made on the spot. The travelling trades: ragn'bone, wheelwrights and corn poppers, you name it, and a bicycle would be there.

Left: *"Women hold up half the sky."* so said Mao. Actually, it was a tad more than that, since they not only did the same manual labour as the men folk, but were also expected to do all the usual domestic chores (and still the 'unofficial' policy of female infanticide prevailed in the countryside on the grounds that male offspring supposedly worked harder - not to mention the dowry costs incurred by having to 'sell off' daughters).

Below: The dark flames of industry. A woman welder in the Datong Steam Locomotive Factory.

Right: Communication could often prove problematic – not just for the 'Long Noses'. Here a post office scribe fills in forms etc. for those from the countryside challenged by the written word. Literacy amongst the city folk was usually much higher, however, when people hailing from different provinces were in conversation, they frequently had to resort to pen and paper in order to be understood; the various dialects normally sounded like foreign languages.

Below: Fishing for ideas.

EPISODE TWO
Hazard Is a Tempting but Dangerous Thing

The mix, however, was as yet incomplete. Some months prior to the forthcoming expedition, our standard-bearers of Euro-lunacy had had their ranks bolstered by the darkly luminescent soul of Sister Ruth 'Lemony' Stirrup. When Sister Ruth, all those moons ago, had plunged over the precipice during an early morning brawl with her Mother Superior at the bell tower of their Sikkim convent - whilst the all seeing Kanchenjunga looked on - most had, quite reasonably, assumed: *"Well, that's that then!"* Little could anyone have suspected that the three-hundred-year old guru meditating below would break her fall! Result: one dead philosopher and a change of habit.

She was a bit of a strange fish: liked riding horses and the occasional Chinese. Ruth, or 'Lemony' as she now preferred to be known, had hightailed it to China on a volunteer programme in an attempt to evade the attentions of a Jesuit hitman, and feared at the time of departure that perhaps the Vatican searchlight was panning her way. She hadn't helped in diverting attention from herself by having become outrageously inebriated at a British Embassy soirée, going for a plunge in the ambassadorial pool fully clothed and returning to the bar in the guise of some kind of decorative oriental seaweed to demand yet more refreshment! What better then than to cover up her identity by joining forces with a couple of Mongol loving Polo Mints? And off they went.

EPISODE THREE
The Events Are Random in the Land Of Lost Mirages

When the hunger pangs struck in Huhehot, Ricardo-Coutts, Stirrup and de Ath fell into the nearest hostelry. The maître d' was keen that such foreign dignitaries not be overly exercised by the spiritual depravity so abundant on the ground floor, and duly ushered our intrepid trio aloft. Upon emergence, it became immediately apparent that hell was far from freezing over upstairs. The fact is that when one Mongol gets drunk, the entire neighbourhood tends to become paralytic. It must be said, however, that there was a sincerely earnest attempt to establish some kind of decorum. The poor chap though eventually gave up with an exasperated wave: *"The pleasure is entirely yours!"* seemed to be the message. It soon became apparent where the difficulty lay. The domo had innocently assumed that all would be well on the upper floor having previously introduced the level above to his only other interloper of the day: a certain Frenchman going by the soubriquet of the Marquis Claude de Vol-au-Vent. Unused to having to cope with one foreigner a year, he now found himself saddled with four! Damn! Not only that, but it was a Sunday, and the establishment was packed to the gunnels with horsemen. Our travellers quickly sized up the situation, as feet flailed in a frantic attempt to cover up the stupefied evidence beneath the top table. To no avail however. Let's face it, once you start to lose at drinking games with Mongols, you're stuffed! There it was then, for all to see: constrained behind the best defences that Mongol riding boots can provide lay two horsemen and the unmistakable form of a louche Frog wearing a pith helmet at an unusually jaunty angle.

After a rather self-conscious lunch, a hand appeared from below, soon followed by a growth of flame-red hair and a slurred utterance sounding vaguely like: *"Mes amis!"* Shortly thereafter, both hair and hand submerged into silence, much to the relief of the assembled clan. Only when de Vol-au-Vent had come to terms with the fact that the wagon his newly found acquaintances had hired to escort him from his dementia was not resting on its roof, did he begin to exhale something resembling coherence: *"L'auberge!"* he spluttered, pointing in the general direction of Paris.

The remedy seemed clear: a couple of days on the steppe, riding a horse and brandishing a reflex bow. *"That ought to sort the bugger out!"* thought the trio.

EPISODE FOUR
Dinner in Yurtsville

It should be mentioned that, despite their slightly unfair reputation, the Mongols try extremely hard to accommodate. Translation though can occasionally become a trifle awkward. And, whilst the Chinese, like the Indians, have had many centuries of experience when it comes to diets alternative to the prevailing norm, cuisine on the steppe is quite a different matter altogether. Sister Stirrup learned the hard way. Bless her vegetarian soul. She hadn't intended to be difficult; it was just that when the masses ensconced themselves in the wilderness to gorge themselves stupid on the local lamb hotpot, she baulked at the prospect of gnashing her way through the whole flock. However, Stirrup was not the only waiter's nightmare on hand. Indeed, both de Ath and de Vol-au-Vent knew only too well how to bring a noshery to a grinding halt. They were normally the types who never even bothered to unfold the menu: the types who preferred to waft their hands in the direction of the surrounding guests in order that the more conformist requirements of their compatriots could be cleared off the stage before the awkward squad launched into their deviancy. Thenceforth, they would attempt to squeeze absolutely nothing that was to be found on the list, à la carte or anywhere else, out of thin air. If they suspected that there was likely to be any limitation in the kitchen department, they would always start off with something slightly less challenging like: *"Vichyssoise, perchance?"* then gradually build up to delivering the sucker punch! *"You couldn't possibly rustle up a couple of dozen raw oysters on ice with a caprese salad and some steamed bread with a basil infused extra-virgin olive oil dip? I'd be most appreciative."* The others present simply cringed behind their menus. Whenever de Ath and de Vol-au-Vent actually did deign to glance over the list of fare on offer, they would always gravitate towards something that they would find worth querying: *"The John Dory. Indeed. Would that be 'actual' John Dory or some Catfish variant, one wonders?"* the waiters looking on in utter disbelief. *"Mon Dieu!"*

In this particular case, however, both de Ath and de Vol-au-Vent were encountering sufficient difficulty in remaining vertical on their chairs to even dream of challenging the chef, and decided that the local cuisine should remain the order of the day. Not so Stirrup!

Conversation ill-advised on the grasslands:

"You haven't, by mere happenstance, any greenery available?" .... Stirrup. Rough translation into Mongolian: *"Look chaps, I'm not sure that I can manage an entire sheep at one sitting."* Result: Stirrup, isolated at a separate table, confronting a pristine white plate garnished with a roast mutton hind quarter affront! Meanwhile, the 'Hot-potters' chomped on through their lamb, greens, bean noodles, and various spicy condiments. There does come a time folks when it really pays to just bite the bullet, and call for the dessert trolley! Particularly when you're in the middle of the steppe with a clan of Mongols breathing down your neck! Hey ho.

After a few nights in a ger (yurt, according to the Ruskies), and several afternoons altering his anatomy whilst experimenting with Mongol weapons' technology, de Vol-au-

Vent began to find the insect community quite: *"Intolerable!"* (or however one says intolerable in French). Therefore, the pistons pumped south alongside the Yellow River.

Ning Xia (Tangut territory of old) proved illustrative in helping to understand the Chinese sense of humour, as de Vol-au-Vent pointed out at the time (referring to the Hui Muslims of northern China: largely descended from Turkic tribes): *"If you've got a shower ov Mohammedans, stick zem in ze desert! Zey like zat kind of sing, don't zey?"*

Eventually, the entry to the Gansu Panhandle (the Hexi Corridor): Lanzhou. They had arrived at the starting post.

EPISODE FIVE
Historical Intermission: 'Smith and Co Unlimited' (or: The Genghis Blues)

Before venturing further, it is perhaps worth embarking on an historical excursion to the Mongol Steppe to dispel one or two myths about those bloodthirsty, jolterhead 'barbarians' from Xanadu.

So, once upon a time, a tent-dweller called Smith (Temujin translates to 'Iron Worker' or blacksmith in English) is brought up in penury after the murder of his father, living off whatever can be scraped from the land by a fugitive outcast with a price on his head: a variety of steppe marmots, fish, juniper berries, and perhaps the odd gazelle on a good day. His mother is a tough, virtuous and strict disciplinarian, who instils a strong sense of honour, morality, and upright religious values in the lad. This unfortunately does not prevent him from murdering his half-brother: for which he receives a ruddy good clip round the ear from mum. The excuse which is offered as justification for his conduct on this occasion is that he had done it because his almost-semi-sibling refused to share the spoils of his hunt with other members of the suffering family. Clearly commendable values, but a tad over the top: 'Give me the boy…….and I will show you the man.' Later, he marries, and his wife is promptly kidnapped by a neighbouring chieftain; this he remedies by persuading one of his father's old mates to help him liberate his beloved, and give the transgressor a thoroughly bloody nose. As a result of these shenanigans, the issue of who exactly the father of Smith's first son, Jochi, is remains something of a question-mark (and indeed is the source of much family wrangling within and without the Borjigin ger throughout Temujin's life).

There you go then, life on the Steppe! So, deciding that he is sick to the back teeth of the trials and tribulations of life, he decides to go on a solo pilgrimage to the top of the sacred Mount Burkhan Kaldun to have a chat with Tengri, the 'Eternal Blue Heaven God': much revered by the Shamanist Mongol and Turkic tribes. The long and the short of it is that Tengri seems to have been a fairly perceptive talent spotter, with the result that our supplicant friend clearly availed himself of some pretty solid pointers to future success. From then on, Temujin never looks back. The man develops some considerable mastery of matters military, political, social, and psychological. So much so that he eventually cuts quite a dash amongst the locals: changing a region once notorious for its feuding tribes (both Mongol and Turkic) into a unified nation under his banner - not least because he establishes a non-tribal military structure within his army. Having done this with such devastating élan, he is duly elevated to the post of king, takes on the moniker of 'Genghis Khan (Great Universal Ruler)', and the rest, as they say, is history.

So, what exactly are we dealing with here: civilised or barbarian? You decide. There is only one 'insignificant' little proviso, and that is: we must take it as read that mass murder, mayhem, rape and pillage have always been, and doubtless always will be, cornerstones of international relations whatever our self-righteous religious, political and cultural tipple might be. Most, after all, who aspire to greatness and immortality, often incline to seeing life through the lens of the megalomaniac, and Genghis certainly appears to have been no different from others in this respect, especially once persuaded of the benefits of getting out and seeing a bit more of the world. Par for the course folks, par for the course.

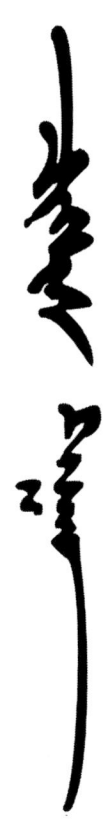

Having climbed the greasy pole from abject waifdom to supreme kingship then, our man, for it was **He**, establishes a nation, adopts a written script for his previously orally based culture, and lays down a legal code (the Yasa) that, amongst other things, attempts to provide something approaching marital and societal rights to the womenfolk. In fact, the Mongol convention was that the widow of the dead khan should become regent until a new khan was elected. As with the Celts, before the 'civilised' Romans got their hands on them, Mongol women had some degree of power: although the Mongol version of sexual equality fell some way short of that which had prevailed amongst the Celts. Celtic women could divorce their husbands, own, inherit, sell property and goods, and lead armies into battle; in short, the very equals of their male counterparts. Because of the high degree of interdependence that prevails in the nomadic tradition, there also tends, in the main, to be a fairly egalitarian culture when it comes to the distribution of labour; nevertheless, when it came to marital contracts, the mediaeval Mongols operated a polygamous and patriarchal system which required the payment of dowries by the bride's family to the groom's. Interestingly, within the camp, there seems to have been a quite rigid protocol in terms of the location of gers. Insomuch as the head of the household had his own ger, so did each of his wives, and all these gers were arranged hierarchically: east to west in descending order of seniority. Some contemporary historians also report that once the man of the house had had his way with his wife of choice on a given evening, all the other wives gathered together with the happy couple for a celebratory drink. One wonders what this may suggest about the virility of Mongol males (unfortunately, neither Marco Polo - a notoriously unreliable source - nor any others seem to touch upon this rather delicate subject). Even when the head of the household died, there still maintained a strong sense of identity within the remaining family; remarriage was rare, and the norm was for the older children to protect and care for the well-being of the widowed matriarchs (note the story of Sorkaktani: commander of thousands). All this was certainly a million miles away from the sexual discrimination that was laid down under the Roman law of the Pater Familias: where the wives hardly rated a notch above the slaves, cattle, and other livestock.

However, to resume. Genghis also introduces fiscal literacy, structures his society around the guiding principles of promotion through merit over noble blood (something that heartily peeved not but a few tribal leaders), demands tolerance of the religious beliefs of others, and generates a culture of mutual respect and honour. Further, he creates a highly organised, disciplined, and world beating army, which is serviced by the world's first pony-express communications system (with riders covering some 90 to 100 miles a day). And finally, he lays the foundations for a superpower the like of which had never been encountered before: becoming the most extensive continuous land empire ever - probably encompassing around half of the contemporary world population. Putting to one side then a level of brutality matching, if not exceeding, that of the Romans, and his notoriety for razing vast swathes of Central Asia and northern China, I'm sure you'll agree that the aforementioned amounts to a reasonably acceptable day's work at the office for someone who lived in a ger in 'a far away country surrounded by a people of whom we know nothing'. All right, this will doubtless do for the moment.

Yes of course, one can always criticise and say: *"But it was all built on those old tried and tested mafia principles of ultimate respect for the don's family and dealing with adversaries by 'making offers that couldn't be refused'*, wasn't it?" Of course it was. But where else was (or indeed 'is') it any different? In fact, the policy of 'surrender or die' was, and still is, both militarily and psychologically quite astute. Alexander of Macedon, for instance, was also an occasional exponent of this strategy, and is he not referred to as 'The Great'? Assuming that the white flag was raised, and therefore, an orgy of urbicide avoided, Genghis could sensibly preserve his troops to fight another day, and the vanquished would come to respect him as a reasonable and merciful leader: a man of his word no less, like him or not. Later, Kublai softened his grandfather's policy to great effect by only executing those nobles and ministers who had been foolhardy enough to cock a snook at the Mongol pile driver. It was well-known that the Mongols would show no compunction if their offers were spurned; it was a matter of honour and respect, pure and simple. An etiquette quite unlike the conduct of the Christian Crusaders: who claimed they would be merciful if their Islamic adversaries surrendered, then promptly slaughtered the defenceless Muslims. Not to mention the practices carried out by the ilk of Julius Caesar, Trajan, the Spaniards in the New World, and Western industrial powers since the end of the First World War: through Lloyd George, Adolf Hitler, Winston Churchill, Dwight Eisenhower, Anthony Eden, to George Bush and Anthony Blair, etc. These particular vampires took over foreign parts because they needed to resolve their actual and impending economic difficulties by abusing and raping the lands of others: those cast as 'barbarians', who possessed the, usually mineral, wealth that these rapacious 'civilised' thugs sought in order to keep their pockets full, and, concerning the later names on the list of the world's most wanted, their Las Vegas style economies ticking over. In the case of villainous war criminals such as Julius Caesar and Trajan, the lure was gold, in Gaul and Dacia respectively (Trajan, though, wasn't concerned with enslaving the Dacians as Julius had done with the remnants of the Celtic population that he'd negligently left alive after his campaign into Gaul, Trajan simply wiped the Dacians off the face of the planet). And the

Conquistadors? They, of course, also committed genocide in search of gold. Eldo-bloody-rado! Where are the Caribs now? Lloyd George and Clemenceau? Middle-Eastern oil, and anything else that could be filched from 'uncivilised tribes' worldwide under the auspices of the Versailles Treaty. Hitler? Well, you can read all about his master-plan in 'Mein Kampf'. Churchill, Eisenhower, and Eden: speak to the Iranians about what happened to their Prime Minister, Mohammed Moussadeq, in 1953. And the unconscionable mendacity of the Bush/Blair clique? Why not spend your next summer break in Iraq or Afghanistan? What we are dealing with here is a blindly voracious economic system acting in concert with a political culture so connivingly duplicitous, and untrammelled by such inconvenient issues as moral principle that it wouldn't even recognise a straight bat if it saw one, let alone know how to play with the thing! (**"Perhaps we are wandering from the plot just a touch here." Ed**)

But to return to the steppes. (**"Must you?" Ed**) Despite his appalling reputation, the norm it appears with Genghis was to despatch ambassadors and merchants to distant worthies to see if mutually beneficial channels of communication could be established for trade and the exchange of knowledge. Let's call it 'arrangements'. Unfortunately, these sophisticates were, all too frequently, afflicted with such stupendous arrogance when it came to associating with mere nomads that a surprising number of them made the misguided error of despatching the heads of the khan's representatives back to him in a basket: with predictable results. Note what happened when the great Sultan Mohammed of Khorezm regarded Genghis as some kind of upstart, sheep-shagging joker. Smug numbskull! Sacrificed everything because he was so self-satisfied, and simply refused to credit that a bunch of shepherds could possibly pose any threat whatsoever, when all that was needed was a bit of peaceful negotiation and unhampered free movement for Silk Road merchants. In fact, Genghis went out of his way to make it clear to the Sultan that he had no military aspirations with respect to territorial gain in Central Asia, or anywhere else for that matter, apparently. Despite his previous success in China, it has been suggested that 'The Great Universal Ruler' thought a war in Transoxania might have been trying to bite off a little more than even he could chew; after all, the Khorezm Sultanate was a military force to be reckoned with at the time. However, both at home and in China, Genghis clearly had faith in Tengri's support: frequently allowing his reputation to precede him by inviting, often numerically superior forces, to survey the results of his handy work enroute. After mature consideration, many of these potential adversaries did the sensible thing: turned coat and threw in their lot with the Great Khan. This resulted in a kind of snowball effect which added to the forces he'd already assembled prior to the commencement of a campaign (and who had had their imaginations lubricated by the potential of rich loot); all this combined with his inimitable tactical intelligence to invariably save the day. For the Sultan's part, however, he saw things rather differently to Genghis. It seems that he himself actually coveted Genghis' territorial gains, and perhaps thought that he if could club the Great Khan, the doorway would automatically be open to the whole of northern China. So, using the flimsiest of excuses: that Mongol caravans were full of spies, he not only executed members of a particular caravan, but also Genghis' diplomatic emissaries. One says flimsy since, generally speaking, local rulers along the Silk Road knew full well that all the caravans were riddled with merchants of espionage, and these leaders tended to tolerate the situation because of the mutually beneficial results that the trade in intelligence afforded. Although hindsight is a wonderful thing, it is truly hard to credit that Sultan Mohammed could have been so blindingly cocksure of his ability to deal with the Mongol threat given that he was aware of what had already happened to the Chin of Northern China (Zhong Du: 1215) only five years previously. Eventually, to cut a long and bloody tale short, Genghis mopped up Bukhara, Samarkand, Otrar and other

Khorezm centres, Mohammed died isolated on an island in the Caspian, and Genghis gave chase to the new Sultan (Mohammed's son: Jalal ad-Din) as far as the river Indus, in today's Pakistan. After being astonished by Jalal ad-Din's heroics here, Genghis said: *"A father should only have sons like this!"* then promptly gave up the pursuit and returned home - taking in one or two sights on the way. Previously, upon entering Bukhara, Genghis had had the opportunity to refine his oratorical skills in order to clear up any previous misconceptions that the ruling classes of the great city obviously had about him by addressing them thus: *"I am the wrath of God. If you had not committed great sins, God would not have visited a punishment such as myself upon you!"* It is fair to say that after his Central Asian excursion, everyone from far and wide got the message! To look on the bright side though, the local Iranians doubtless welcomed the Mongols as saviours by thumping the Khorezm Sultan Mohammed, since these particular Turks, whom the Sultan represented, had been making everyday life in that part of the world a misery for years.

But, to backtrack a year or two, another person who also suffered from this same disorder that afflicted Sultan Mohammed - with regard to the apparent impotence of the Mongols - was the Chin Emperor of Northern China. At the time, Genghis likely had two things uppermost in his mind. Firstly, having been recently elevated to the post of 'Great Universal Leader', it was hardly befitting for a man of such stature to be paying tribute to the Chin Emperor (as the Mongols had been doing for many a year), not to mention what his friends and newly acquired allies would think of him if he continued to tolerate Chinese suzerainty over the Turko-Mongol steppe nomad tribes that he ruled. And secondly: being renowned for his generosity, it was going to be hard to maintain the cohesion of his power for long without the lure of some considerable booty. So then, in 1211, Genghis took up the cudgel and began his campaign against the Chin. By 1214, he was at the gates of Zhong Du (the Chin capital: modern Peking), where he was met with a spirited resistance during which the plucky defenders utilised not only incendiary, but chemical and biological weapons too. The result of this and other factors being that Genghis ultimately withdrew to Mongolia: his troops starving and disease ridden. Did this put him off? Not a bit of it! Having received intelligence that the new Chin emperor had thought it prudent to move his capital further south, away from the marauding hordes, the Mongol army returned again a year later. The upshot was that, as a result of some stunning military trickery (on a par with the legendary Wooden Horse of Troy episode), Zhong Du capitulated, apparently without an arrow being fired. The Mongol troops were then given free rein to raze the city to the ground and annihilate its remaining inhabitants - Genghis, surprisingly, being elsewhere at the time. Even years later, visitors to the city were greeted by piles of blanched human bones, streets slippery with the fat of corpses, and air so polluted that it was barely breathable. With all this evidence, what could Sultan Mohammed have been thinking in 1220 when he took that fateful step in despatching his bloody invitation to Genghis to pop in and exercise his rhetoric? Whatever it was, from then on, the name Genghis Khan was writ large over gravestones throughout Asia from China to Europe.

None of these adversaries really appreciated that when the Mongol 'new order' went on a campaign, they did so big time; it was like an entire nation on the march! A Mongol cavalryman was expected to turn up for duty with a minimum of five horses, and the army's support cast in the accompanying van could easily consist of upwards of a million sheep and cattle. Let's face it, they just wanted to broaden their horizons a bit, and, to be frank, the steppe can be mind-numbingly tedious in places.

And yes, you can also say: *"Weren't there bouts of internecine struggles for power between members of the royal family and their followers?"* Naturally, but that simply goes with the territory wherever you hail from. By contrast however, one would have to look quite hard to find a nation (in for instance, that bastion of 'civilisation': thirteenth century Europe) where succession to the throne was based, not on the expedient of the crown's automatic transfer to the first born male, but on a consensus arrived at during a Khuriltai (Mongol Grand Conclave) of the princes and Mongol clan barons, which elected, yes elected, a new Great Khan from a menu of all the sons of the royal family. The only exception to this being the appointment by Genghis of his immediate successor: Ogedei. The system had its downside though as the code required all khans to return to the heartland for the election. This proved to be something of an Achilles heel for them in terms of maintaining the cohesion of the empire; thus explaining why they occasionally had to re-establish their territorial gains all over again after the new Great Khan had been chosen.

In addition, where else at the time (except of course in the Islamic states of the Middle East) could one find a culture so religiously tolerant that Shamanists, Buddhists, Zoroastrians, Manichees, Daoists, Muslims and Christians existed cheek by jowl? Genghis' daughter-in-law, Sorkaktani, was not only a Nestorian Christian but rose to become one of the most powerful people in the empire (nae, the world even. Has anyone in the West even heard of her?), and during her latter years, this Christian woman bankrolled a variety of Muslim projects throughout Central Asia. Remarkable. Of his grandsons, all from a Shamanist background, namely: Kublai Khan (Great Khan after Mönkhe) married a Buddhist, and both Mönkhe Khan (Great Khan after Guyuk) and Hulegu Khan (Khan of Persia and scourge of the 'Assassins') married Nestorians. Let us not forget, of course, that all this was taking place at the same time that those deranged murderers we call Christian Crusaders were slaughtering Muslims, Jews, and even Christians too (remember the outrage of the Albigensian adventure, and what happened to the Cathars): all to slake the thirst of power-mad, Godforsaken pontiffs and blood-crazed, European nobility.

The pastoral nomads, however (unlike their more 'civilised' European counterparts), also knew a thing or two concerning how to cherry-pick from the more sophisticated settled communities that which would advance their own interests in the fields of scientific disciplines such as medicine and pyrotechnics, etc. In fact Genghis' practice, following his many successful military actions, had been to preserve the women, scientists and artisans to utilise their talents back home in the motherland. Furthermore, they seem to have accepted good counsel in terms of the most profitable methods of raising taxes without biting off the hand that fed them. They did, however, occasionally lapse by allowing the misguided policies of a more traditionally conservative persuasion to take over (emanating from members of the 'Let's Turn the Whole of Northern China into Livestock Pasture Brigade'), but once the consequent toll on the empire's coffers became apparent, the Mongols soon got the message: leave well alone. A lesson the likes of Stalin and Mao could have learnt from before forcing Kazakh and Mongol nomads to convert pastoral steppes to arable land. Unconscionable bloody morons! Not only that but, these great figureheads of communism fell into the same trap as capitalist corporations so frequently do; they deceived not only their public, but also themselves into believing that agricultural output traced an ever ascending spiral when, in fact, quite the opposite was the case at ground level in the communes: just like the insatiable greed for higher and higher dividend returns on the roulette wheels of the stock markets leads to the cooking of the corporation books. It all rather reminded de Ath of the times when he did occasional free-lance press photography for the Shah's rags in Iran during the 70s. Such was the fear generated by the powers that inhabited the palaces of northern Teheran that deception was the only option; estates of thirty new houses were transformed in the darkroom to a sprawl of three-hundred. The camera never lies. **("If this guy meanders much further, we'll be exploring the therapeutic effects of Dadaism on the clinically depressed before long!" Ed)**

All good things must, however, come to an end: even for someone of Genghis' stature. Since Genghis was a man who had spent almost his entire life on military campaigns of one sort or another, Tengri had few options open to him, and so ultimately decided to deprive the world of the Great Khan's presence some three days after he had successfully routed the Tangut chief's forces at Ning Xia (the Tanguts had unwisely slighted Genghis by declining to send troops to assist on the Khorezm Campaign). Even in death his spirit lived on to take thousands on the journey to the Eternal Blue Heaven with him; Ning Xia was razed and its population annihilated. Although there are many stories surrounding this death, it appears that he most likely expired as a result of a heart attack consequent to a raging fever he had been suffering from throughout the Tangut campaign. He was no longer a young man, after all. And, not only is the precise nature of his death open to question, but because he wished his earthly departure to remain a secret, any who witnessed the cortège on its return to Mongolia were killed. His final resting place also remains shrouded in mystery to this day. Is it somewhere in the Ordos Mountains (where his bier became bogged down in the mud: this being taken as a sign that he wanted to be buried there), or was he interred back in the homeland at Mongolian Shamanism's Holy of Holies: Mount Burkhan Kaldun? No one knows. Nevertheless, whilst the location of his grave is unknown, his memory, unsurprisingly, continues to carry considerable resonance amongst his people; Genghis is still the most popular boys' name in Mongolia.

Genghis' people remember him as someone for whom duty and honour were uppermost. Duty to avenge insults thrown at either the Mongols or himself (ostensibly one and the same), and duty to support and serve his people. Genghis was renowned for his magnanimity towards those whom he trusted, generously rewarding the faithful service he received from them with lands and money. Moreover, his patronage of the poor, and the orphans of those who had fallen whilst on campaign, was legendary. So too was his conduct amongst the troops. He ate and drank with his troops the same rations that they were provided with, and shunned the use of titles and kowtowing to rank.

Finally, according to Genghis, a man's greatest pleasure was: *"To chase and defeat his enemy, seize the entirety of his possessions, leave his married women weeping and wailing, ride his gelding, use the bodies of his women as a nightshirt and support, gazing upon and kissing their rosy breasts, sucking their lips which are as sweet as the berries of their breasts."* Some people can be just so delightfully easy to please, don't you think? Interestingly enough though, his greatest fear seems to have been incurring the displeasure of his mother: something for the psychologists to mull over perhaps.

Anyway, without eulogising overly much, and going back over work previously published by this author in: 'The Gourmet Khan (Kublai's Recipes for Perfect Pasta)' and 'Hulegu and The Curse of Alcoholism in the Mongol Royal Family (Popular Gout Remedies during the Il-Khanate and the Yuan Dynasty)', you have probably got the picture that the writer has something of a soft spot for nomadic culture by now, so, time to move on. Now where were we?

("Christ almighty! I've got it! They were all just a bunch of cute little bunny rabbits! Yes? Ed)

EPISODE SIX
We Are All Speechless in the Land Of Babel

For the first time during their sojourn in China, our travellers realised that the Chinese were just as 'Confusionised' as they were. Lanzhuo, renowned as an industrial hub, but with many more visitors than Taiyuan, proved educational. The import of comprehending the script though became immediately apparent as up and down the main thoroughfares, the Chinese, hailing from various locales, were to be observed painting invisible characters with their index fingers across opposing palms in an effort to be understood: because they couldn't comprehend a single word that they were saying to each other.

Feeling somewhat saddle-sore, the cavalry straightaway registered at the nearest and most salubrious establishment that they could find. Despite the somewhat austere Stalinist exterior, the hotel redeemed itself by possessing absolutely no Mongolian flies, a well-stocked bar, and, wait for it, yes, a billiards room! Oh yes! A billiards room! De Ath almost relieved himself with ecstasy there and then! The only other time that he had seen the sacred green baize throughout his stay in 'The Garden of Hyacinths' had been on a side street in Huhehot, where a bunch of Mongol kids had been utilising a junior version as a commercial break (scuse the pun) between hiring comics from a local pavement newsagents. Truly, this was heaven! A full-sized table, six pockets, and yes, a red and two white balls - one with a spot! Heaven! It soon became apparent that the boys had become a tad overwhelmed by their toy, so Ricardo-Coutts and Stirrup duly retired to a neighbouring snug to discuss methods of disposing of the opposite sex.

"*Pourquois?*" queried de Vol-au-Vent, with furrowed brow, "*C'est impossible! Non?*"

"*Ask no questions, old bean.*" replied de Ath, as he sidled off in the direction of a rack of shrivelled and twisted cues.

It was hard not to resist the thought that the architect had copied the blueprint of a joint that he had seen in Leningrad, couldn't figure out what to do with the room, happened upon a photo with this strange green table occupying the centre ground (accompanied with a bar that Jack Nicholson in 'The Shining' would have been proud of along one side), and thought: "*That's precisely what we need, comrades!*" Funny how the ball rolls.

How do you fit triple-expansion locomotive boilers into a billiards break? No idea. But hey, life's like that, don't you know. By the time that Dame Emily 'Lister-Jag' Cholmondeley entered the saga, with Wing Commander Reginald Plantagenet Arbuthnot-Arbuthnot in train (so to speak), de Ath and de Vol-au-Vent were having trouble locating the scoreboard - the bar posed absolutely no difficulty at all! Nevertheless, whilst attempting to prop themselves up with their tools, they had already embarked upon a meaningful discourse on historical developments in Chinese interior design. The first thing that struck our amphibian friend was the way that Cholmondeley sashayed onto the 'Planet of Indolence'. Being, by contrast, a well-bred Cantab Grad, de Ath's cue remained resolutely vertical.

"*Where do we go from here, old chap?*" he whispered to de Vol-au-Vent just as our Parisian chum was preparing to embark on a detailed inspection of the underside of the table.

"*Fancy a game, old bean?*" de Ath ventured in the general direction of Arbuthnot-Arbuthnot, as he attempted to shovel de Vol-au-Vent deeper under the slate. Realising that chaps will be chaps given half a chance, Lister-Jag immediately gravitated to the conspiracy in the shadows.

It should be said that de Ath tried, with all the effort he could muster, to maintain a double life; on the one hand (realising where Arbuthnot-Arbutnot's interests lay), he tried to sound knowledgeable on matters ranging from Gresley versus Stanier through to A4 Pacifics, Black Fives and the benefits of super-heated steam and split-funnelling: "*250 pounds per square inch! Bloody bomb on wheels, old man, what!*" whilst on the other, desperately attempting to render de Vol-au-Vent unconscious (à la Inner Mongolian eatery). De Ath, constantly aware of the instability that lurked beneath, rounded off with a couple of well-directed trajectories at the very instant that Arbuthnot-Arbuthnot delivered a quite devastating cannon involving no fewer than three cushions, going in-off and potting the red into the bargain! Fluke! Thus it was then that while the air force demonstrated how its pilots had refined their billiards skills between sorties, de Vol-au-Vent drifted into the land of mythological empiricism.

EPISODE SEVEN
Memories of Madness

At first, it was indistinct, but not until the others were cosseted in the land of nod, did it gradually begin to come together. *"Lamb Shambles, Lame Brambles, Sham Lamas, Non, non, non, mes amis! Shambhalah! Ah!"* came the whisper from beneath the frozen balls. That was it! As the message wafted through the air-conditioning system to the upper levels, it all made sense. The contingent was almost complete now, though they knew not why they had coincided, nor who they were, however, they knew where. The road lay ahead.

EPISODE EIGHT
"Unt, Vhen Did You Last Zee Your Vater, Young Man?"

We are already familiar with Ricardo-Coutts, de Ath and Stirrup, but less so with de Vol-au-Vent, Cholmondeley and Arbuthnot-Arbuthnot.

Wing Commander Reginald Plantagenet Arbuthnot-Arbuthnot was unquestionably a thoroughly endearing type. Impeccable breeding, in short, a jolly good egg, despite the somewhat tiresome effect his chatter on the subject of steam locomotion had upon most of the gathered assembly (de Ath, naturally, couldn't get enough of it though). Reg carried himself with a distinctively military bearing which betrayed his ancestral heritage: his great-grandfather having dropped off the coil, and on to the sharp end of an assegai at Rouke's Drift. The Brits could never really come to terms with Shaka's rules.

By contrast, Dame Emily Lister-Jag Cholmondeley hailed from thoroughbred motor-racing stock. Nevertheless, all those years spent traipsing to and frow between Spa, Brands, Le Mans and Monza had taken their toll. The aroma of Castrol R40 had somehow lost its magnetism. She sought pastures greener. A stone built home, perhaps adjacent to the sea, reflecting the warm and secure embrace of nature's elegant simplicity, was what she yearned for.

The Marquis Claude de Vol-au-Vent, however, could best be described as a loose-cannon. He greatly respected his old man: Le Duc Victor de Vol-au-Vent had been a driving force in the St Malo Maquisards when Schicklgruber embarked on his 'Grand Tour'. Victor later escaped to the UK with de Gaulle and his entourage, and thereafter found himself posted with a Spitfire squadron to an Assamese airfield alongside the Burma border. Thus it was then that son Claude had decided to chase his father's tail plane. He had absolutely no idea how he had ended up in Inner Mongolia, and nor did anyone else.

EPISODE NINE
The Deed Is Done

The world looked darkly grey to de Vol-au-Vent. It wasn't until the vacuum cleaner had intruded for the third or fourth time or so under the billiards table that he realised he was not reinacting the Blitzkrieg. The charmaid stepped back in horror upon observing the heavily camouflaged pilot emerge from beneath the baize brandishing a side-arm.

Claude stumbled into the innocent bystander and whispered, addressing the vacuum cleaner directly and in the most earnest of terms from behind his fogged up goggles: *"Ecoute ma amie!*

Ve are all bones at ze Somme!" before releasing his vice-like grip on the puzzled mechanical comrade. He then proceeded to shamble his way towards the light, bouncing off a variety of objects like a pinball as he progressed.

Happily, the light had been coursing its way to him via the breakfast-room, where the other members of the troop sat at the round table tucking into acrid nouvelle smoked dofu garnished with some over-salted Chinese version of sauerkraut. It came as something of a distraction to the assembled combatants to see de Vol-au-Vent stumble into the room and promptly fall gracefully flat on his face in a desperate attempt to disentwine himself from his parachute webbing.

"Ze audacité ov ze verité!" he exclaimed. The weapon he was wielding immediately discharged sending its projectile pinging around the periphery of the room before encountering de Ath's case-hardened beard and tinkling to rest aside a perfectly drilled knife and fork.

Having just polished off his devilled kidneys, de Ath found his mien to be quite unflustered by the intrusion: *"Bloody Frogs! Men can't shoot straight and all the wimin are neurotic!"*

"Quite so old chap." Arbuthnot-Arbuthnot agreed.

Later, around dinnertime, the party, by some bizarre coincidence, found that they had triangulated. All eyes glinted across the table as the raiders, in séance mode, chanted in unison: *"Shambhalah, Shambhalah, Shambhalah!"* The waiters winked knowingly. Although to the average Westerner Shambhalah has a somewhat esoteric flavour, in the East, the perspective is more pragmatically sure-footed. Strangely, so was it with our friends:

"What is all this Tibetan hogwash?"
"Shangri-la?"
"The Lost Horizon?"
"Island of the Blest."
"Mystic bunkum!"

"Forty days and nights in the desert with a pole up your anus, you're bound to conjure some kind of delusion up."
"Mais oui, but consider ze path!"
"The Sogdians, the Parthians, the Chinese, the Turks, the Mongols, the Road!"
"The trade!"
"The city!"
"The Jade!"
"The Silk!"
"The chair!"
"The chair?"
"It's there!"
"The Silk Road!"
"Forget about the Buddha in the clouds."
"It existed?"
"Like Troy?"
"Chateaux on ze Rhone!"
"A local warlord!"
"A protection racket!"
"The offer you can't refuse!"
"Manna from heaven!"
"It's waiting!"
"Turpan!"
And so it went on.

("Help me out here!" Ed)

It had become irresistible, irretrievable, irreversible. There was only one direction: The Taklamakan! They immediately resolved to journey up the Panhandle. It unfolded ahead in their imaginations: Jia Yu Guan, Dun Huang, Crescent Lake, Hami, Turpan, Yarkhoto, Urumqui, Heavenly Lake and Mount Bogda Feng. They knew what they had to do. Kind of.

At the railway station, the following day, Lister-Jag found herself in a queue behind a Hong Kong film crew who had given up on waiting for appropriate weather conditions to record their punchobatics. Fortunately, a couple of People's Liberation

Army (PLA) recruits were on hand; the seas duly parted, and the ticket booth immediately materialised before her.

"Six singles for the Urumqui Express, please." requested Lister-Jag.

"You don't want to come back?" came the concerned response.

"Fact is, old chap, we're not too sure as yet." added Arbuthnot-Arbuthnot with an air of mild apprehension. The deed was done.

EPISODE TEN
I Think I Can, I Think I Can, I Know I Can, I Know I Can

The gleaming jet black loco was a joy to behold - it looked like Mae West cruising into town: flags in all hues of red festooned the front of its boiler. Once de Ath and Arbuthnot-Arbuthnot had dragged themselves away from sniffing the burnt engine oil and coal fumes, they resolved to conjoin with the other members of the squad. The quest had begun. Onwards and upwards, and downwards occasionally.

Left: *"Drink, drink, glorious drink."* Diners in Mongolia play the equivalent of 'paper, rock and scissors'; the loser's penalty is to take a shot of the local fire water. Strangely, once one starts losing, it becomes a streak, and before long, the tiles get ever closer.

Below: Yurtsville.

Right: Kublai prepares his favourite pasta. Note the dough resting on his left forearm whilst shavings are cut off with a flattened-out section of tin can, and fly straight into the boiling water. Another method involves stretching and folding the pasta until one obtains an immensely long and thin spaghetto: referred to in the trade as the 'Everlasting Noodle'.

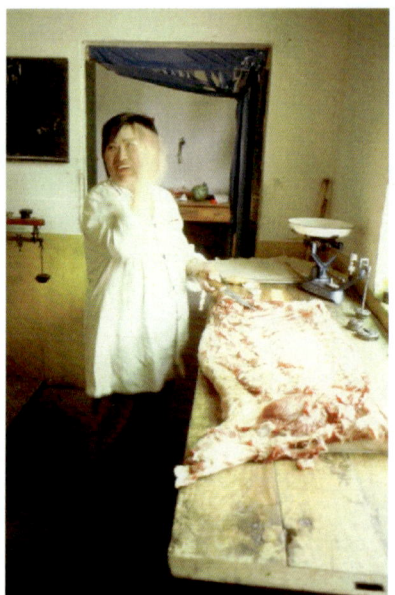

Left: Mongolian nosh. Whilst vegetarian dishes are quite common amongst the Han Chinese, it is difficult to avoid animal products on the steppe. In fact the nomadic Mongols and Kazakhs are amongst the few groups living within the Chinese borders who indulge in dairy products, but even they normally have to ferment milk into chigee (kumis); the process converts the lactose to the more digestible, and slightly more entertaining, lactic acid.

Left: *"You wanna talk bout summut, mister?"* Genghis as a sign of things to come. Primary school kids in Huhehot, the capital of Inner Mongolia.

Right: Young Mongol blades take a comic break between billiard games. Here, the lads rent comics from street agent who also hires out a tiny billiards table for use whilst his customers await the availability of desired reading matter.

Above: Le Duc Victor de Vol-au-Vent sporting the haute couture of the period during his stint as 'Protector of Burma'.

Right: *"Bloody bomb on wheels!"* The work force at the Datong Locomotive Unit prepares a QJ to take our travellers up the Hexi Corridor. This factory was the last in the world to produce steam locos.

Right: The 'Palace of Dreams'. Note driver utilising seat-cum-leg-locator as he steams up QJ.

Below: 'The Adoration of Mao by the Peoples' in a provincial railway station. As with the ubiquitous megaphone, portraits of the 'Great Helmsman' were to be found everywhere, particularly in the 'autonomous' regions – much like the recruiting posters of Lord Kitchener.

Above: All dressed up and ready to go. QJ wearing her little black number with the red shoes for the Panhandle Party.

EPISODE ELEVEN
The Boater Rolls into Town

Special Agent Titus Burgermeister III pedalled onto the platform just as the Urumqui Express was steaming up for the coming challenge. He dismounted from his trusty Flying Pigeon beneath, and tipped his boater towards the assembled masses whilst wheeling his treasured bicycle over to the nearest Chinese waif: *"Listen buddy, won't be need'n this no more."* The kid was dumbstruck. A bike that would have cost his parents a couple of month's salary at least, however could he explain it? Titus headed for the guard's van and climbed aboard. The whistle pierced the airwaves.
"Let the propaganda roll." whispered agent Burgermeister to himself as the massive 2-10-2 QJ locomotive unleashed its 2,980 horses on to the rails, and defied the darkness.

EPISODE TWELVE
Fidelity, Bravery and Integrity

Titus had been working incognito in the 'Land Of The Lost Souls' for some time. Not only that, but de Ath and Titus were not strangers to each other. They had met some months previously whilst on an expedition up Hua Shan, adjacent to Xian. Sacred Chinese mountains were renowned for their stairways to heaven, and the pair had spent many hours discussing the make-up of the inhabitants during their ascent.
　　"Bunch of fukin Kuo Min Tang livin in caves waitn for the second comin!" Titus spewed forth as they addressed the climb.

"Well, they've got him now haven't they? Deng Xiao Ping. If you hang around long enough, eventually fashion goes full circle and leeches are all the rage again." reasoned de Ath.

"Hell of a wait though. Should've sent in the marines years ago to put them out of their misery." added Titus.

"I'd have gone for the Black and Tans myself." said de Ath.

They were quite right of course. During the war against Chiang Kai Shek, the PLA had staged a quite audaciously bonkers raid upon Hua Shan: sheer cliffs and all the rest, in an attempt to dislodge some of the last remnants of the Kuo Min Tang. The whole thing was an utterly pointless, pyrrhic affair, resulting in the right-wing survivors being granted, by Mao, a lease of life to exist in the Hua Shan caves ad infinitum. After all, what harm could they do rotting in their prehistoric lounge? They were going nowhere. For the remainder of their lives, they pretended to be Daoist monks, and to this day, their descendents line the stairway to salvation eking out an existence selling mandrake, fried bread and soda pop.

Titus just couldn't resist that ultimate game of poker though. Knowing little of the pursuit, other than the ground rules, de Ath chanced his luck. He never forgave himself. Burgermeister had put his entire month's salary on the line (in dollars). When the cards hit the deck, Burgermeister blanched. Fate is so tempting when you think you have the winning hand. De Ath never fully came to terms with the fact that he had won, and tried to back down on the bet, but, to no avail, Titus was a man of honour, truly, and refused to accept any concession. To make matters worse, it all took place in front of the all-seeing gaze of Yu Huang Da Di. All day, the peasants from beneath had been prostrating themselves before the Yellow Jade Emperor in the darkness atop the mountain as the local High Priestess unfolded what appeared to be empty smack bags at the feet of the God; thus apparently, she released the accursed ailments of the suffering relatives down on the plains below in the hope of some curative remedy as the intoxicating incense fumes wafted under the nostrils of the Daoist God of the Mountain. One simply did not renege in such ethereal company, even if you were the winner.

On a later occasion, following their gambling episode, our special agent had approached de Ath in the hope that he might put the dear doctor's conscience to rest. Through his investigations, Titus had picked up on the fact that de Ath had had some experience in the art department.

"*Listen buddy, you wouldn't mind doin me a blue-print for a tattoo, would ya?*"

"*No problem, matey.*" came the response.

"*Wanna be the elephant n' havin the goose flyin overhead. Loads a clouds n' mountains et cetera, okay? Know what I mean?*" requested Titus (well, request is perhaps a tad euphemistic).

"*Your wish is my command, old chum.*" responded de Ath.

So was it then that our favourite special agent eventually came to drop his pants in the lobby of the Peninsula Hotel in Hong Kong to apprise Ricardo-Coutts' mother of the accomplished workmanship that her son-in-law had decorated across Burgermeister's buttocks. It was the beginning of an enduring relationship.

The thing was that Burgermeister had become romantically transfixed by a local concubine (the goose in the tattoo). He (the elephant in the tattoo) was as soft as a marshmallow, despite his formidable form. Built like a drum of steroids, though he never indulged himself, and naturally, emblazoned with tattoos, he gave the impression that he knew how to cope with most situations when he walked into a room full of strangers. After all, he'd been brought up in Cicero (Capone's fiefdom in Chicago). One day, he actually met the great 'Furniture Dealer' himself outside one of Al's soup kitchens: "*What the hell does this douche bag Ness want with me? Couldn't even catch a goddamned cold if he tried! The IRS? Who the hell are they? I'm just playin' the game. Listen kid, capitalism is the racket of the ruling class, an'don't you forget it, buddy.*" quipped Alphonsus. Little did he realise the impact that his observation would have on the young lad standing in line. Not that Capone had ever intended it, nevertheless, the youthful Titus from that moment on developed a fateful attraction to 'The Other'.

EPISODE THIRTEEN
Back off the Rails Again

Titus tossed his gear on to the bunk, as directed by the rather cutely delectable little PLA guard, polished his spectacles, and asked for directions to the dining car. He'd had plenty of experience on Chinese trains: *"Like walkin' through barns of battery chickens."* thought our special agent to himself. All very social stuff, even music to go. Couldn't escape from a damned megaphone anywhere! He sauntered past the racks of bunks with their febrile comrades, through one carriage after another till his hand finally sensed the warmth of food radiating from a door-handle. Then, he knew he'd made it! The Chinese took a lot of pride over the presentation of both their trains and food, you just kind of knew where dinner was, unlike that to be stumbled upon on British or Soviet trains (but more of that later). The first thing that confronted him was a shoal of what appeared to be party secretaries on a freebee, so inebriated that they wouldn't have noticed the Titanic sinking right in front of their eyes!

"*Probly jus downd the first course.*" reflected Burgermeister.

"*More ice!*" came the demand from the crustaceans.

Titus moved on. In the distance, towards the back end of the car, he soon began to recognise a species that he had something in common with. Yes, for it was truly them! Ricardo-Coutts and de Ath rose immediately and declared in choral unity:

"*Titus! What brings you hence?*"

"*Throw of the dice and the lure of food, guys! So Callista, the good doc finally got you on to the night train to nowhere.*" replied Titus.

"*Yes, he wouldn't stop playing his damned harmonica into the early hours until I agreed.*" she said with resignation.

After much back-slapping and reminiscences over their catastrophic efforts to assist our favourite special agent with his early morning weight-lifting exercises, the two Scots finally got round to introducing him to the gang. Prior to Titus' arrival on the scene, however, our group had expanded by one more member: Rolf 'The Austrian' Harris Tweed Schultz.

"*Interesting cuff-links.*" commented Burgermeister III - ever observant.

"*Indeed. Given to me personally by St. Ignatius Himself.*" volunteered Rolf.

EPISODE FOURTEEN
Harris Tweed

Now, Rolf had been somewhat of a casual acquaintance to Ricardo-Coutts and de Ath upon an earlier railway adventure to Kun Ming, in the south of the country. They had found discussions with him peculiarly riveting: ranging through Loyola to Darwin, he had expounded with considerable erudition. Apart from the fact that he rarely attired himself in anything other than Savile Row Harris Tweed suits, whatever the temperature, it wasn't until he had died and was brought back to life again by a passing geography tutor, who happened to be visiting China on the Vatican University Exchange Programme, that they had begun to suspect something might be amiss. One evening, when Rolf had lapsed into his habit of speaking in tongues, it dawned on de Ath that either the unfortunate Jesuit was possessed or perhaps suffering from a serious medical condition. On arrival in Yunnan Province, and once suitably refreshed (Rolf loved his dose of juice, you understand), they ventured forth to sample the fare at the local market.

Now, before going any further, the reader needs to know that Rolf was pretty fluent when it came to the vernacular of the region. Indeed, on one occasion, de Ath had been traversing some rice fields with 'The Austrian' when they requested directions from a couple of farm hands. Rolf launched casually full frontal, and in faultless Mandarin, only to receive glazed and gawping looks in return. As de Ath and Rolf walked off, scratching their heads in an attempt to set their own bearings, they couldn't help but hear the two peasants in conversation with each other.

"*Funny, I could've sworn that wog was speaking Chinese.*" said one.

"*No chance, he's a big nose. Not possible.*" responded the other.

It tended to be a bit like that in China. In fact, one of the best techniques de Ath had developed to deal with the inherent belief that existed amongst the Chinese community, who were convinced that no foreigner could possibly master the complexities of their language, was to creep up behind them and start talking before the victims had had the opportunity to see the length of his nose. The resultant shock was such that conversation often flowed like nervous rapids from the unsuspecting targets - whose main concern by then was usually how to pull their pants up from around their ankles. It all seemed a bit rich to de Ath. *"These people can't even understand each other! You spend years trying to learn their language then they take one look at you, and the impenetrable curtain of incomprehension drops! What kind of twisted comedian is this God character? Creates us all so we can't communicate with each other. Then, he floods the playing field because he doesn't like the pitch made from his own turf. Whereupon, he turns us into pillars of salt because we've worked out how to enjoy ourselves. And, not satisfied with that, demands that we murder our first born to prove that we have some kind of respect for him. Bugger off! Go burn in your own infernal bush, mate!"* Neither could de Ath come to terms with what he perceived as God's schizophrenia: *"How come in the Old Testament he is nothing but fire and brimstone, yet in the New Testament, he is sweetness and light? Maybe, he learnt something from us for a change! And another thing, how in the name of the sacred Archangel Samael did this twaddle about God's creation of the world taking place after the agricultural revolution ever catch on?"* The doc frequently wondered to himself who was more retarded: the fruitcake soothsayers that promulgated all this fallacious gobbledegook or the cretins that swallowed it? Indeed, despite the Hospitaller heritage that his family seemed so steeped in, he'd never really been able to come to terms with all this romanticising of The Crusades: *"A bunch of megalomaniacal clerics and their Frankish henchmen raining murder and bloody mayhem down upon any communities that were not followers of the Latin Church from*

Germany to Jerusalem. And all in the name of reinventing the Empire of Rome." He did, however, take some solace from the fact that, along with humans, religions too had a limited shelf-life. Like a favourite pair of warm slippers, know what I mean? Eventually they wear out. How many worshippers of Ra, Ahura-Mazda, Invicta and the Greek Pantheon (since the Muslims clubbed Zeus out of existence in Afghanistan over a century ago) were around anymore? (**"Eh, hem. Could we possibly get back to the Kun Ming market before it closes down for the night, and I have to call in the exorcist?"** Ed)

Anyway, let's leave de Ath's religious question marks for the moment, and return to the matter in hand: Rolf's curriculum vitae. The long and the short of it was that Rolf's condition was easily explained. He was a Jesuit, and had been decorated with the medallion of the Sacred Order of Diabetes for his self-sacrifice and unswerving devotion to the Holy See. This became apparent to de Ath when accompanying Rolf round the aforementioned market in the capital of Yunnan Province. De Ath had become somewhat casually distracted by a local spice saleswoman - as was his wont - but upon hearing a commotion nearby, he turned to find Rolf brandishing his limbs in a contorted manner before a quite innocent, and clearly concerned, seller of Communist Party flags. The doc immediately recognised the pleas for help emanating from the salesman's dilated pupils. This was obviously not a mere linguistic misunderstanding. He had had some experience of his own father's hypoglycaemia during his upbringing, and suspected that, since lunch was approaching, perhaps Rolf might be requiring a little light refreshment.

De Ath tapped 'The Austrian' on the shoulder and suggested: *"Listen, old bean. Fancy munching on one of these delightful oranges I've just recently purchased?"*

"Mein Gott! Ist zo orange, ja?" Rolf promptly wolfed his way through its entirety: skin, pith, fruit, pips, the lot, with drooling abandon! Within minutes, he had returned from Zog. Magic!

On another occasion during the same jaunt, de Ath, Ricardo-Coutts, Rolf and a number of random acquaintances, including a pleasantly rotund party secretary from Hunnan, were arrayed about a restaurant dining table when it became apparent that Rolf was in dire need of sustenance. He may have been encouraged into a false sense of security by the somewhat exuberant but confused secretary, who had just deposited his false teeth on his side-plate: perhaps in anticipation of a rather soggy starter (his real teeth had apparently been lost in a bathroom brawl during the Cultural Revolution). In any event, Rolf immediately proceeded to climb the 'Tower of Babel' yet again. Such incoherence often occurred when dinner was delayed. Everyone glanced sideways. He then reached for the, it has to be said, thoroughly unappetising steamed bread roll languishing beside him, proceeded to break it in sacramental style, and utilised it to wipe his forehead free of the profusion of sweat pouring forth from his overworked cranium. Thenceforth, he chomped his way through this contribution to Chinese nouvelle cuisine. De Ath signalled to the stunned waiters that it might be a good idea to plant something more substantial on the table, pronto! The first dish duly arrived. No sooner had Rolf finished stuffing the remainder of his steamed bread down the inside of his shirt than he pitched face first into the decoratively arranged starter! The horror was soon dispelled from the faces of the surrounding diners when it was explained to them by Ricardo-Coutts that this was a traditional Jesuit grace performed exclusively by select members of the Austrian élite - at which point, the other guests stood up and launched into an enthusiastically resounding frenzy of applause.

("Phew, that was close!" Ed)

EPISODE FIFTEEN
Unlucky for Some

Stirrup (Sister Ruth of old) glanced down at Rolf's cufflinks and reached for her bicycle clips! So, the Vatican had finally caught up then! She knew immediately that her days would be numbered if she didn't do something, and soon! But what? Her eyeballs, encircled by that Sikkimese Black Narcissan mascara, combined with Stirrup's by now ashen complexion to cast something of the manic over her face. Although she would have liked nothing better than to indulge in the hooch that was flowing so copiously round the table, she determined to remain resolutely sober whilst racking her brains for a solution to the dilemma. Plots ricocheted around her grey cells, but nothing credible emerged. She awaited her opportunity. It came sooner than expected. The firewater available in the dining car was a brand (Fen Zhou) commonly found in the north of the country, and definitely not to be consumed on empty stomachs; it also happened to be one of Rolf's favourite beverages: went down like a dose of caustic soda! Before very long, it became clear that none of our valiant crusaders was going to be mobile without considerable assistance, except of course Stirrup herself. Unseen by the others, Sister 'Lemony' Stirrup had been surreptitiously pouring the contents of her glass onto the floor, and replacing it from the water jug. So then, once the group had become sufficiently well-oiled, she feigned nausea and excused herself for the evening. Despite the fact that the Basque's (Ignatius Loyola's) retainer had probably clocked her, she still felt relatively safe given his current condition - he was almost certainly going to be in no fit state to pull a fast one post repast.

Sister Lemony had always suspected that the Holy See would eventually rumble her and her mischief. They were clearly resorting to extreme measures by employing one of Loyola's sidekicks! Prior to her last dramatic act in Sikkim, however, she had already checked up on the options available to the pontiff. They all had their Achilles heels though, usually sexual; but somehow, she got the impression that Rolf definitely wasn't in the rutting season - which rendered her cute little red number and high heels utterly redundant. In this particular case, as a result of previous casual conversations with de Ath about expats he had met on his travels, she had discovered that Rolf (prior to identifying him as a potential assailant) was a diabetic, and additionally, would likely have a coronary condition given his insatiable love of the juice.

Even if she had known where his bunk was though, she couldn't afford to be seen rummaging around through his kit in order to tamper with his insulin; these were open sleeping cars and packed to the gunnels. Neither was she in possession of something handy like an ampoule or two of digitalis that could be slipped unnoticed into his booze, and nor was Foxglove on the dinner menu at the time. So then, it was beginning to look like she might have to devise a set of 'self defence' circumstances and get the axe out!

Meanwhile, back in the dining car, the others were thoroughly engrossed in an animated discourse upon the merits of Barbarian versus Roman culture; the party secretaries had long since sunk beneath the waves, and were being transported to the first class sleeping compartments by a collection of random peasants from the cattle wagons. As 'The International' died off into the distance, the field was left to the 'Big Noses', who were still knocking back the moonshine.

"Vercingetorix?"

"Mais oui. Ze only reason zat zat merde Julius Caesar vent on is crusade into ze Celtic lands vas to placate is creditors and enhance is position wis ze gold. Zey adn't mint anysing of value for years, zen, suddenly, ze gold price plummet by quarter of ze previous price after ee ad taken over ze Gaul! Merde!"

"Ah yes, the great Julius! Never has history thrown up such a leader: a veritable paragon of altruism and nobility. So concerned was he for the well-being of the Celts that he proclaimed himself their protector in order to save them from themselves, then proceeded to pillage, murder and enslave at

will. Hah! Therein lies the worth of war. If you've got minerals and can't defend yourself, you're stuffed. Look at that bugger Trajan, committed genocide in Dacia for exactly the same reason, and still the Italians celebrate their ignominy with that wretched column in Rome. Damned Dagos took a leaf out of his book when they went to the Americas. Completely wiped out the Carib. Nothing new under the Sun. Then it was aurum, now we are mainlining ourselves up to oblivion on black gold like cross-eyed junkies: 'Your minerals, or the full might of civilised, law-abiding, democratic savagery will be visited upon you and your kin.' Humans don't change, they just get old and die, only for the next generation to scribe another loop on the spiral."

"Exactemont!"

"God, the pair of you are so depressing. Hooey! Humans do change. After all we aren't cannibals anymore, are we? And another thing, I think that that Eric Blair chappie was right when he questioned as to whether we are irretrievably programmed into the blindness of the greed gene. It's scarcity that brings out the worst in us. Whenever there is an abundance of a commodity, you can hardly give the stuff away."

"Yes, okay, I agree with you. However, it doesn't say much for our heartfelt sense of community when we deliberately devise circumstances that encourage our descent into the law of the jungle by manufacturing scarcity: like de Beers do with their confounded bloody diamonds. Damned things are as common as muck. The fact is that there is always much more lucre and power to be derived from keeping the carrot at a temptingly useful distance from the mule rather than filling its feeding trough with them."

"C'est vrait. Precisely, mon ami. Gaul ad ze mines, Italy ad shite. Ow you say zat?"

"Ich bin ein barbar!"

"Yes old boy, I think we've gathered."

"Barbarians. Really! Who cares?"

"Really? Ven did a Roman voman ever rule ze empire? Ven vas a voman even allow to own anysing, inherit anysing? Ven did ze Celts ever toss zeir children unwant on to ze dump for ze rubbish?"

"You can't be serious?"

"Mais oui! Ze Romans vere a shower of bloodsirsty, villainous, dictatorial porcs; got exactly vat vas comin to zem. Ze Partian! Vivre Surena et les Partian!"

"Absolutely, stuffed that acquisitive property speculator Crassus at Harran. It was simply beyond the comprehension of the thugs from Rome that you could run an economy that wasn't based on slavery, a professional army and a centralised state. The thing was that Parthian culture didn't depend on slavery, but had a feudal structure, which wasn't adopted by the Europeans for centuries. They had no central capital. Any peoples that they took over were treated with a tolerance and respect that even the home-grown rulers rarely showed to their own."

"And ze Romans didn't even get stuff good and proper by Alaric like zey tell you in ze istory lessons. Ze Gots only spend a couple of daze zere and ardly touch it. Look at ze Coliseum: mass murder, sousands daily, for entertainment's sake over ze centuries! Imagine Himmler he sell to ze people ov ze Sird Reich ze billet for to vatch ze gas chambre in action comme le Saturday afternoon soccer match! Is dat vat you call ze civilisation?"

"But, what about the architecture?"

"Vat architecture?"

"The roads?"

"Ow you sink ze Celt ever manage to trade over such distance enormous, trade intercontinental, mon dieu! Long before ze Mafiosi Romani arrive, heh? Zer communication stretch over area zat ze the scum in Rome could only, ow you say, slaver over. Peace, cooperation, trade mutuel, sausedgity egalitarian, at least relative, non? Far exceeding to anysing Rome ad ever conceive. Massematical and communications system and a calendar zat vas centuries ahead of anysing ze Romans could ave dream ov, even if zeeze 'civilise' type could ave found a translation sufficient in zer dictionaries. Sacre bleu!

Ze bloody Roman calendar vas zo, ow you say, out of ze kilter zat zey eventually manage to progress spring to autumn! Never happen with ze Celt! Spring start at ze time same every year, and you could make ze calculation for undred of year vers l' avant."

"But what about the histories, the poetry?"

"Would you believe the history of the vanquished written by the victor? Maybe, given what they'd been responsible for, it salved their souls to write about it. The only one worth his salt was Tacitus, and he was probably a Celt anyway."

"You mean vat ze bastard in Rome wrote? Zey may ave ad ze dictionaries, but little else."

"What do you mean?"

"Vere vere zer massematicians, zer scientists?"

"Yes, they had no interest in anything other than that which could provide an immediate profit, and the easiest way of doing that was to steal and create a climate of fear for the subjugated. Caesar massacred and enslaved over a million Gauls during his Celtic adventure. 'Aurum est potestas', and also helps to keep your creditors happy. But on top of that, of course, they were always keen to adopt any technology that would enhance their military effectiveness. Having said that though, the thugs went and murdered Archimedes. He had wrecked their fleet with mirrors, mechanised grappling irons and a variety of other imaginative war machinery. In fact, the Hellenes dreamed up just about everything that the Renaissance liked to claim credit for: the orrery, the ...."

"Give it up, doc. You'll be saying they invented the steam engine next!"

"They did! And what's more, the Parthians invented the electric battery and their own distinctive brand of concrete!"

"God, now I know you've had too much of the hooch!"

"If it hadn't been for the wisdom of the Muslims in preserving as much as they could of Hellenic scientific developments, and that of other cultures, from the suffocating ignorance of Rome, the Renaissance might never have taken place."

"But the cuisine!"

"Would you be meaning the recipe for Parma ham filched from the Welsh by the Romans, or the one for making pasta that Marco Polo later brought back to Venice from Yuan Dynasty China? Only thing the Italians invented was the professional army. Oh, almost forgot, they also invented the gross fiction of Christianity. Would you believe a scripture cobbled together by a Roman emperor?"

"Heil Arminius!"

"Stuffed the bastards at their own game! Hail Herman!"

"Up yours!"

"Vercingetorix!"

"Down the hatch!"

"Alaric!"

"Cheers!"

"Hannibal ad Portas!"

"Slàinte!"

"The Parthians!"

"Bottoms up!"

"Ze Celts vere not ze varmongers, it vas Roman who vere ze zavage."

"Boils on the sphincter of history. Where would we be now had 'civilisation' not intervened?"

"Smart buggers though. Quite why so many around the world have faith in this fantasy dreamt up by bloody Constantine is entirely beyond me."

"SPQR."

"Sono Porci Questi Romani!"

"Stronzi!"

"I'll drink to that old chap!"

And so the spirit flowed ad absurdum.

Eventually, the delights of 'Silk Rail' cuisine terminated their erudite ramblings. Just in time, as it happens, since Rolf was beginning to exhibit signs of launching into obscure and stratospheric tales of his campaigns with Napoleon, and fishing trips with Jesus: monologues which inevitably preceded a coma if not saved by a handy orange of course. The remedy arrived, and our group of gourmets proceeded to sate themselves on some really rather excellent railway fare; the most delicious of the offerings, they agreed unanimously, had been the 'Beef with Mahogany Shoots'. From then on conversation turned to matters of more immediate interest.

"*So where're you guys headed?*" Titus chipped in.

"*Turpan.*" came the choral response.

"*What gives at Turpan?*" puzzled Titus.

"*Shambhalah.*" came the reply, beginning to sound like a mesmerised gospel choir.

"*You mean Shangri-la?*" Titus queried.

"*Non, non, mon ami, Shangri-la est un mirage, Shambhalah est un realité.*" clarified de Vol-au-Vent.

"*Oh yea? Well, I heard it from the horse's mouth during one of my nightmares that there's this lamasery place called Kum Bum up in Qing Hai Province, where the monks can fix you up with painless tattoos and elixirs of endless ecstasy, not to mention taking my vows, and learning one or two shortcuts to reaching Nirvana. Figured I'd check it out before it's too late. Some things ya just gotta do in life.*" explained Titus.

"*Yes old chap, but some things are just hocus pocus. Apart from anything else, you are going to have to hang around until all sentient beings have been saved before you can reach Nirvana: fat chance of that happening anytime soon. But, I suppose these monk types can doubtless organise some 'Cheap Day Return' deal for you to check out Nirvana – see if it's worthwhile. Why don't you just let Callista and myself help you out with your weight-lifting like the good old days, probably do you more good?*" suggested de Ath.

"*Whatever you hit me with, you Limey boogger, I've gotta check it out. Anyhow, what's with this Shambhalah/Shangri-la stuff? What's the difference? I'm going to Kum Bum and you're off to Turpan. What's the deal though? I mean the rain evaporates before it even hits the ground out there, what kind of paradise on Earth could that possibly be?"* said our favourite special agent, with a degree of incredulity.

"Well, we've decided to exhaust reality before resorting to the fantastical. After all, everyone thought that Troy was a myth until Schliemann came along. Turpan may be the world's second deepest depression, it also may be like a furnace, but, it isn't as parched as it's made out to be; it's actually quite lush because underground cisterns feed the land with the runoff from the nearby Bogda Mountains, just where the Tien Shan Range peters out." Cholmondeley informed Titus.

"And that isn't the only factor concerning its location. The thing is that it is situated bang on the Silk Road at the most northerly point of the Taklamakan Desert: which has a reputation for being probably the most ferocious on the planet, apparently the Turkic translates into: 'If you go in, you never come out'." added Arbuthnot-Arbuthnot.

"So, what does all this mean?" asked Titus.

"Well, look at the map." said Ricardo-Coutts as she unfolded her trusty Bartholomew's of the region. *"Merchants never went through the Taklamkan, they went round it, taking their caravans either by the southern or northern routes. If they were travelling east to west, they would stop at Dun Huang to pay homage to the great Buddhas for safe passage to Kashgar, which lies at the far end of the desert, and meets up with the challenge of the Pamir Mountain Range. Then further on, we encounter Bamiyan in the Hindu Kush, where there is a huge cliff face riddled with Buddhist caves, and two gargantuan statues of the Buddha carved out of the rock face - one being the tallest in the world. They were built around two thousand years ago, and most likely designed by the Kushan descendents of Alexander's entourage, which explains why their robes and many images of Buddha in China and elsewhere are in the Classical Greek mode. Interestingly, it wasn't until quite recently that some of the more isolated eastern Afghan tribes converted from their worship of the ancient Greek Pantheon to that of Allah. Here then, at Bamiyan, the caravans would camp again; this time to give thanks for the protection afforded them*

on their fraught journey. The same homage would be paid in reverse, first at Bamiyan then later at Dun Huang, when journeying from the West to China."

"Not only zat," as de Vol-au-Vent took up the baton from Ricardo-Coutts. "Mais, Dun Huang est at ze end vest of ze Panhandle Gansu, and ver ze road divide into ze souse and ze norse route. On ze route souse, zome caravan vent on to Kazgar, but ozerz took ze zpur Khotan over ze Pass Karakoram into ze India. Zis est ow ze Buddhism came to ze China, and vat est behind ze Monkey King tale. It vasn't only ze commodities zat zey traded, but also ze philozophy, non?"

"Quite." continued de Ath pompously. "In the same manner, if they chose to go by the northern route, they could refresh themselves at Turpan then continue to Kashgar or take the north-western spur on to the Kazakh Steppe and from there to Russia."

"Okay, but........" Titus tried to establish a foothold on it all.

"The thing is, old bean, that where you get a trade route, the merchants need to restock on supplies for the journey, and if you happen to be situated on such an artery, it gives you an ideal opportunity to extort whatever you could get away with in the form of goods, and more particularly, taxation and 'protection': especially if you had a healthy agriculture and good relations with the local Turkic tribes. Let's not forget that The Silk Road was the longest and one of the most well travelled communication arteries in history - not to mention the value of some of the cargoes." responded Arbuthnot-Arbuthnot.

"Yeah, I know all that about protection rackets." chuckled Titus.

"Precisely mein freund, ze Mafia ov Zentral Azia. Just like doze schlösser am Rhein: 'Give to us ze geld or ve blow your fukin arse aus von fukin das wasser'!" contributed Rolf, roaring with laughter in his singular manner as his unique blend of English and German became increasingly scrambled.

"So, you see then why Turpan became such a wealthy location when the Silk Road was in full swing." Cholmondeley added.

"What we reckon is that there is a jolly good argument for suggesting that the ancient earthen city of Yarkhoto (or Jiao He, as the Chinese would have it) in the Yarnaz Valley at Turpan could have been Shambhalah: particularly given its obvious size and wealth at the time. The fact is that it was capital of the local Cheshi State and in close proximity to Heavenly Lake and Bogda Feng (the Mountain of God) in the Alpine scenery of the Altai Range." backed up the wing co.

"'Intelligence exists where two rivers meet', as the old Indian proverb says, and that is exactly what happens at Yarkhoto." concluded Ricardo-Coutts, the resident 'Keeper of the Maps'.

"Indeed, there is considerable verity in this; check out demography relative to water resources, particularly in challenging terrain such as deserts, old chap." de Ath added.

"Okay, sounds convincing, but I've made my commitment to the Lamasery, so, gotta go. Anything for a free tattoo and everlasting ecstasy. Apart from that, you never know what might happen if you let some of these monks down!" said Titus.

"But surely, you've overshot the route a tad, haven't you?" Arbuthnot-Arbuthnot wondered.

"True, it's a bit circuitous, but the Infant Buddha in my dream told me that I must first prostrate myself at the feet of the Great Buddhas at Dun Huang before climbing up on to the Tibetan Plateau and heading for Kum Bum. Sounds a bit like your Silk Road Merchants, don't it? He also told me that the monks at Dun Huang would supply me with a very reliable guide to guarantee my safe passage." explained Titus.

Thereupon, lubricated by copious amounts of fiery libations, the banter became more random and deranged. Eventually, Lister-Jag and Callista decided to pay Lemony a visitation, just to make sure that all was well, at which point, they all figured that it was probably an appropriate moment to call it a day: particularly if they were going to be in any fit state to appreciate Jiayuguan in the morning.

The ways in which booze reacts with the individual can vary from person to person and is dependent upon the quantities consumed: some become playful and silly, others maudlin, one or two like nothing better than to indulge in a ruddy good punch up. Rolf, however, was exceptional in that he became quite speechless, stared straight ahead, and his body tended to set itself like reinforced concrete. It was as if he had seen some monstrous apparition. And thus it was that when the gang struggled to their feet and began to move bunkwards, the Austrian failed to react. They tried everything to elicit a response, but to no avail. What to do then? Fortunately, de Ath and Ricardo-Coutts had seen him in such a state at a provincial Communist Party banquet during a previous hallucination.

Callista turned to the doc and said: *"Looks like it's time for the sedan-chair."* The others looked at each other bemused.

"Worry yourselves not, my faithful comrades, it never fails." soothed de Ath before disappearing into the galley.

Moments later, he returned with two broomsticks and some lengths of baler-twine. The twine, he utilised for securing Rolf's ankles and wrists to the chair, and whilst he was doing this, Callista slotted the broomsticks under the seat, one on each side, and tied them on to Rolf's seat with the remainder of the twine. Hey presto, an Austrian pumpkin! And what's more, he, being the upright Austrian type that he was, hadn't so much as batted an eyelid during the entire process. With Cholmondeley up front as the advance guard, and Callista taking up the rear, the others took a corner each, and off they went. There was some initial concern as to whether four inebriates could manage the task, however, Rolf's weight in the centre drew everyone together and balanced things out. Perhaps there is some Indian proverb that goes something along the lines of: *'When five drunks collide, there is stability'*. Being ahead of the procession, Cholmondeley found herself constantly having to satisfy the curiosity of the Chinese travellers as the party moved from car to car. The natives seemed happy however with the explanation that Rolf was a member, albeit a minor one, of the Austrian nobility. Upon receipt of this information, some of the very elderly even bowed their heads in the direction of the tweed suited figure when he passed by. He, Rolf (for it was **He**), in full accordance with protocol, stared straight ahead making no acknowledgement of the masses whatsoever. Finally, they made it. Wherever else Rolf was, at least he was in bed, just like the rest of them.

There was no rest for the locomotive, however, as it slogged on through the night. Nor was there for the dark hand of fate as it stalked the Hexi Corridor between the Gobi and the Tibetan Plateau.

EPISODE SIXTEEN
Radio Jia Yu Guan

Sun-up. No need for an alarm clock here. Our intrepid adventurers emerged from their slumbers thinking that perhaps fire had broken out, but no, it was simply the general clamour of the planet's most populous nation desperate to answer the call of nature in circumstances where the toilet facilities were at something of a premium. Who on earth would want to be on a track maintenance gang! Special Agent Burgermeister III glanced at his Rolex. *"This can't be right."* he puzzled. Burgermeister had forgotten that, for the foreigner looking in, there was a multitude of confusing facets to the country and its culture of difficulty - time being one of them. The fact is that there is 'China Time', and there is 'Rest of the World Time'. China straddles the equivalent of some four or five time zones if you happen to be on the Siberian Express travelling through the good old USSR (or 'The Vlad Lands', as it is more popularly known today); but in China, wherever one happens to be geographically, it is always Peking time. Despite the obvious simplicity of this, the result for the foreigner observer is still confusion. Inversely, the question of whether to zone or not to zone across a country had arisen with the advent of rail in the UK. Take Brunel and his efforts to produce more accurate Great Western railway timetables for instance; perhaps the Chinese, like the British, had decided against employing such a finicky system, and opted for the ultimate time carpet, who knows? In a country covering the longitude of the UK, incorporating the minutes it would have taken the sun to traverse Great Western territory into a timetable had a negligible effect, however, by not applying time zones to a land of China's dimensions, discrepancies became a little more apparent. You just had to take a step or two back and look at one's watch from a different angle altogether. Unavailable then to those tardy party secretaries who may have journeyed from far afield to the Congress in Peking was: *"Sorry comrades, forgot to adjust my watch."* Once Titus' mind had kicked into gear, he reflected to himself: *"Imagine flying from Peking, with the sun just edging over the horizon, and arriving in Urumqui shortly thereafterwardski, where the locals are still deep in slumberland, and you are fresh as a daisy on your version of Peking time? Guess those folks in Kashgar et cetera are used to havin sunup at midday. Must have a word with Albert about this when I get back to Princeton."*

Once the gang had completed their ablutions, and were preparing to set off for the dining car, Stirrup ventured: *"Anyone seen Rolf this morning?"*

To which Cholmondeley responded: *"Not yet. Better check him out. He was in a bit of a state last night, probably still sleeping it off."*

At this point, Cholmondeley, Stirrup and Ricardo-Coutts peeked round the corner into the neighbouring hutch. Initially, they couldn't see Rolf since his bunk appeared to be surrounded by a 'frenzy' (the popular collective form for journeyists of the Chinese persuasion, by the way) of travellers, who seemed to be talking in urgent tones and shaking some human-like object vigorously. Eventually, once the gathering had taken in the presence of the threesome, the sea duly parted to reveal Rolf - whose complexion had assumed a distinctly alabaster cast. Not only did his pallid hue cause concern, but, he was sitting bolt upright, staring straight ahead and pointing at some invisible (to all but himself) object in the distance. He was utterly rigid. By the time that their jaws had hit the floor and bounced back up again, the males of the species had rolled up to join in.

"*Good Lord!*" exclaimed Arbuthnot-Arbuthnot.

"*Yes, I imagine he is having a cosy chat with someone in a black habit right now.*" responded de Ath, searching for Rolf's pulse whilst shining his handy pencil torch into Rolf's eyes, and holding his vanity mirror in front of the Austrian's mouth and nose.

"*Ladies and gentlemen, I'm afraid that our Austrian representative has succeeded in reaching the frozen peak of 'Mount Forlorn Hope'. Rigor mortis has clearly set in.*" he concluded.

Just at that moment, two train guards appeared in the company of a tall, gaunt looking gentleman wearing a white shirt and PLA green trousers. The senior guard issued a string of staccato orders to the surrounding masses, at which point they evaporated. The man in the green trousers advanced and began to examine the late Rolf whilst one of the guards explained to de Ath that the gent conducting the examination was a PLA major in the medical corps. The guards then apologised for any inconvenience, but required that our travellers should assemble, together with the Chinese sharing Rolf's compartment, in the dining car; there were certain formalities to be gone through under these most awkward of circumstances, you understand.

"*Awkward! Is that how these guys describe death?*" Titus thought to himself.

It was all fairly perfunctory. The train crew were a paramilitary branch of the PLA, so, in the absence of the police, it was their duty to take witness statements. All were gathered in the dining car awaiting their turn to help the guards with their enquiries in a neighbouring compartment. During the interim, our adventurers passed the time exchanging tales of their more bizarre experiences in the Middle Kingdom, interspersed with periods of silence. They were all called up individually to relate their connections with the deceased, and what had happened the previous evening; the business of the sedan chair seemed to create some amusement. Ricardo-Coutts' interview, however, appeared to take an inordinately long time.

"*They like her. Must be the red hair.*" ventured Cholmondeley.

"*No, they probably reckon that because most murders are committed by left handers, she's been up to no good.*" chuckled de Ath.

"*D'ya ever get the feelin' some dapper little Belgian bastard with an immaculately trimmed moustache an' a three piece suit with a pocket-watch is gonna waddle in an' announce 'and now ladies and gentlemen, I will reveal who dunnit'?*" said Burgermeister III.

"*You are utterly unspeakable! How can you make light of a situation like this?*" Stirrup rebuked them. Was she trying to cloak some evil-doing under a smokescreen of grief? Only the post mortem would tell.

By mid morning, the train had arrived at Jia Yu Guan, and a posse of flatfoots were on the platform ready to accept the sheaf of witness statements from the guards. Rolf was still as stiff as a board, so had to be tied to the sedan-chair again. While he was being carried along the platform to the waiting ambulance, de Ath couldn't help but be reminded of the legend surrounding the dead El Cid strapped to his saddle, and leading his troops out to do battle with the Moors in defence of Valencia. The chief of police informed the group that Rolf would be taken to the local hospital for further examination, but in the meantime, perhaps they would like to visit the famous fortress in the company of one of his officers, who could answer any questions about the Great Wall that they may have, after which, if they would be kind enough, they should all reassemble at the hospital.

"*Sounds fine to me.*" Titus chipped in, and off they all went.

The great fortress of Jia Yu Guan certainly lived up to its reputation as 'The Strongest Fortress under Heaven'. The original Great Wall, which began its construction during the Warring States period, and was completed by book burning strong man Qin Shi Huang Di some two thousand years ago, was an attempt to hold back the nomadic Xiong Nu tribes to the north (often believed to be Huns by the Europeans), and appears to have been relatively successful - at least until Genghis and his chums arrived on the scene in the Thirteenth Century. The old wall posed absolutely no problems for the Mongol and Turkic army: they simply went round it at the east end. Once in China they took over completely and established the Yuan Dynasty of Kublai Khan fame. Following the demise of the Yuan came the Ming. The Ming Dynasty decided to reinforce the wall and extend its western frontier from Lanzhuo out into the Turkic lands as far as Jia Yu Guan, at the west end of the Panhandle. Here, they punctuated it with an immense fortress where the wall meets up with the natural obstacle of the Tibetan Plateau.

Our visitors were suitably impressed with the structure. Who wouldn't be? It covered an area of two and a half square kilometres surrounded by over six hundred metres of wall standing nine metres tall. Within the enclosure lay a giant keep and various other towers, all topped with upturned flying eaves supported by blood red columns. Any visitor who had been accepted into the Middle Kingdom had to pass through a huge arch called the Gate of Sighs; presumably they were expected to be impressed at being given passage to the civilised world (the Chinese were so unconscionably xenophobic). Jia Yu Guan was clearly intended as a statement both architecturally and politically. Such travellers, however, must have yearned to return home upon journeying down the barren Hexi Corridor!

"Know what I reckon?" mused Titus, *"The only reason this stuff was set up was to keep the Chinques occupied and inside the wall, never mind about the nomads beyond; they were just a ruse, at least until Peking decided to insult them. Put the fear of shit into the locals, stir it up a bit, and they all wake up with nightmares of Temujin n' Timur, then you can manipulate according to your fancy."*

"Welcome to China!" reflected Cholmondeley looking up at the battlements, *"Something tells me this would have been about as effective against Tamerlane as the old wall was against Genghis. Just as well for the Ming that the amir kicked the bucket at the beginning of his campaign."*

As she was reflecting upon over eight hundred years of tortured history, their police guide's radio crackled into life. Sergeant Pe Luo De approached de Vol-au-Vent and said: *"We go to hostipal. You like come with me, prease."*

From behind the sombre veil came three green shrouds. The tall gentleman leading the procession apparently was the pathologist. The other two, presumably nurses, were carrying what seemed to be a box roughly the dimensions of a loaf of bread, which was draped in a white cloth. It all had the aura of a rather sinister, surrealist magic show about to start.

After the formality of introductions, the pathologist took a deep breath and explained all thus: *"Comlades, I aflaid to say that accolding to findings, ferrow traverrer suffer from weak hat, diabetes, and la bu no lea, had crealy indulge in spilitual ribations for some time. Prease accep deepes sympathies."*

At this point, the two nurses advanced ceremoniously, and carefully deposited the box into the waiting hands of Arbuthnot-Arbuthnot, since he was standing closest to them. As they engaged reverse gear, they pulled back the white cloth to reveal a pristine, top of the range 'People's Radio'!

"This is most kind of you comrade, but we already have the pocket-sized version: more convenient for us travelling types, you see." contributed de Ath, most diplomatically.

To which the pathologist responded, *"Perhaps you misunderstand. Mr Loa Le Fe* (the Chinese habitually transliterate the names of foreigners rather that translating them. Tai Te Se reckoned this helped them to distinguish the 'big noses' from the native 'civilisation' when in conversation, since very few foreign names ever corresponded to the only one hundred Chinese surnames.) *clemate, and this ladio contain lemains."*

Despite her feelings concerning what she thought were Rolf's true intentions, Stirrup's Catholic background surged to the fore, and still in a deeply lachrymose state, exclaimed: *"But the Vatican forbids cremation!"*

Ricardo-Coutts immediately came to the rescue. *"I'm sure they didn't mean it, Lemony."*

"After all sister, when in Rome et cetera." added Burgermeister sensitively, almost setting Stirrup off again.

"Just as well. How in God's name would we have managed a coffin his size?" whispered de Ath to de Vol-au-Vent.

Once things had settled down, Arbuthnot-Arbuthnot suggested that they simply accept the casket, and pay their respects somewhere more appropriate. They all duly conformed and conveyed their thanks to the pathology team, the Chief of Police and Sergeant Pe Luo De for any 'inconvenience' caused, and all the trouble they had gone to under such 'awkward' (they were learning, you see?) circumstances.

Just as they were on the point of departure, Cholmondeley thought she would chance her luck: *"Indeed we are most deeply appreciative of all your efforts, but, if we might enquire as to where we could obtain a 'People's Wagon' in order to transport dear Rolf to Dun Huang. He always used to say that some day he would like to retire there."*

"Matta of fac, I believe that we will despatch some donor olgans to Dun Huang in one of amburances soon, prease arrow me momen to check." replied the pathologist in understanding tones.

"Hope they didn't come out of Rolf, or the recipient is going to be in for a big fukin surprise!" Burgermeister thought to himself.

During the interim, de Ath inspected the radio. Inscribed across the top, in immaculate Pinyin (Chinese Romanisation), were the words: **Koa Me La De Luo Le Fe Ha Li Se Te Wee De Shu Le Te Se.** Initially, the doc was somewhat bamboozled (such damned complicated stuff this Chinese business), but then suddenly clicked: *"'Comrade Rolf Harris Tweed Schultz'! Most thoughtful. Smart buggers these commies."* mused de Ath to himself. After a little tinkering with the dial, he also worked out that it was a real box of tricks: since it seemed to be able to receive not only the better known quotes of Chairman Mao, as if on an endless loop, but, another rather more obscure station - something quite incomprehensible until Stirrup clarified.

"*I know what it is, it's the sermons of Saint Ignatius of Loyola in Basque.*" she said.

"*Sacre Bleu! Maybe Rolf ee can still speak to uz!*" enthused de Vol-au-Vent.

After fifteen or so 'Peking' minutes, the pathologist returned with good news, "*I happy to say, one of vehicles will reaving within hour, and will able to accommodate you all.*"

"*You are so kind, thank you.*" gushed Cholmondeley.

"*Preasure entiely mine. I wish you all safe and comfotable journey, someone will arong shotly to correc you.*" said the pathologist, and disappeared behind the dark curtain.

"*A 'Volksradio', a 'Volkswagen', all we need now is the 'People's Mutt', and we'll have the whole damned set!*" chortled Burgermeister to Arbuthnot-Arbuthnot – carefully maintaining Sister 'Lemony' out of earshot.

Above: No leaves on the lines here, and full employment too.

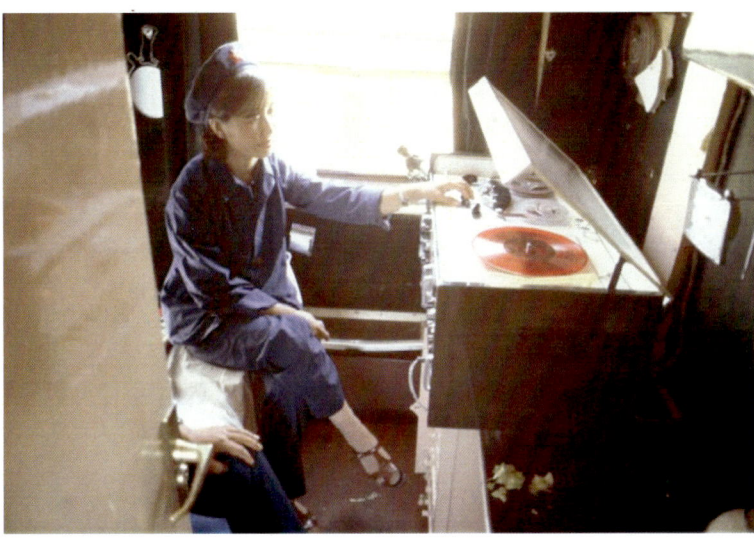

Above: PLA disc jockey. Note the red vinyl. Constant amusement ranging from party policy statements to Peking opera was available over the airwaves in the work place, on mountain tops, and on trains too.

Above: Hua Shan. Yes folks, those Chinese paintings are for real too.

Above: *"Anyone for Kuo Min Tang soda pop?"* The fate of Chiang Kai Shek's followers on Hua Shan.

Above: Yu Huang Da Di (The Yellow Jade Emperor) plays a mean hand at One-Eyed-Jacks.

Above: So, this is where all the sorghum goes: the Fen Zhuo distillery. Cheers!

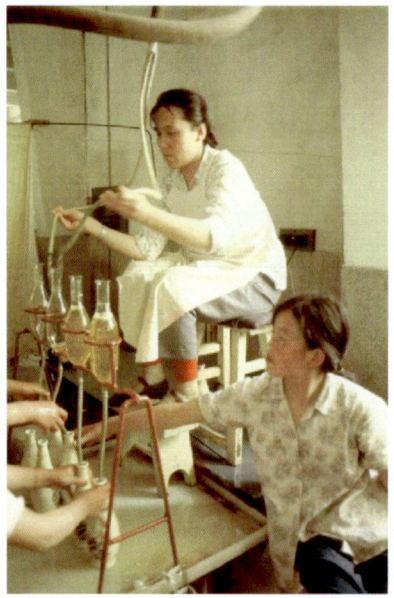

Left: *"Fancy a drip feed Rolf?"* The Chinese, and the odd foreigner or two, avoid the fluoride in the water supply by adopting Colonel Jack D. Rippa's solution: the water of life.

Left: Aladdin's cave at the distillery. The bondsman and unit manager inhale the angels' share.

Below: The Nine Dragon Screen deflects evil spirits preventing their entry to what lies beyond. Such spirits have their limitations you see, since they can only travel in straight lines. Silly coves.

Right: Grasshopper burglar alarm system. The idea is that if one purchases some five or so grasshoppers, and places them in one's abode, they will merrily fill the night air with their inimitable music, until at least they suddenly fall silent upon hearing any unusual sound (eg: that of an intruder). The resultant lack of insect symphonia immediately awakens the human inhabitants from their slumbers. Cute, no? A bit like the white spaces in Chinese pictures signifying as much as the painted parts.

Below: Jia Yu Guan. The walls of death - just in case the grasshoppers fall asleep. At least that was the idea.

EPISODE SEVENTEEN
The Road to Dun Huang

Forget the blood n' tears et cetera. For the most part, our intrepid voyagers simply wished to climb in and cosy up with the donor organs in order to staunch the profusion of sweat flooding from their brows. No revelations, no deluded fantasies, just show me the deep freeze comrades! None had ever been so far detached from the sea in their lives, and there they were, driven, with a radio full of Austrian ashes and refrigerated cases replete with human organs, by a certain notion that there was some place called Shambhalah at the end of the rainbow. When night fell, things cooled down, and they all lapsed into their mutual comas.

Dun Huang arrived with sunrise; it was going to be another scorcher. The ambulance driver and his mate dropped our what by now could only be described as rabble off outside a rather drab looking hotel; its saving grace being that it was probably the only one in town with air conditioning. In fact, most of the town looked like it might have seen better days when the Silk Road was active. No matter, they had things to do. Titus had an appointment with a monk at the 'Caves of the Thousand Buddhas', where he would be assigned a minder, and from whence he would journey on to Shangri-la in search of eternal ecstasy and free tattoos. The others also had to go on their own pilgrimage to the caves to pray for safe passage along the Silk Road and success on their quest to find Shambhalah. So, after freshening up, and a brief consultation with the manager, they were directed to a well-stocked stable that met with their requirements in the camel department.

"One cannot simply roll up at a shrine like that in a bloody mini-van for God's sake! Where is your sense of decorum, occasion, atmosphere........?" exclaimed Lister-Jag.

"Okay, as long as they are Bactrians, I always fall off dromedaries." qualified a concerned Callista. She needn't have worried though, there wasn't a dromedary in sight.

When the caravan left town, heads turned, and Dun Huang came to a silent standstill. All eyes followed the procession as if they were watching a funeral cortège.

"*They've probly never seen 'Big Noses' riding camels before.*" said Titus.

"*Must say old chap, finest damned Bactrians I've ever planted my arse on! Feel like I'm on a Kushan catwalk!*" added de Ath.

"*Mais, perhaps zay know somsing, non?*" suggested de Vol-au-Vent.

"*Who? The camels?*" puzzled Stirrup.

"*Non, ze fan club.*" clarified de Vol-au-Vent.

To which Lister-Jag responded with exasperation: "*Good Lord Claude, don't be so bloody paranoid!*"

In actual fact, the funereal aura was not too far off the mark given that our travelling circus had, out of respect, also hired a camel for poor Rolf. The good folk of Dun Huang, however, were not to know of the radio's contents, they had simply never before encountered a camel whose only burden was a 'People's Radio' strapped between its humps.

"*Must be the latest model.*" was the whisper that went around the multitude.

Left to right: Lady Callista Ricardo-Coutts, Dr de Ath, Rolf 'The Austrian' Harris Tweed Schultz (inradiocognito. Latest model of course) and Special Agent Titus Burgermeister III (clasping his automatic).

EPISODE EIGHTEEN
Rites of Passage

As the caravan approached the caves, the vegetation grew more sparse, and the dunes increased in altitude: heralding the climb up on to the Tibetan plateau. Only one of our troupe of comedians was contemplating that particular route though.

After the others had decided to make a small detour in order to take a peek at the nearby Crescent Lake, Special Agent Burgermeister III said, glancing at his watch (still trying to come to terms with Zhong Nan Hai time): *"Listen comrades, I'll give the lake a miss, don't wanna keep the abbot waitin'. See ya up at the caves."* and with an *"Eee yaa!"* he gave his steed a firm thwack or two on its hind quarters and galloped off in a cloud of dust towards the narrow valley at the foot of the colossal dunes.

The problem was that the racy enthusiasm shown by Burgermeister's camel was instantly picked up on by Rolf's mount: perhaps they were related. In any case, Rolf atop, said beast carried the remains of our 'Austrian' west at some speed in the general direction of the Crescent Lake. The other six attempted to keep up, but after a couple of dunes, they lost sight of the camel and its cargo, and were restricted to tracing the animal's hoof prints. The thing was that with only 'Radio Rolf' on board, it was much lighter.

"Power to weight ratio." explained Lister-Jag to the others as she recalled all those tedious days trackside watching her father going round and round in circles.

Eventually, after a mile or two, they reached the summit of a dune, and before them were revealed both of their objectives. So, two birds in the hand and none in the bush. Good gallop's work if you ask me. At the foot of the light gradient was the appropriately named Crescent Lake, and, approximately half way between our pursuers and the lake, there stood a solitary camel.

"That's strange," commented Arbuthnot-Arbuthnot, *"where's the saddle? Where's the radio?"*
"Perhaps it's a different camel." offered de Ath.
"No, that's it." said Sister 'Lemony' (for she knew a thing or two about animals).

Our heroic band approached, and as they did so, the camel, clearly recognising its chums, advanced to join the group again. In moving from where it had been standing, the camel revealed something even more bizarre. There was no escaping it, everyone saw it. There, where it had been, was a jet black iron cross rising some four feet out of the sand!

"Mon Dieu!" exclaimed de Vol-au-Vent as he read out the inscription on the cross:

Here lies Rolf Harris Tweed Schultz.
Devoted Storm-Trooper of the Holy See.
GO NO FURTHER!

Closer inspection of the area behind the sinister monument showed that the dune leading down to the lake was littered with what appeared to be pockets of quick sand, and that any attempt to 'go further' would be fraught with hazard. This also explained what had doubtless occurred to the hapless Rolf-like remnants. The generally accepted assumption amongst the group was that the camel, sensing danger, had come to a sudden halt, thus throwing Rolf et al at the mercy of the voracious Taklamakan sands.

Surrounded by dunes, Crescent Lake in the distance was mirrored by our heroes and their mounts - forming a sombre arc in front of the iron cross. Throughout the brief service conducted by Sister Stirrup, Arbuthnot-Arbuthnot's mind drifted back to his time with Carter in Egypt during that accursed 1920s Valley of the Kings expedition. So many had popped their clogs in dubious and unexplained circumstances. His task had been to deliver some of the archaeological treasure trove back to Cairo in his trusty Vickers Vimy transport. He almost went for a Burton on a few occasions: when being shot at by irate local fuzzy-wuzzies peeved at foreign meddling in their region. Once, he landed at Luxor with what seemed to be more bullet holes than ply and canvas, but the Vimy was a tough old bird: *"What's good enough for Alcock and Brown is good enough for me. Even if they did end up by pranging it."* he would reassure himself. He also had the comfort of a Lewis machinegun and the 360 horse power of a couple of Rolls Royce Eagles to hand. Nevertheless, he counted himself fortunate; he just hoped that things weren't going to become any more peculiar on this particular trip. Stirrup's *"Amen."* shook him abruptly out of his brown study.

When they reached the top of the dune, as they headed off to join up with Burgermeister following Rolf's send off, they turned to take in the view for one last time.

"Look!" exclaimed Ricardo-Coutts, *"What's that?"*

In the distance, a limpet mine atop a dark hand surfaced from the lake. Commander Crabbe had been seeking out Khruschev for some time and gone a smidgen off course since Prime Minister Garden issued the orders.

He peeled back his mask and spat out his mouthpiece, scrutinised his surroundings, and bellowed: *"Come and get me, you commie blackguard!"*

The last they saw of him was a pair of flippers submerging in the general direction of Cuba. The plot thickened. Dun Fu Min (a local Chinese entrepreneur) later established a watering-hole for visiting foreigners at the spot called 'The Cross and Crescent'. Passing ex-pat Brit travellers however, who were usually more au fait with the mysterious background associated with the site, simply referred to it as: 'The Lone Frogman'.

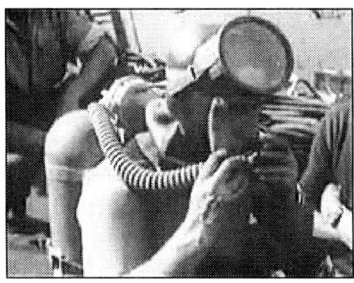

It was at that very moment that the 303 round screeched overhead, with the result that de Ath turned a deeper shade of puce; immediately, he delved into his case of photographic equipment, withdrawing what looked like the wooden shoulder stock of a rifle from which he extracted his well-oiled 9mm Mauser M 1916 service pistol, clipped on the shoulder stock, and barrelled down the dune towards the distant plume of blue smoke that was rising in the still air some way off in the direction of the cave complex.

Being somewhat more level-headed, and familiar with such situations, Arbuthnot-Arbuthnot exclaimed: *"Hell's teeth! Looks like Balaclava all over again. He's completely cracked! Quick, dismount and take cover!"*

They all conformed, but took turns at observing the mad Scot's progress.

"Is this kind of rampant lunacy normal for him?" enquired Lister-Jag of Ricardo-Coutts.

"Unfortunately, he does tend to rise to a challenge sometimes, regardless of the odds. Most of his front teeth are false." she replied.

"Front teeth! Is that all?" Stirrup remarked, injecting a flavour of optimism to events.

As things turned out, whether it had been because of the fusillade he had let fly with, the withering flow of expletives that issued forth from him as he charged after the as yet unseen sniper, or the cloak of dust that seemed to envelop his advance, no more shots were heard from their assailant. What was heard though was the unmistakable sound of a bugle announcing the all clear. The others then trotted down to de Ath's position whilst he reloaded, and then placed the pistol back inside the stock before returning both stock and bugle to his photographic equipment case.

"*You have certainly come well-dressed for the party.*" Arbuthnot-Arbuthnot saluted de Ath.

"*Absolutely, Biggles old bean. School motto, what: 'Ready Aye Ready' n'aw that. Reckon we've seen the scoundrel off. Incidentally, what have you chaps done with Frog-Topi-Wallah?*" responded a jovial de Ath.

They looked round. The camel was noticeably de Vol-au-Ventless. All points of the compass were scanned: nothing.

"*Lord, it never rains but it pours!*" said an exasperated Cholmondeley. Having then gained a better vantage point, she exclaimed "*Look, he's there!*"

De Vol-au-Vent, even at that distance, was unmistakable in his trademark headgear. However, no sooner had they spotted him than he disappeared below another dune.

"*Where the hell is he going?*"

"*In completely the wrong direction.*"

"*Imbecilic, custard-brained amphibian!*"

"*If the Taklamakan doesn't get him, the radiation at Lop Nor almost certainly will!*"

"*Okay, let's get him, and, if we're lucky, we might actually make it to the Buddhas by the end of the millennium.*"

Thus the exchange went.

The sight that confronted them when they reached what they had decided could be none other than the bleached remnants of the errant Frog was bizarre in the extreme. But, they were getting used to the unexpected, and took it all in their stride. It could only be him. The neatly structured pyramid of whiter than white human bones might almost have been mistaken for a modern, abstract expressionist interpretation of a sci-fi public institution: much along the lines of some Le Corbusieresque maquette, but with a skull on top. This in turn was capped with a pith helmet, quite obviously belonging to the marquis since the de Vol-au-Vent family cipher appeared embossed upon its peak. There was no possible alternative conclusion, and yet, there seemed to be no credible explanation as to what had occurred. In fact, events were becoming less and less credible with every step they took. Following much head scratching and debate, not to mention the realisation that their daylight hours were becoming numbered, they gang decided that the best course of action was to gather up de Vol-au-Vent's earthly remains and head for the Great Buddhas in search of some answers.

Upon their approach to the narrow poplar-lined valley leading to the caves where the two Great Buddhas were, they began to be aware of a noise resembling the audience natter in a packed Albert Hall prior to the arrival of the orchestra on stage. The valley became increasingly constrained, and its walls more vertical as they walked their camels up towards the source of the din (in fact, it was a minor miracle that the place had not been submerged under the gargantuan sand dunes after all these years). The camels themselves seemed quite unfazed by the atmosphere; this encouraged our adventurers (although, it had also occurred to the more paranoid amongst them that the beasts may have been in on something unsavoury and weren't letting on). Then, just as the cacophony had increased in volume to almost ear-splittingly loud proportions, they rounded a kink in what was now more of a crevasse, and all became clear. How clear indeed. The bottle-neck opened out, and took on the appearance of a natural, elliptical amphitheatre. The sheer west cliff faced a mirror image of itself on the east, but differed in that here there were two immense sets of open wooden doors. In the recesses beyond the thresholds: the twin Great Buddhas of Dun Huang. The first was sedentary, with blood red lips, a dazzlingly white complexion, and matching robes. The second was standing powerfully upright, but had a swarthy complexion and correspondingly darker robes when compared to the seated Buddha; he mesmerised one with his expression of sinister sobriety. In both cases, the style of their attire was typically reminiscent of that which adorned the Grecian looking Great Buddhas of Bamiyan in Afghanistan. Milling around on the floor of the amphitheatre, and on a level below the two huge sets of open doors leading to the Buddhas, was a veritable ants nest of yellow hat monks, all of whom appeared to be deeply engrossed in some kind of perambulatory, philosophical discourse. It was all very febrile: everyone shouting and gesticulating at the same time. There were pairs, trios, quartets, quintets, any number of groupings, except that when there was a clutch of roughly eight plus, they stopped, formed circles, and traded notions (or was it insultomaticisms) in the round with each other. De Ath found it all a bit confusing, he only wished that they would whip out a sax or two, and get themselves wrapped around a few decent jazz standards instead - but hey, dat's life. Despite the apparent pandemonium, it didn't take long to locate our favourite special agent; apart from anything else, he was one of just two people in the coven not to be wearing a burgundy coloured habit. The other person to stand out, due to his absence of habit, was standing beside Titus, and was attired in white pantaloons and shirt, black riding boots, a black cummerbund, a matching turban, and a long, striped satin coat in purple and emerald green (of the type that tended to be all the rage in northern Afghanistan). Our special agent seemed to be deeply involved in a discussion with the only monk to actually be sporting a yellow hat: one had to assume that this was a mark of rank. Eventually, Burgermeister's eye was caught. He turned back to the monk and gestured towards the new arrivals. Immediately, Titus' Buddhist companion clapped his hands together three times. The effect was quite dramatic! This was no ordinary 'single-hand clap' - total silence prevailed. Then, like cockroaches scuttling down a drain when the kitchen light was switched on, the valley cleared! Only about half a dozen or so, presumably retainers, stayed on aside the cleric in the yellow hat. Our travellers approached, and in doing so, de Ath couldn't help but notice the SMLE 303 Number Five bolt action rifle dangling from the shoulder of the thick set gent wearing the turban.

The doc's reaction to this observation must have been obvious as Arbuthnot-Arbuthnot turned to him and said: *"Yes, I noticed too. Stay calm, old man, most of these monks are doubtless well practiced in the martial arts."*

For once in his life, de Ath actually conformed, but not without comment: *"No bloody wonder he missed. Couldn't hit a barn door with one of those buggers. Definite contender for the chocolate spanner award! Feel safer carrying a tooth-pick!"*

Titus did the honours. The diminutive 'Yellow Hat' turned out to be the abbot, whilst the somewhat beefier 'Turban' was called Hassan Babur, and apparently had been assigned to be our special agent's minder for the trip to Kum Bum. The abbot gave a hint of a bow in the direction of the team, to which they corresponded. The turban was more vocal.

"It is my great pleasure to meet you at closer quarters (de Ath toyed with the catches on the aluminium case hanging from his shoulder). *I must offer you my most sincere apologies for my previous behaviour. The fact is that I mistook you for someone else, but now I can see that your mustachio is quite different from Stein's."* Babur said holding Arbuthnot-Arbuthnot with a quite disarming smile.

"Stein?" the good Sister 'Lemony' enquired.

"Yes, of course, that's it. Aurel Stein! Hungarian archaeologist, worked for the British government during the Great Game: when just about every European wandering around Central Asia was invariably embroiled in espionage. He managed to con the keeper of the Dun Huang Caves out of hundreds of priceless Buddhist texts, including the Diamond Sutra: the oldest printed book in the world. It's all in the British Museum now, languishing alongside the rest of the booty he filched from here and Afghanistan et cetera." clarified Ricardo-Coutts.

"And the moral of the story is: always count your fingers after shaking hands with a Magyar!" de Ath added flippantly.

"*Think you really ought to have a shave darling.*" said Lister-Jag turning to a now rather pallid looking wing commander.

"*So, where's Frenchy?*" asked Titus.

There then followed a somewhat protracted and confusing account of events following the special agent's separation from the group. Everyone had a contribution to make, but nevertheless, he got the gist of it.

"*I have an idea.*" he said, and went into a conclave with the abbot.

No one could work out what was being said, however, when they had concluded, Titus asked for the bag of bones to be handed over to the abbot, reluctantly they agreed, and the abbot departed with his retinue and said sack.

"*Suppose things can't get any worse for de V.*" said the wing commander.

"*Funny things happen in this part of the world. Reckon if anyone can help, these are the guys.*" reassured the special agent.

"*Help? How precisely does one 'help' a bag of excarnated Frog remains?*" queried an increasingly perplexed de Ath.

Shortly thereafter, the abbot appeared at the head of a solemn procession of heavy duty looking monks emanating a liberal helping of gravitas. Immediately behind the abbot, one of them was carrying the sack containing the Late de Vol-au-Vent. There then followed two more, supporting a substantial, three-legged, bronze, Chinese pot. Finally, bringing up the rear, came three monks: one of whom was holding out front what seemed to be a large book draped in a cloth of bright, chrome yellow silk. The other two were clearly the keepers of the scrolls. Without so much as a glance in the direction of our friends, the train of monks disappeared into the residence of the Great White Buddha. Strangely, the huge wooden doors, entirely free of human intervention, slowly closed behind them.

"*What on Earth is all this about?*" asked Lister-Jag.

Titus and Babur formed a double act, explaining that the pot contained some weird kind of narco-gunk which would be smeared all over the bones of de Vol-au-Vent. The book was in fact a copy of Gray's Anatomy, and the scrolls contained the appropriate mantras for the occasion. To say that eyebrows were raised would be to wildly understate the reaction. Of particular concern was the copy of Gray's.

Babur, however, put their minds at rest: *"The old man, unfortunately, is not quite as adept as he used to be. It became obvious that his talents were deteriorating a few years back; occasionally, his reconstructions had started to become, how should I put it, somewhat abstract. Not enough practice you see. It took some time to persuade him to get a copy, now he swears by it. Anyway, to matters of more current import. Perhaps I may show you to your quarters so that you can freshen up, then, I would be honoured if you would join me for dinner. I'm afraid we shan't be seeing the abbot and the others again for some time. Nevertheless, I feel confident that we can manage without him. He's not really much of a conversationalist."*

Babur, as it turned out, happened to be something of a curiosity. Born, as he had been, rather abruptly in the middle of a poppy field, he was descended from a long line of Assassins going back to Isfahan at the time of the Crusades (the Assassins were followers of The Old Man of The Mountains, who were sometimes called the Hashishin by westerners). Indeed, one of his ancestors had apparently been responsible for the 'Poisoned Cake' episode that persuaded Saladin to see the light, and take a more mature and considered attitude towards the sect. Throughout the Crusades, they conducted a justifiably murderous campaign against the Templars **("I knew it, I just knew it! Can't anyone write anything these days without the bloody 'T' word coming up?" Ed)**. However, it wasn't until the arrival of Genghis' grandson, Hulegu Khan, in Persia, that they met their match. From the Mongols on, the surviving Assassins remained a secret weapon of the Ismailis. The fearless and demented Assassins, reputedly permanently high on a cocktail of opium, hashish and alcohol, who had quite extraordinary talents when it came to eliminating political 'inconveniences' with silent invisibility; it was always wisest to have them on your side. Babur's grandfather, however, had, to some extent, broken the mould, at least insofar as the liquidation of irksome and misguided demagogues was concerned. The family eventually moved east to the hills overlooking Jalalabad, where they converted from Islam (which they had found was becoming a trifle claustrophobic) to worshipping the Greek Pantheon: Afghanistan being its last outpost. Their personal lifestyle didn't change too much though, since intoxication was almost a prerequisite where the Greek Gods were concerned. Whilst both Babur and his father involved themselves less and less in the more unsavoury aspects of the family trade, they did occasionally keep their eye in by going on an annual trip up the Khyber to 'deal with' any British officers who had been getting out of line. They had no compunction about doing this, particularly since the duplicitous Ismaili leader, the Aga Khan, had defected to the British Raj to enhance his personal fortune. Consequently, they had come to regard him as a traitor, and sought revenge, second hand or not. The British commanders down in Delhi constantly obliged by providing an endless stream of cretinous ya-hoo ex-public schoolboys who thought they could teach the wogs a thing or two. Oh dear. For the Babur family, it had really become more of a sporting activity, little more than mere target practice if you like, by that stage.

The family had also, over the decades, nay centuries, amassed a not inconsiderable fortune accruing from generous bounty payments, particularly during the Timurid period, not as employees of The Great Amir but through plotting against him. Thus, when Hassan Babur, by now in his mid-thirties, or two-hundred and eighties (numbers have never really been my strong point), decided to journey around the Middle East and Europe in order to broaden his world view, he was well provided for. He travelled extensively throughout these regions, and embarked on an in depth study of their cultures, scientific developments, political institutions, religious traditions and languages. He was clearly a natural linguist, as could be noted by his superb command of the English language. Whilst sojourning in Paris, he became a much fêted and sought after figure at the soirées of the great and the good. In London similarly so. In fact, he was invited to present a paper to the Royal Society entitled 'The Zen of the Artful Assassination', as a result of which, he received one of his greatest accolades: an evening spent in the company of one of the city's most renowned sleuths (a certain Mr Holmes), who was keen to pick Hassan's brains on some of the more subtle techniques employed by his sect. Mr Holmes' valet and secretary, a gentleman going by the name of Dr Watson, constantly noted down the minutiae of Hassan's tales as he and the great detective rambled on throughout the long cocaine-fuelled, and highly entertaining, evening: *"Definitely, a seven percent solution occasion."* as Mr Holmes described it at the time.

Following his residence in the West, he retraced the Silk Road back to the Orient to see what it had on offer. He, by that stage, took only scant interest in the worlds of politics and mainstream religion, other than in the elimination of the occasional ayatollah, bishop or prime minister - but naturally, only when the bounty was commensurate with his talents and the risks involved. He always kept a low profile in such sensitive matters; in short, he had become something of a class act. Except for his meditations upon the Kabbalah, he found the Judeo-Christian tradition symbolically quite sterile. He spent a fruitful time in Yazd and later in Mahan, near Kerman, as a student of the Zoroastrians and the Sufis respectively. Indeed, it was when he resided with the Sufis in Mahan that he first encountered a certain Mullah Nazrudin: an instructor who had clearly made a great impression on him. But apart from that, he felt that the orthodoxy of Islam, Christianity and Judaism were little more than devices for dictatorial, emotional delusions concerned with propagating a form of collective ignorance and superstition instead of challenging one to develop a deeper understanding of the inner-self in a manner that would lead to a more perceptive and well-rounded hitman. Hassan reckoned then that he would give the traditions of China a whirl prior to returning to the poppy fields of Jalalabad - which was how he had ended up as a student of the abbot at Dun Huang.

Even though Hassan had little time for the Mongols, and didn't relish the thought of getting any closer to their heartlands than he had to, particularly after what Hulegu had done to the Assassins, he felt quite sure that the Great Universal Ruler himself would never have dreamt of defacing the Buddhas of Bamiyan as the Muslims later did, and calculated that given that most of them had long since converted to Buddhism, his presence as a novice in Dun Huang would doubtless go unnoticed by the Devil's Horsemen. He also provided the shrine (in return for board, lodging and tuition) with his expert services whenever the monks required a peaceful and pre-emptive solution to any 'misunderstandings' with the outside world. He was always of the opinion that such matters usually reached a much more expeditious, elegant and satisfactory resolution if opposition leaders were 'persuaded' of the error of their ways before things got out of hand. A true diplomat!

"So my new found friends, we have learnt much about each other this evening." concluded Babur as he laid down his napkin. *"I'm afraid that your French companion is unlikely to be reincarnated before dawn. So, might I suggest that you repair with me to the Den of Dreams for a bast or two of the finest Persian opium prior to retiring for the night?"*

Whilst there were one or two sideways glances at the suggestion of a more filled out de Vol-au-Vent, everyone was amenable to the invitation, and withdrew to a neighbouring cave. It should be said that one simply does not argue with a beard as well trimmed as Babur's. After a few pipes, de Ath's suspicions of the Assassin had totally evaporated (as had most of his other senses); indeed, despite his family's ancestry, he had warmed to 'The Turban' quite considerably.

"Listen Hassan," said the doc, stretching his legs out over the vibrant red, silk, Turcoman carpet, *"it is clear to me that Titus could not be in better hands on his quest for Shangri-la, however, I am a tad concerned about the quality of your*

weaponry. Far be it for me to question someone with your background, but, the Short Magazine, Lee Enfield, Number Five, 303, Bolt Action Rifle is notoriously unreliable. I would therefore be honoured if you would accept my Mauser as a replacement. At least for the duration of your journey to Kum Bum. Despite its lack of range, it is deadly accurate, very compact (fitting neatly into the shoulder stock when not in use), and has excellent provenance having come from the collection of Ahmet Muhtar, also known as King Zog Ist of Albania. Indeed, the said king gave it to my father (after the old man had retired from the RAMC) for services rendered on the occasion of an assassination attempt upon him during his period of exile at the London Ritz. I'm sure someone of your undoubted talents will find it rather handy."

"You are most kind, doctor, but I couldn't possibly deprive you of such an elegantly designed and most murderous piece of kit." responded Hassan, somewhat embarrassed.

De Ath was of course fully conversant with the etiquette in such circumstances. Thus, after the pantomime of offer and refusal had gone round for the requisite three times, Hassan was finally obliged to submit and accepted the weapon. In fact, he couldn't wait to get his hands on it, and was truly over the moon! De Ath, for his part, was somewhat relieved to be rid of the thing, since he reasoned that there was probably a marginally increased chance of his surviving the expedition alive if it were not in his possession. Before heading nodwards, Lister-jag enquired of Babur if he could speculate as to what may have happened to de Vol-au-Vent to render him into such a disassembled state.

"Speculate, yes, that is the best I can do madam. Many spectres haunt the Taklamakan, but there is only one that I know of that leaves such a calling card, and though he died some five hundred years ago, his distinctive mirage still lurks within the sands." Babur paused. "You must ask your friend what he can recall once he has been recomposed." And on that note of mystery, the group retired with spirits immunised by the opiated vapours.

The moonlit shade of the Goddess Morphia caressed the valley throughout the night.

"*Mes amis, where have you been?*" asked a wide-eyed de Vol-au-Vent the following morning as he seemingly floated out of the Buddha's residence dressed in burgundy robes, and wearing his singular headgear of course. The combination of monk's habit and pith helmet looked altogether quite chic.
"*This could set quite a trend on the Paris catwalks, what d'ya reckon, doc?*" chortled Titus.
"*We might ask you the same question.*" retorted Sister Stirrup with reference to de Vol-au-Vent's curiosity.
He responded immediately with unrestrained exuberance, "*Moi? Ah ave been debating wis ze 'Buddha Infant'. Most stimulating, very enlightening, ighly illuminating, oui! Ze sagacity extraordinaire dans one zo yousful. And, apparently, ee is descend from Isaac Newton! Incroyable, non?*"

Just to confirm that the poor amphibian hadn't lost his marbles completely on the abbot's operating table, they all peered into the darkness of the shrine. It was completely deserted.

EPISODE NINETEEN
Captain Ahab Goes Fishin

A distant dust plume began slowly to ascend skywards towards the sun. Below, it seemed fired by a wide, shimmering waterfall of light that the parched sands on the horizon soaked up leaving no trace. De Vol-au-Vent had become transfixed by the threatening beauty of the scene: the sea of sand stretching to the horizon, and the silvery mirage that divided the desert from the billowing dark cloud. Before long though, another band appeared. This time in obsidian black. It emerged undercutting the mirage, and extended straight across his entire field of view. Like water that turns to wine when poured from jug to glass, as the band of rippling silver narrowed, the black strip grew in stature. Soon, the cloud had cast de Vol-au-Vent into its shade. Strangely however, the mirage maintained - at least until overcome by the now much more defined black. Our French friend was only too aware of what he was confronted by. He became riveted to the spot with fear, or was it curiosity? Nowhere to run, nowhere to hide. He felt like T. E. Lawrence watching as Sherif Ali approached over the sands at the beginning of the film. The only problem was that this time there were thousands of Omar Sharifs, and this was no film!

Regimental banners fluttered furiously atop lances as armour glinted in the obscure sunlight. The leading rank detached itself from the horde (which had come to a halt some one hundred yards distant), and, lowering their weapons in his direction, encircled our hero. He had begun to feel like the bull's eye on a target range. Immediately in front of him, one of the horsemen dismounted. This figure was clearly a man of some considerable consequence. Encased in the lamellar armour much favoured by the Avars, Mongols, Turkics and Chinese, he also wore a bronze and black steel helmet shaped like the copula of a Timurid mosque with a nose guard, a tough leather and steel drop protected the back of his neck, and from its pointed summit there sprouted an incongruous fan of turquoise and violet peacock feathers. This was the top dog. His body armour was obviously well-tooled (as was the circular shield attached to his left arm) and its protective knee-length skirt was something that Cromwell would have drooled over. Finally, draped from shoulders to black riding boots, he sported a bespoke long-sleeved gown of emerald green, in the Samarkand mode, embroidered along its silken edges with red and gold Turkic script. This was clearly no ordinary front line member of the ranks. This was the embodiment of the entire army! Sartorial elegance, eat your heart out! He advanced upon de Vol-au-Vent with a pronounced but confident limp, withdrawing his sabre from its gem-studded scabbard as he did so. It had now dawned on de Vol-au-Vent just what he was facing; he didn't need confirmation from the sharply trimmed beard or the blood-shot eyes: he knew he had a category one challenge to deal with! The spectre approached, both eyebrows raised. **("Listen, enough of this dammed, half-baked, purple prose stuff, just get on with it!" Ed)**

The tip of the blade came to rest on our favourite Frenchman's shoulder.

"So, my young infidel friend, at last we meet."

Although de Vol-au-Vent was not conversant with the Turkic tongues, he noticed that his adversary had obliged by providing a simultaneous translation running along the length of his gleaming sabre blade. Our hero had initially contemplated begging for mercy, but thought the better of *"Please don't kill me!"* on the grounds that it would doubtless bring about an instant reorganisation of his anatomy. The marquis had never encountered a foe on such terms before, and pondered to himself: *"There must be a way of slithering out of this in order to play for time and rally the troops for a counter attack."* After all, how could he possibly hold his head high while explaining his conduct to Marshal Ney when they, sooner or later, met up beyond the Styx? And right then, it was looking like sooner if he didn't try something. It simply wasn't worth thinking about: to be consigned to a Paradise where no one spoke French! Purgatory without end! Little did he appreciate that he had already entered quite a different time and place zone. Then it struck him! Immediately, he delved into his satchel. In response, the cavalry archers' draw strings were tensioned, but before they had time to convert the marquis into a Saint Sebastian look-alike, he whipped out a Champagne bucket, replete with ice and a bottle of Madam Ponsardin's best - a tin of Beluga caviar resting comfortably beside it.

"The pleasure is entirely mine. Delighted to make your acquaintance, General Chaos. Perhaps I may offer your eminence a flute or two of this extra special vintage, which I

always carry with me in anticipation of occasions such as this. In fact, it dates back to 1815, when our bravest of the brave were slaughtered by the shopkeepers from the 'Islands of the Red Herrings'." said de Vol-au-Vent with as much casual alacrity as he could muster.

The commander leant forwards. *"Ah, a well-bred miscreant! However, it would be unwise to indulge in front of the troops; they might get the wrong idea. We Mohammedans never drink on duty. Later perhaps. I assume that you also have an appropriate coterie of nymphets in your saddlebag to accompany the refreshment."* he whispered along the sabre. *"Whilst your flattery is most gratifying, it currently cuts little ice! Now, answer with the greatest of care, for your future hangs in the balance. What precisely have you done with my compass?"*

"Your compass, sire?"

"Yes! My compass! Play no games my fiend; the balance is beginning to tilt. Where is it?"

"I could never be less than candid with one so distinguished. Perhaps your Indefatigable Greatness might be kind enough to assist my memory by describing this compass. What did it look like?"

"What did it look like?! Were you born tomorrow?! It looked like a spoon, you dunderhead!"

"A spoon?"

"Allah! Yes, an infernal bloody spoon! What in the name of Beelzebub did you expect it to look like?"

"A spoon? Ah yes. Of course! That would be one of the Chinese variety. How remiss of me not to recognise the description."

"Odious perfidy! What do you mean: 'Chinese variety'? My compass was made in Hong Kong? Hong Kong! Now listen here, garlic breath, the sands are rapidly running out for you."

"Your Eminence. My deepest apologies. I am not explaining myself very well. I meant to say that it must be one of the original Qin Dynasty lodestones. Clearly you are a man of infinitely sophisticated taste in compasses. Unfortunately, I have not seen one of that style for centuries; they are unquestionably extremely rare, and much sought after since they represent the very first types of compass known to……."

"Silence! Allow me to make myself clear too. At the present time, my interest in the antique market is not particularly high on my list of priorities. My primary objective is to locate the Ming that I may teach them just precisely how black can be the colour of the brightest day! If I ever get my hands on them, then I shall construct a pyramid of skulls so high that it will take a lifetime to climb! Now, you are clearly a man of some erudition, therefore, you may have some inkling as to how I may find these arrogant scorpions who spurned the descendents of my father-in-law: 'The Great Universal Ruler'!"

In the forlorn hope that he might be able to persuade his adversary to simply bugger off over the horizon before the champagne became unpalatably warm, de Vol-au-Vent looked about himself for a sign saying: **'Ming, this way →'**. No joy. Then, it hit him! *"But of course!"* he thought, fondling the cork.

"Your Supreme Highness, Lord of the Fortunate Conjunction, it gives me great pleasure to be the first to inform you that the Ming were crushed by the Manchus many moons ago."

Upon receipt of this bombshell, the 'Iron Son-in-Law' blanched, the whites of his eyes instantly turning from crimson to scarlet as he raised the multi-purpose, polyglot communications device high above his head. By the way, don't you think it did wonders for de Vol-au-Vent's pronunciation of whatever tongue he was speaking in?

"Borrocks!" was the only thought to go through the commander's head (in fluent Chinese, strangely).

Obviously, a not dissimilar thought had gone through the mind of de Vol-au-Vent. The sabre suddenly began to rattle as the lame leader clutched at the armour over his heart, his entire body now seemed like quivering jelly, then he keeled over backwards like a felled oak. Just for a brief moment, de Vol-au-Vent caught a glimpse of a remarkable piece of jewellery on the hand being held over the heart of the falling villain. It was quite unmistakable: the ring of a Templar Grand Master! After that, things became a tad hazy for our hero.

("Ere we go a-bloody-gain! Next stop Holy-Effin-Grail, I suppose!" Ed)

Above: De Vol-au-Vent heads dunewards away from the Great Buddhas of Dunhuang and off to meet the 'Spectre of the Taklamakan'!

Above: King Zog I of Albania's Mauser; now residing at the REME Museum, where it is reputedly the curator's favourite exhibit.

Right: Grecian robes grace the Hindu Kush at Bamiyan. The artisans of the Kushan and Gandharan empires carried on the traditions left behind by Alexander of Macedon: traditions that have prevailed throughout the Buddhist world right up to modern day representations of Buddha. The Muslims (the Taliban in particular), however, seem to disapprove; despite the lack of evidence in the Koran outlawing depictions of the human form. The Iranians too appear to have been unable to locate such a prohibition as their many, and beautiful, paintings would seem to suggest.

Below: Buddha overlooks the bazaar at Bamiyan.

Left: *"Try takin me back to Holborn, matey!"* A little something that Aurel Stein and others found a tad awkward to pinch.

Below: Which way is right again? The other of the two Great Buddhas of Dunhuang that did not end up in the British Museum, or the Berlin Ethnographic Museum for that matter.

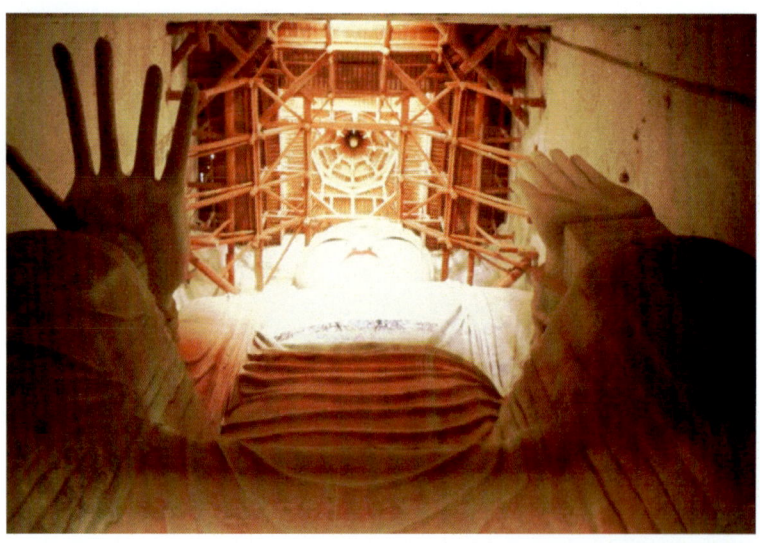

Right: The Abbot of Dunhuang extols the virtues of Gray's Anatomy prior to his successful reassembling of de Vol-au-Vent.

Left: Hassan Babur, descendent of a long line of Assassins, as he appeared some two centuries ago. Today, he is the CEO of 'Old Man of the Mountains Inc'. De Ath's trusty Mauser is carefully concealed beneath the robe draped casually over his forearm.

Left: Amir Timur, aka: Timur the Lame, Tamerlane etc. After the exhumation of the 'Uzbek from Hell' in the 1940s, Mikhail Gerasimov reconstructed the Iron-Son-in-Law's features from Timur's skull using putty and toothpicks. This technique is now employed by police forces worldwide to identify the corpses of the unknown.

Below: The Infant Buddha raises an eyebrow or two over one of de Vol-au-Vent's assertions during their overnight debating session. Note the double crown, peculiar to members of the Illuminati.

Above: Hulegu Khan enjoys a well-deserved bowl of Chigee (fermented mare's milk) after the hunt. Nice boots Huli, like the bow too mate, not surprised you're concerned about the beverage though. Frankly, thought you had more taste.

Above: Mao entrances some of the masses at least as they await the arrival of their pumpkin.

EPISODE TWENTY
The History You Haven't Heard Yet

"Are you quite sure that that was what he said? I mean: 'black being the colour of the brightest day', 'a pyramid of skulls', and this obsession with his 'compass' and the 'Ming' Dynasty et cetera, not to mention all that 'Great Universal Ruler' stuff?" Arbuthnot-Arbuthnot was something of an aficionado when it came to the algebra of language, and was keen that things should be just so before applying his not inconsiderable knowledge of codes, ciphers and such like obfuscation to the material.

"Methinks you detect a Dagobertine, Templaresque missive from the future here." ……de Ath.

"Pretty tenuous, thinks me." ……Lister-Jag.

"Mais, not strutching at claws." ……de Vol-au-Vent.

"I'm lost." ……Lemony.

"Snap." ……Callista.

The clan had regrouped, and was now back to the original sextet of its inner council. Having bade farewell to Special Agent Burgermeister III and Babur, and thanked the monks for reviving de Vol-au-Vent, they had returned the Bactrians to the camel stable, and eventually remounted the iron horse to Turpan at the western extreme of the Gansu Panhandle. Once clear of Dun Huang, things had gone fairly uneventfully for a change, though by then, they were prepared for almost any outlandish twists that fate might deliver their way. De Vol-au-Vent was moderately content with the deft workmanship of the abbot and his initiates. The only concern our errant Frenchy had was that he seemed to have survived the operation with two left hands instead of the rather more commonplace one left and one right configuration. Apparently, this peculiarity had occurred as a consequence of the abbot's attention wandering from his copy of Gray's to the finger arrangement of the Great White Buddha sometime towards the end of the narco-gunking process (prior to the 'Recitation of the Mantras' stage). Our man's worries were, however, put to rest when the abbot pointed out that the new design would almost certainly guarantee the marquis increased success with the ladies. This was indeed a most fortunate slip in de Vol-au-Vent's case, since two right hands had an entirely different significance altogether. Luckily, it seems that the abbot had had the presence of mind not to mix up ladies with laddies.

"*So, you recognised the amir's phantom then?*"........Colmondeley.

"*Mais oui, immédiatement!*"........ de Vol-au-Vent.

"*Wonder what the bugger was on about. Pretty rum business.*"........ de Ath.

"*Reg is on the case, just have to wait and see what he can come up with.*"........Stirrup.

"*Bunk probably, look at all the inconsistencies. I'm sure Tamerlane died of a fever, or plague, or something, not a heart attack. And, he wasn't actually Genghis' son-in-law either. Then there's the ring! What about the ring?*"........Ricardo-Coutts.

"*What does it really matter any way? The villain was a total nutcase, the only good thing is that he's pushing up the cacti. Look what he did at Smyrna. Took the citadel, massacred the inhabitants, including, I shouldn't wonder, quite a number of your ancestors' chums, doc. Then, when the Knights of St John sent in reinforcements to save the day, he went and used the decapitated heads of their comrades as missiles on the arriving fleet!*".......Cholmondeley.

"*Yes, the family had many a tearful brandy and cigar over that one.*".......de Ath.

"*Bonkers, oui. Mais, brave et generous aussi.*".......de Vol-au-Vent.

"*Brave and generous?*".......Stirrup.

"*Oh yes, he certainly couldn't be accused of being mean when it came to the doling out of dosh to his mates. His accountants must have had their time cut out.*".......Ricardo-Coutts.

"*Tongues too probably.*".......Cholmondeley.

"*And then there was that crazy stuff at the siege of Urganch.*".......Ricardo-Coutts.

"Urganch?"……..Stirrup.

"Yes. The local chief, Yusef Sufi, was vacillating about whether or not to throw in his lot with the 'Lord of the Fortunate Conjunction'. So Timur, deciding he'd had enough of this shilly shallying, figured he should help the poor bugger make his mind up. However, when Timur arrived to lay siege to Urganch, Yusef Sufi sent a message to the effect that instead of wasting the lives of all these good Muslim folks, surely it would be better for the pair of them to have it out in single combat in order to resolve the issue once and for all. Yusef clearly wasn't banking on what happened next. Upon receipt of the despatch, Timur immediately threw on his armour, leapt on to his trusty steed, and galloped down to the walls of the citadel: much to the distress of his generals, who had just aged ten years in as many seconds at the sight of their commander disappearing off into the dust. Timur then spent the rest of the afternoon or so limping around at the foot of the citadel walls, and ranting for Yusef to get his gear on and honour the challenge; not only that, but all of this took place within easy range of the hundreds of archers lining the battlements – none of them daring to take a pot-shot. Yusef, for his part, remained in his palace, unable to move - a quivering wreck of a man. Eventually, Timur grew weary of all the amateur dramatics and rode back up to his army to do what he knew best. Needless to say, the story is a bit one-sided since it was passed down courtesy of Timur's troops: no one was left alive on the other side to confirm its veracity."……..Ricardo-Coutts.

"Looks like you got off pretty lightly, Claude."……..Stirrup.

"Wish Hassan were here, feel sure he could provide some background to all this Grand Master stuff. In fact, I think I recall his mentioning something about the Assassins getting a bloody nose from the Templars after their attempt to convert to Christianity when Amalric Ist was ruler in Jerusalem. In addition to which, sure he said that they didn't have a particularly great press with the Mongols and some of the Turkic tribes following their reported plot to assassinate Mönkhe Khan. Which of course was why Hulegu Khan *eventually paid Alamut a visit to set the record straight, wasn't it? Almost wiped them out. I was just thinking, perhaps there may be grounds for speculating that a group of Templars did a flit following Philip IV's 'Friday 13th' persecution of them, and ended up offering their services to the Mongols and eventually to the Lame Uzbek. After all, the Mongols were annihilating Muslims in the Middle-East just like the Templars were. Even Timur spent most of his life killing Mohammedans despite the fact that he was one himself. What do you reckon?"........de Ath.*

"Balderdash! The Assassins trying to convert to Christianity? Pull the other one! You'd probably have stood more chance of persuading Genghis Khan to throw in the towel in favour of a career in bloody calligraphy!" ....Cholmondeley.

"Yes, imagination has certainly never been one of your short suits, dear."........Ricardo-Coutts.

"Always suspected he wasn't playing with a full deck." ....Stirrup (under her breath)

"Well frankly, it wouldn't surprise me. I mean, if some were willing to flee to Rosslyn and the bogs of Scotland, it's not unreasonable to think that others may have preferred the desert sands of their old stomping grounds, and took a hike to the Middle East and thence to Samarkand in the second half of the fourteenth century; apparently property prices in Central Asia were quite reasonable at the time. Better than surrendering to a diet of mince pies with a garnish of torrential rain in Glasgow, or being burnt at the stake in Paris just because they'd refused to let the French king get his mitts on their loot! ....de Ath

"I like zis idea."........de Vol-au-Vent.

"You would!" ....Ricardo-Coutts.

"Narcoleptic baloney!" ....Cholmondeley.

What was it about night trains? They always seemed to stimulate these kinds of off-the-wall theorising and whacky discourse. Meanwhile, the team's resident cipher boffin was still struggling with Timur's ramblings; the wing co, having immediately ruled out Bacon for obvious reasons, first applied Atbash, then Caesar, followed by any other systems he was conversant with, but nothing appeared to make sense. In fact, poor Reg was beginning to think that he was in need of some psychiatric assistance, even an evening in conversation with the Infant Buddha, perhaps: otherwise, he was probably going to end up with a one way ticket to Doolally.

As the loco fumed its way through the cool desert air towards their object of desire, they dreamt of ancient mirages.

EPISODE TWENTY-ONE
Chapter 69 (Sex Scene for the Editor. Or: Footsie with the PLA)

("Moi? Sex? What!" Ed)

As we know, for Ricardo-Coutts and de Ath, visiting Kashgar had always been high on their list of fantasies, now it was within reach, but, at the same time, frustratingly elusive. The expeditionary force decanted from the train upon arrival at the Turpan Zhan halt (which was situated on the northern lip of the depression some five hundred odd feet above its floor), and made straight for the bus station. The sun had just cleared the horizon, so the temperature was moderately pleasant; but they were all only too aware of the searing heat that was headed their way, and wanted to reach sanctuary down in Turpan city before they all ended up looking like dried foreskins. Lady Callista and the doc parted company with the others upon arrival at the bus station after being informed that if they wanted to include Kashgar on their itinerary, there would be a wait of a couple of days before they could depart; moreover, the journey to Kashgar alone was likely to take at least three days.

"Bugger!" exclaimed a dejected de Ath. *"Three days there, three back, plus two hanging about here, and the time there: it's all a bit on the tight side. Was really hoping to make the missing link with the Pamir."*

At that moment, a notion sparked a hopeful light within Ricardo-Coutts: *"Listen, there must be some kind of truck caravanserai around here. Why don't you all get the early bus, and we'll see if the truckers can come up with a better offer, then we'll catch up with you later in the day?"*

Everyone seemed amenable to the suggestion, and so, Callista and the doc waved off the foursome on their descent against an impressive backdrop of the 61 mile long fault belt escarpment of the Flaming Mountains, which formed the south wall of the depression: rising from the depths to 2,723 feet above sea level. The mountains took their name from the effect the setting sun had on them as it played along the vertical rib-like erosion patterns of their steep faces.

The pair soon located the caravanserai, and socialised with the drivers. It became apparent however that, despite the willingness of the truckers to accommodate them, the journey was still looking totally impractical. De Ath should really have appreciated this from the first. After all, it was virtually the equivalent of driving the length of Turkey from Istanbul to the Iranian border, but on even more challenging roads. That was that then. Dreams of Kashgar were in remission and would continue to haunt them from the bottom of their luggage.

"Suppose some places are meant to remain mysteries for a while. Keeps the curiosity alive. Bollocks! Anyway, never mind, Kashgar can wait for us even if we have to wait for it. For now, Shambhalah calls from the fiery depths. Feeling a trifle peckish, sure there must be some kind of noshery here to service the drivers, what do you reckon?" he said turning to Ricardo-Coutts in an attempt to raise his deflated spirits.

She had never quite clicked with his love of deserts, but at least a few days down in the depression seemed a more attractive proposition when compared with a week or two skirting the Taklamakan.

"Good idea, let's see what the dumplings are like." she replied.

The transport café was the usual rough and ready establishment that they had come to know and trust. It reminded them of the workers' café they used to frequent just outside the impenetrable walls of the university back in Shanxi: basic but dependable. In fact, the only time de Ath had had a problem with the fare in China came in the form of a cockroach in his guo yuo ruo at one of Peking's swankier restaurants whilst being entertained by his parents-in-law. Another thing he liked about your no-nonsense Chinese café was that the locals would actually talk to you unsolicited and out of interest, not because you might be of some kind of use to them in the future. A number of the academics in the university never really got it; didn't think it appropriate for Callista and the doc to be mixing with the lowlifes of the working class, let alone eating and drinking with them. God forbid comrade toady! Maybe the reaction of the lecturers was just some kind of backlash resulting from the recent Cultural Revolution, but de Ath and Callista suspected it all ran a lot deeper than that: something chronic in the psyche. China hadn't really changed that much, the veil of snobbery and corruption that seemed to prevail more or less wherever one went on the planet was no different there, and never had been. Whether they referred to each other as 'comrades' or 'court officials', nepotism and the 'backdoor' were still just as essential to those on the make as they had ever been. A handy backdoor was often of greater use to a student than good exam results if trying to avoid being assigned to a post in Xin Jiang (Turkic China), Inner Mongolia or Tibet, all of which were regarded as a virtual death sentence: largely because of the repression that had been wreaked on these regions by the Han Chinese themselves. In fact, prior to embarking on the expedition, the university minders made it clear that they were at a loss to understand why de Ath and his good lady wanted to visit uncivilised locales inhabited by the likes of Turks, Mongols and Tibetans. Callista and the doctor, however, had no such complications.

So, there they were then, just about to put in an order for the house dumplings, when a military green wagon came to a halt in a cloud of dust outside. It was like the 'Hole-in-the-Wall Gang' entering the saloon. In sauntered Lieutenant Wong Xu Zi and her charges: Chinese copies of AKs slung over their shoulders. They had that kind of jovial confidence about them that came with the knowledge that they could get away with murder if they so wished; just as they and their predecessors had been doing for decades. It didn't take long for them to acknowledge the alien presence in the room. *"Maybe this could be one of those situations where I won't regret having given the Mauser to Babur."* thought the doc. Lt. Wong gave a casually dismissive gesture towards one of the larger tables, the troops obeyed by shambling over to it, unburdening themselves of their weapons, and making themselves comfortable. As she approached the hatchway, where our duo was in conversation with the cook, de Ath fingered the Aliens Permit in his pocket, just in case she was planning to feel his collar. He, of course, knew full well that Callista and himself were both clean with respect to authorisation to be where they were. Funny business really, this:

"Why are you here?"

"I dunno, where are you when?"

Shortly after arriving in China, he had cracked the system though. The thing was that whilst the Peking and Shanghai police forces had a comprehensive list of all places 'out of bounds' to the 'Big Noses', the provincial plods were rarely aware of the forbidden locations other than those under their own jurisdiction. So, the trick was that, if one wanted to visit a banned locale, one did not apply for the permit in the same province but in a neighbouring one; or even better, a distant one, where the cops were even less likely to be aware of, nor care about, the status of the place. This, however, was the last thing on Lt Wong's mind as soon became apparent.

"Good morning, lieutenant." de Ath thought it beneficial to get in the first word.

"Good molning. I see you conversan with lecognition of lanks, you mus have rive in our countly faw some time."

responded Lt. Wong displaying a full set of fluoride etched teeth. Perhaps she hailed from Shanxi Province, where the chemical, which occurred naturally in the water supply, tended to leave its unmistakable trademark of brown decay on the enamel.

"Yes indeed Ma'am. You are most astute yourself." de Ath played the game (trying not to be too smart by suggesting that she may have been a native of Shanxi).

When it came to the subject of identifying the rank of officers in the Chinese military, de Ath was reminded of the WWII silhouettes of combat aircraft on the recognition cards he used to play with as a child (*"Was that a Messerschmitt or a Hurricane?"* he'd puzzle over in his youth); they all looked much the same but, of course, with subtle differences. So it was with the Chinese military, but they weren't that fancy. One simply had to count the pockets on the uniform. Oh, and, also do look out for the number of pens in the breast pocket. **("Is that the sex bit then?" Ed)** This code prevailed up until one became a resident of Zhong Nan Hai: the seat of the leadership. A rather more disingenuous approach applied to these neighbours of the Forbidden City, where it no longer became possible to assess the social status of the marsupials simply with regard to their pouches.

"Where you go?" enquired the lieutenant with an enticing smile.

Studiously omitting any mention of Shambhalah, Ricardo-Coutts explained that they were planning to meet up with their comrades down in Turpan.

"You join us, we go to ballacks in city." invited the lieutenant.

Just to prove that they were fully versed in the local etiquette, there followed the ritual polite refusal, offer, refusal, offer, and finally, embarrassed acceptance.

"Prease, you come have dumpring with us then." proposed the PLA.

Following a second bout of this ritualistic palaver: 'attack – parry riposte – parry reprise – parry riposte – parry remise'.

"Touché!" De Ath and Callista knew when they were beaten. *"Foo Engrish aw lound!"* fired Lt. Wong in a volley of shrill military staccato towards the kitchen.

Being a road house of the most exacting standards that almost exclusively catered for the Mohammedan community, bacon was at a bit of a premium. However, the local cured beef, or was it boiled (can't quite remember), was a more than adequate substitute. In fact, all in all, it turned out to be a reasonably good approximation of UK transport café fare. De Ath had been instructed to accommodate himself beside Lt. Wong, and duly obeyed, whilst Callista found herself surrounded by a coterie of male troops, who seemed completely entranced by her red hair. The conversation was moderately uncontentious; de Ath carefully restricting himself to topics that couldn't be construed as being linked, even remotely, to organ donations, female infanticide, The Cultural Revolution, Muslims and Lop Nor, et cetera. At least that was plan A. Lt. Wong quite clearly had other plans.

The thing was that whilst the good doctor usually turned into a veritable Mr Hyde once he had managed to get the leg over with a member of the opposite sex, his daytime persona by contrast was plagued with feelings of inadequacy and self-doubt when it came to the animal attraction stakes; he could never really get a handle on all that courting regime stuff. He was no Bird of Paradise that was for sure. Even despite the fact that he'd been together with Callista for years, he still couldn't understand what she saw in him. Prior to meeting her, he'd tried almost everything, ranging from such hackneyed subtleties as: *"I'm sure we must have met before?"* right through to the more risqué: *"Got some absolutely spiffing etchings back at the ancestral pile, you wouldn't by any chance fancy a peek?"* It was only when a female colleague sensitively pointed out to him: *"A woman would have to sit on your face before you would clock to her having the hots for you!"* that he simply gave up. **("There goes the Blue Peter contract then!" Ed)** As destiny would have it, immediately following this momentous decision, Callista arrived on the scene to share his carriage enroute from nothing to nowhere. Maybe it had just been a case of fear of the other and trying too hard to overcome it, combined with a dose of sexual myopia. Who knows?

Taking all of the above into account, imagine his surprise when this far from unattractive, indeed, really rather delectable (apart from her teeth, it should be said) PLA lieutenant began to express her hormones beneath the breakfast table. Initially, de Ath thought it must have been an accident when Lt. Wong's leg brushed against his. He couldn't have been more mistaken! There then ensued an onslaught of steamy sideways glances, accompanied by intricate footwork below from Wong, which de Ath attempted to deflect by avoiding direct eye contact, nervously stroking his beard, and maintaining what had now become a seriously faltering conversation (*"God! These Chinese can be so damned complicated sometimes."* de Ath thought to himself). Nor did the sexual mischief come to a halt once everyone was ensconced on the open top wagon heading down to Turpan. Callista had become flanked, yet again, by youthful Chinese testosterone at the rear of the vehicle whilst the doc and the lieutenant stood leaning, casually as you like, forwards against the back of the cab. Eventually, Lt. Wong resorted to a more direct approach in the hope of engaging de Ath by turning to face the back of the truck and stretching lasciviously in the doc's direction. *"Brazen hussy! Bloody cat on heat!"* he fretted silently to himself. Apart from the fact that the situation had the potential to result in his being turfed out of the country for lewd fraternisation with the natives (or worse still, espionage, given the military connection), he couldn't bring himself to think of the potentially deleterious consequences that this dangerous dalliance might have on his relationship with the admirable Lady Callista. As the temperatures rose to almost unbearable levels, Lt. Wong, meanwhile, was stroking herself in the most inappropriate regions of her anatomy (well, let's leave all those fingers alone for the time being). (**"Why so prudish all of a sudden?" Ed)** De Ath couldn't take it any more, feigning discomfort with the scorching heat that was blasting into his face (not to mention elsewhere), he successfully extricated himself from his PLA vamp to join Callista and the besotted troops. Wong maintained her position up front: unamused. It took an awkward hour or so to bottom out at their destination, and fortunately, at least the driver was on the ball on the way out to the barracks. He drew up outside the only hotel that had been granted licence to put up with foreigners. De Ath had some vague recollection of its placard proclaiming their arrival at 'The Oasis', or something apt like that, but at that precise moment, his only concern was to establish a demilitarised zone between himself and the spurned lieutenant. After much smiling, handshakes and thanks, Callista and de Ath parted company with the troops and aimed for the hotel reception, or in the doc's case: sanctuary. Lt. Wong gave another of her sultry looks, accompanied by a disdainful wave, as only she knew how, and off the troops went.

"Lord, you've really caught the sun!" commented Callista on the crimson hue that the doc's complexion had turned. Accrington Stanley: one. Manchester United: nil.

("Have to do a tad better than that if we're going to sell this to Hollywood. After all, we've already stuffed up the kiddies TV slot!" Ed)

EPISODE TWENTY-TWO
Swingin with the Natives

By expedition norms, their residency at the rather appropriately named 'Oasis' was fairly uneventful. The only incident of note occurred early on the evening of the first day, and only night, there. Not only was the establishment entirely unafflicted by the weightier aspects of soviet architecture, but it was also adorned with white Moorish arches and a reed canopied terrace out front. In addition to which, it had a resident, and indeed much vaunted in those parts, big band. Oh yes! Just what the doctor ordered! The musicians ran through a couple of Uighur jazz standards: Turkic arrangements of 'C-Jam Blues' and Thelonious Monk's 'Epistrophy', if recollection serves, they might even have deviated from the genre by including some pandemonics from Captain Beefheart's 'Lick My Decals Off, Baby' before being accompanied on stage by the Billie Holiday of Turpan for a rendition of 'Let's Do It' and much more. Most members of the gang were firmly of the 'Sun-over-the-Yard-Arm' persuasion when it came to spiritual indulgence in desert climes. Not so de Vol-au-Vent! He had by then adapted only too well to his uniquely novel anatomical reconfiguration, and developed some most effective strategies for coping with imbibing. To say he was saturated by the time the good 'Lady in Satin' had taken hold of the microphone would be something of an understatement in his case. Unfortunately however, he could still stand. And that is exactly what he did, topi and all! The thing was, he'd got it into his head that the vocalist's name was Salome, and reckoned that a spot of belly dancing was on the menu. When this appeared not to be forthcoming, he took it upon himself to provide some encouragement and launched into his own inimitable fandango. It wasn't so much the outlandish gyrating of the hips, nor the rhythmic flexing of the arms, but more his efforts to click the fingers of his two left hands in time with the beat that caught the eye of his by now astonished counterpart. Stirrup quickly cottoned on to the situation; racing through her mind were visions of disturbed natives, rampant mayhem, a lynch mob, the whole band of brothers dangling from the limb of a tree by their thumbs, thus jeopardising the entire mission. It simply didn't bear thinking about. Accordingly, the good sister came to the rescue by having a deafeningly quiet word in de Vol-au-Vent's ear about his having exceeded his pleasure quotient for the evening. It obviously did the trick. Our errant Lionel Blair, persuaded that unveiling was not on the cards, reluctantly assumed a less provocative sedentary position. Despite being mesmerised by the 'Hand of Beelzebub', the young lady bravely struggled through the remainder of her repertoire. Clearly, the sexual cachet attributed by followers of Tantric Buddhism to possessing a misplaced thumb did not seem to prevail amongst the Mohammedan community.

Later the same evening during a meet-the-management-get-together (in attendance: band leader, hotel manager plus secretary and, of course, the plucky songbird herself), it fell to Sister 'Lemony' to account for de Vol-au-Vent's 'condition'. With her crucifix prominently displayed in order to enhance her credibility in the piety stakes, she appeared appropriately meek and spoke in hushed, sincere tones. She explained, to the increasingly agog gathering, the sad tale of the Frenchman's injury: resulting from an unfortunate encounter with a giraffe. This misfortune was then compounded, it seems, by shoddy surgery carried out by an alcoholic French surgeon. And it didn't end there! Oh, no! Poor de Vol-au-Vent had, with quite unconscionable insensitivity, been tarred with 'The Order of Quasimodo' by his countrymen: resulting in his having to lead a life of ignominy wandering the by-ways of France as a beggar until he was spotted by a circus talent scout, and so on, and so on....... The reaction of Lemony's enraptured audience exceeded even her wildest dreams. They'd swallowed it hook, line and sinker; they were falling over each other in a competition to see who could express the most generous helping of sympathy. The welter of apologies was usefully accompanied with an: *"Our house is your house - Payment is not an issue - In fact, it would be an insult. - Your wish is our command, et cetera."* 'Lemony', quite dumbfounded by her own accomplishment, eventually managed to break free from the clutches of piety and excused herself to reflect on her guile with a feeling of sublime elation and relief. To be fair, she did suffer a slight pang of conscience at having deceived the natives, but reasoned that, firstly, her intercession on de Vol-au-Vent's behalf had probably accumulated huge numbers of paradise kudos points for her Uighur audience, and secondly, to have told the truth could really have put the kybosh on everything. Anyway, nothing that a few hail Marys couldn't redeem.

EPISODE TWENTY-THREE
Bingo!

The following morning, as the troupe headed out of the hotel to their waiting pumpkin, the manager was on hand to see them off. He was a pleasantly rotund, delightfully endearing chap, and detained de Vol-au-Vent for some time, harrying the groggy and bilious amphibian with a barrage of niceties; it wasn't really the best time of day insofar as de Vol-au-Vent was concerned. Things did become momentarily awkward when it came to handshakes, but de Vol-au-Vent, who was by now beginning to feel increasingly nauseous, took the matter in hand, as it were, and climbed aboard. As they pulled away, they could see the flummoxed gentleman receding into the distance through the rear-view mirror inspecting his digits in some detail: first the palm, then the back, then the palm again.

"*What does he expect? Horns to grow!*" commented de Vol-au-Vent settling into the seat between de Ath and Lister-Jag. Their grail was now just a mere six miles away.

Six Miles or not, sometimes it felt like sixty. It wasn't so much that the road undulated. No. You could have laid a spirit-level from the town of Turpan all the way to Yarkhoto, and the bubble wouldn't have budged from dead centre. The thing was that it was so rutted and littered with potholes that one could be forgiven for thinking that an air raid had recently taken place. The driver seemed quite unconcerned by these hazards, and the terminal damage being done to the suspension, let alone the effect the ride was having on his passengers; it was like the fun fair ride from hell!

"*Reckon this guy is on Mercury Oxide or something.*" quipped de Ath, referring to the ancient Chinese practice of dosing up the troops with the poison prior to going into battle in order to induce a kind of maniacal tunnel vision - all the better to kill you with!

No sooner had the words left his lips than the vehicle lurched skywards leaving de Ath temporarily conversing with the ceiling of the wagon. At this particular juncture, three things took place at once (physics is a funny ole business, don't ya dink?): the vehicle made contact with terra firma once more (sooner than desired in de Ath's case), the good doc corresponded by plummeting back down to his seat, and, just to reassure all present that he was actually sentient, the driver hit the anchors! Ah, the magic of the trilogy! The combined effect of this sublime coincidence of natural forces was that de Ath's seat acted not unlike a trampoline at a forty-five degree angle. This in turn resulted in the doctor resembling a human cannonball as he shot forward in the direction his good lady; in potential-collision-slow-mo-time, he saw Callista taking up an increasing amount of his field of vision like some romantic Hollywood clinch, the only difference being that her facial expression betrayed the fact that she didn't appear to be relishing their coming together at all. In real time, his right arm shot out like greased lightning, and he grabbed the first thing that came to hand so as to minimise the impact. Indeed, the impact was reduced to such a degree that it never even happened. However, de Ath's misfortune was that the device he had employed in the emergency was the handle of the sliding door. The driver, by now entirely in synch with the dazed de Ath, decided all was well and he could hit the gas again. In doing so, the doc, still firmly attached to said handle, flew back onto his seat dragging the door open as he went. Strange the thoughts one has in such situations; de Ath had begun to toy with the notion of the driver and himself embarking on a career as ballroom dance partners, so immaculate was their timing. The cries of shock from the others at seeing the open door kicked the driver's brain back into gear, and he hit the brakes yet again, but harder! It goes without saying that de Ath had by then grown accustomed to this novel and dynamically interactive approach to travel, however, by this time he was no longer clutching the door handle. Again, he assumed the role of maverick projectile, but, now that he was in hands-free mode, he lacked any form of stabilising influence, with the result that he promptly ricocheted off the doorpost next to Callista, and flew serenely out into the void.

Now, you are probably thinking to yourself *"Here we go, Dun Huang revisited. Some unspeakably bizarre thing is going happen to the doc."* Well, yes and no. In actual fact (strange word: fact), de Ath's flying lesson came to a rather abrupt end when he landed in the ditch next to the road - if that's the right word. Considering the acrobatics involved, he felt fine, but as yet was unable to assess any damage that may have been inflicted upon his skeletal structure. The reason for his lack of motion was not unrelated to the fact that he had found himself involved in a staring match: eyeball to eyeball no less, with China's answer to the Diamond-Backed Rattler - minus rattle. Inasmuch as the doc really didn't want to encroach on what was clearly the snake's territory, he nevertheless found his muscles quite unresponsive to his wish to give way to his newfound acquaintance. Something beyond his wishes had taken over the neuro-command-and-control-system. The snake, however, determined to take a more active approach to dealing with this immense and uninvited imposition, duly raised its head from its coil, arched its neck, displayed its fangs, and hissed! By then of course, it was much too late for the doc to escape, there seemed barely enough latitude to even flinch and get away with it, and so, he decided not to. He just kept trying to outstare his apparent nemesis; actually, his birth sign on the Chinese zodiac was the snake, so he ought to have known a thing or two about coping in such a situation, don't you think? The snake arched yet further in preparation for the final strike, but had delayed for too long (maybe de Ath did know a thing or two after all.). Unlikely though it may seem, this was the precise moment that the backdrop framing our venomous friend changed from a vista of the ditch stretching out into the distance beyond to a solid curtain of mud encrusted, rusty steel; the snake's head responded to this change of setting by promptly slumping to the ground. Now they were both motionless but, in de Ath's case, he was still breathing. He looked up to find himself being looked down upon by a gnarled, weather-beaten but beaming Uighur face. He wasn't entirely convinced the situation couldn't have been resolved via hypnosis rather than violence, or even employing shock tactics by planting the weapon between the two adversaries, but hey, it wasn't his field. Doubtless it was his astrological sign that induced this feeling of empathy for the snake. Nevertheless, the doctor pulled himself together and shook hands enthusiastically with the Turk.

So, what had happened to bring about the creature's demise? Well, our beaming Uighur-Turk saviour had been pottering around in the field adjacent to the road when he heard all the commotion emanating from the passing minibus, and duly hot-footed it over to the vehicle just in time to see the airborne Scot performing his crash-landing in the ditch. Upon arrival at the accident site, the farmer immediately assessed the situation, raised his spade, and brought it down, with some considerably severe force, cutting straight across the equator of the snake's coil. In one fell smite then, a completely reconfigured collection of dissociated snake parts was despatched to reptilian paradise. *"Shame really."* reflected de Ath as he returned to the vehicle. Whilst he wasn't too keen on the venom, he actually had nothing against snakes as such. In fact, he found most of them rather attractive. The misfortune, he felt, was of course compounded by the fact that the farmer, being of the Mohammedan persuasion, was unlikely to cook the creature for dinner. Something the Han Chinese wouldn't have batted an eyelid over; no squeamishness, religious legislation or waste where they were concerned.

"Well, that was stimulating. Don't suppose anyone fancies a spot of snake for tea?" Having dusted himself off, de Ath was now on board again, door firmly closed behind.

"Such insouciance from one so hot-blooded." reflected Lister-Jag (*"Clearly traumatised."* she thought).

"Can't help thinking that we're not meant to get there." added Lemony reassuringly.

Minutes later, snakes, spades and potholes became a distant memory.

"Look, there it is!"
"Yarkhoto!"
"Jiao He!"
"The Place Where Two Rivers Meet!"
"Shambhalah!"

EPISODE TWENTY-FOUR
'Abduction of a Lady with her Porcelains'

It was far from difficult to see why the Turpan Depression had become such a hub on the Silk Road. Despite its unlikely setting in the ferociously arid context of the northern Tarim basin, the cistern system (much the same as that found in parts of Iran) carried the melt-water runoff from the local mountain ranges: the depression itself acting not unlike a huge well thus facilitating access to the aquifer for the agricultural community from classical to modern times. Quite unlike anything to be found in the barren sands of the surrounding Taklamakan, here: melons, pomegranates, figs, cucumbers et cetera flourished, and to continue, alongside grew nuts and staple grain crops, not to forget of course cultivation of the ubiquitous grape, the use of which - due to the strictures that have applied since the arrival of

Islam to the region - has been limited to the production of raisins. Pity. There were many oases along the arduous route linking East and West, but few could contend with the extensive abundance of this land where the rain never touched the ground. Furthermore, its location on the Silk Road could not have been more timely for parched caravans journeying to and from China, the Middle East and the Central Asian Steppes. Perfect quarry from which to raise healthy revenue.

Of the many survival skills that we humans have mastered in our short history, that of communication surely ranks highest on the list - and if one can make a healthy profit from it so much the better. Therein lies the very keystone of the Silk Road's success story. However, to regard this well-trodden conduit as an artery for the trade in drapery goods from Chang An (China's capital in classical times: today's Xian) to Rome, and Europe in general, over a two thousand year period would be to undersell it on three counts: geographical, historical, and in terms of the nature and significance of what passed along this arduous highway: the bottom line.

Firstly, yes it did link up the classical and mediaeval worlds of Europe and China, but not simply by means of one convenient line on the map that traversed the sands and snows of Asia. Moreover, it wasn't only Greece and Rome that China made contact with; in fact, it was Central Asia and Iran that acted as the main axes of trade to and from all points of the compass. Imagine if you will, a hypothetical caravan trip from east to west during the Han Dynasty (206 BC – 220AD). Having journeyed up the Gansu Panhandle from Chang An, one is confronted by the challenge of the Taklamakan; here, one can either skirt it along its northern or southern edges – both of these routes linking up again at Kashgar to the west end of the desert. If one wished however, the caravan could opt to move north-west from Turpan, and, travelling via Urumqui, pass through the Dzungarian Gates into Uzbekistan to the Kazakh Steppe and Russia beyond. Alternatively, if on the southern route, one could opt to head south to Khotan, traverse the Karakoram Pass, and enter India via Kashmir. But, to continue on our trail westward after Kashgar, whether we have decided to negotiate the Pamir and Hindu Hush ranges, or to follow the banks of the Oxus, another web of possibilities opens up in Iran. Again, we may choose to make our way over the Kazakh Steppe by way of Turkmenistan, and pass via the north of the Caspian into Russia, instead though, to the south, we may prefer to strike out for Isfahan, Shiraz, and eventually the Persian Gulf. Should we, however, maintain our journey west, yet more vistas open up to the south of the Caspian Sea and the Elborz Mountains around Teheran. At this point, we have the possibility of making for Baghdad, and thence to the Arabian Peninsula, Syria, Palestine and Egypt, or we could continue west by skirting either the Mediterranean or Black Sea coasts of Anatolia – ultimately crossing into Europe over the Bosphorus. But there again, we could always head off through Georgia, hug the north-east of the Black Sea, and get to know the Ruskies a bit better. Finally, it should also be pointed out that not only did the Silk Road link China with Europe, the Middle East, Central Asia and India, but it provided Mongolia, Manchuria and Japan with connections to other parts of Asia too.

None of the above, of course, takes into account the maritime trade routes that were operating at the same time: and which were in part responsible for the eventual demise of the Silk Road on land. It has been suggested that as far back as the Han Dynasty, sea routes were active between China, South East Asia and India. There is certainly later evidence of this, even reaching as far as the Arabian Sea, the Red Sea, the Nile, the Mediterranean, and eventually to Byzantium, Venice and Rome. The Chinese were no mean sailors, and by around the time of the Yuan (1279 – 1368 AD) and Ming (1368 – 1644 AD) Dynasties, some historians have it that they, during the Ming in particular, were the first to circumnavigate the globe: with remnants of their ships being located as far afield as the Caribbean. And these ships were not your mere pint-sized little Chinese junks; they were seriously big barques! *"A ship carries a complement of a thousand men, six hundred of whom are sailors and four hundred are men-at-arms; including archers, men with shields and crossbows, who throw naphtha .... The vessels have four decks, which contain rooms, cabins and saloons for merchants; a cabin has chambers and a lavatory, and can be locked by its occupants."* according to Ibn Battuta. Europe never came close to building vessels of such dimensions for centuries. It was the rough equivalent of the Chinese sailing around in ships the size of Nelson's flagship, HMS Victory (crew complement around eight hundred and fifty), at the same time that the Europeans were pootling about in toys little bigger than Drake's Golden Hind (crew complement around eighty to eighty-five). For those who wish to visualise precisely what kind of difference we are talking of here, go to the South Bank in London, and there you will find a reconstruction of the Golden Hind - just a little downriver from the recently rebuilt Globe Theatre. Then, take a trip to Portsmouth, where one can be confronted by HMS Victory. Quite a difference!

From its early days during the Han Dynasty, or so some Chinese historians would have it, the Silk Road became the most prominent and influential conduit for commercial, cultural, scientific, philosophical and religious exchange throughout a period of over 2000 years. 'War is the mother of invention', and no less so in the apparent establishment of this great artery; military expediency, we are led to believe, laid the foundation stone.

The Han Dynasty emperor Wu Di (reigned 141- 87 BC) had learned of the famed 'Celestial Horses' (aka: Horse Dragons of Ferghana): larger, stronger and faster than anything the Chinese of the day possessed, and determined to avail his empire of such an invaluable weapon with which to deal with the restive Xiong Nu tribes to the north. All this does, however, rather beg the question as to how examples of the product of Chinese sericulture ended up in ancient Egyptian grave sites predating Wu Di by almost a thousand years. Nor does it explain how the world's oldest carpet so far discovered, a Persian one, was found in a Siberian grave dating back some three to four hundred years before Wu Di was born. Equally, it doesn't account for the existence of mummies with apparently western features found in the Tarim Basin at Loulan dating back to around 2000 BC, and at Cherchen going back to 1000 BC (this area having been quite lush, and supporting a healthy agriculture back then). But we'll leave it to the Chinese to resolve those particular little conundrums of their own making. In fact, what appears to have happened was that the envoy Wu Di despatched to Ferghana to obtain the Celestial Horses actually discovered that there was already a pre-existing and thriving trade in silk and other goods going on along the route between Chang An and Central Asia. Furthermore, not only did Zhang Qian (Wu Di's roving emissary) happen upon this east west trade, but, on a later journey, he also became aware that the people of Sichuan had been trading in silk with the Burmese for at least two hundred years prior to Wu Di's arrival on the scene; according to recent finds and research, these examples of international free enterprise owed their beginnings not to the silk trade, but in fact to that done in jade. These jade merchants, it seems, go back not just hundreds of years before the Han Dynasty, but thousands! However, what Wu Di and the Han dynasty did contribute to the Silk Road - always with an eye on the main chance - was a system by which to supervise and tax this clearly highly profitable mercantile adventure by using passports and inventories of goods being trafficked. It should be added that apart from the introduction of a tax regime, and the enhancement of Wu Di's stable with the Celestial Horses, China became acquainted with grapes, rhino horn, sesame seed, onions, cucumbers, coriander, and alfalfa for the first time during the Han: the alfalfa was imported for the survival of the Celestial Horses. It is of course not uncommon for nation states to feather their imperialist caps by attempting to take the credit for inventing this or discovering that. Take for example the delusion that afflicts many French people in connection with the establishment of a canal link between the Red Sea and the Mediterranean. Apparently, it was this great European colonialist power that was responsible: conveniently neglecting the fact that it pre-existed Alexander of Macedon – the Pharaoh

Senusret III having constructed a canal linking the Red sea to the Nile as long ago as the 1860s BC! Speak to the French though and you may find yourself being convinced that they invented everything, whereas of course, as anyone with a half a brain and a decent education knows full well, it was the British who invented everything.

Suffice to say that the history of the Silk Road doubtless stretches back to whenever merchants first recognised there were commercial benefits to be gained by taking up the gauntlet, loading up a few camels, and trafficking goods back and forth across some of the world's most inhospitable environments. Indeed, it is also pretty unlikely that goods remained with a given caravan from the initiation of their passage to their ultimate destination. Much more probable is that points enroute (Turpan and Khotan, etc) acted as marshalling yards for reloading merchandise on to other caravans to termini elsewhere. This achieved, the portals to Central Asia, Persia, Syria, Egypt, Europe and India began to open up.

The Sogdians of Samarkand appear to have been amongst the most significant players on the Silk Road stage from the Han right up until the end of the Tang Dynasty (618 – 907 AD). Apart from trading horses, alfalfa and grapes, they also introduced Sassanian silverware and glass objects, Baltic amber, and Mediterranean coral to the Chinese. Additionally, the Sogdians were the first to benefit from the breaking of the Chinese monopoly on paper manufacture, sericulture, and the weaving of silk cloth; thus making them instrumental in the transfer of such knowledge to Europe. Knowledge and philosophy were other commodities that the Sogdians became a conduit for: Persian Zoroastrianism and Parthian Manichaeism to name but two creeds. Manichaeism is of particular interest, since not only did it become the national religion of the then nomadic Uighurs, but it also employed a Syriac script; much later, this script seems to have been passed on to the Mongols, thus introducing these orally based nomads to the wonders of the written word. Buddha too meandered his way along the Silk Road from Nepal to China, dressed in Grecian robes by Kushan and Gandharan artisans (who were so influenced by the Hellenic artistic styles left by the descendents of Alexander's army in India and Afghanistan, and in turn defined the way in which the Buddha is depicted today).

By the time that the Tang Dynasty entered the scene, the Sogdians had become such a regular feature in the mercantile landscape of China that the names Kang and An had become Chinese surnames (Kang signifying someone hailing from Sogdia, or Samarkand, and An being a person of Parthian extraction – An Xi was the Chinese name for Parthia). Just as Chinese silk, Jade, papermaking, and porcelain production techniques, woodblock printing, compasses and gunpowder, etc spread to the West, so Iranian haute couture and cuisine became all the rage at the Tang Dynasty court. Along with sports such as polo, new kinds of musical instruments, exotic Middle Eastern dances, turbans, and Persian knotted carpets, etc, the high and mighty became acquainted with Iranian spinach, sugar beet and pistachios, Mediterranean mustard, cotton and saffron from India, Bactrian camels and Lapis Lazuli from Central Asia, and, possibly most notable of all, the chair. Up until the arrival of the 'Barbarian Bed', as it was known in China, the Chinese had utilised mats for sitting on; it seems most probable that this now most common of household objects may have found its way to China from the Byzantine Empire. More likely though: Egypt.

Even when the juggernaut of the Mongol hordes took over in the early Thirteenth Century – going on to establish the Yuan Dynasty, and an empire stretching as far as the Mediterranean – the Silk Road still flourished. After the initial disruptive bloodletting of the Mongol expansion, considerable political stability prevailed and it returned to business as usual. It was though no longer an artery that linked up the loose collection of nation states and tribes lying along it, but one that traversed and served the giant Mongol superpower. In the 14th Century, however, it often fell victim to power struggles between various members of the royal family. Particularly notable was the feuding, firstly, between Kublai and Ariq, his younger brother, and later, with Kaidu, Kublai's nephew. This latter struggle led to major splits in the empire, eventually producing divisions involving Kublai's Yuan China, Kaidu's realm in Eastern Turkestan (Central Asia), the Il Khans in Persia, and the Golden Horde in Southern Russia. They were all vying for Kublai's position: the ultimate crown, and the supreme position of Great Khan. After all, he'd gone native and become Chinese, hadn't he? But he was just too damned smart for all of them. There was, of course some justification, as they saw it, for the old guard thinking what they did of him, since Kublai seemed to spend virtually all his time preoccupied with affairs in the Middle Kingdom. However, to be fair, the bureaucratic demands posed in managing such a populous and productive region required not only considerable time and attention, but elaboration on, and sophistication of, the administrative structures laid down by his grandfather, Genghis. The competing princes really had little patience with all this nonsense. During Kublai's tenure, nevertheless, China managed to sidestep much of this family bickering, and it remained a desirable place of residence for artisans, engineers, medics, and a multitude of other talents, coming from all over Asia.

The Silk Road eventually outlived its usefulness though once the power of the Borjigin family had declined, and the Europeans had taken to the water on their colonial adventures. In China, it atrophied not long after the collapse of the Yuan and the coming of the Ming Dynasty's isolationist policies – despite the voyages of the intrepid Admiral Zheng He to the Persian Gulf, East Africa and the Red Sea. Neither indeed was its survival aided by the Black Death, nor by the dead hand of religiously intolerant Central Asian Islamic regimes (which had by then cast its crippling shadow over Central Asia and Western China); all of these factors (the most significant perhaps being that of the European navigators) contributed to the Silk Road's withering completely as a major trade artery. This trade had been partially shut down on previous occasions: most notably by the Sassanians during their conflict with the Romans in an attempt to ruin the empire's economy by remote attrition. Once this tactic had proved itself a success though, the route was opened up again. Not so after the Yuan though, by then things had moved on.

"If the Chinese were to lengthen their collars by half an inch, it would keep Britain's mills in business for the next 300 years." So, apparently, said a Yorkshire mill boss during Queen Victoria's reign. In an amusing little footnote to our Silk Road history then, we find ourselves transported to the mid-nineteenth century at the time of The Opium Wars – or was it: 'The Rhubarb Wars'? Britain had for some time been profiting rather nicely, thank you very much, from her concerns in India, and reckoned that China would perhaps be a useful addition to her business portfolio. The Chinese, for their part (always justly mistrustful of outsiders meddling in their affairs), wished to have nothing to do with such 'Foreign Devils', and duly gave the Brits two fingers. London's response to this was to embark on an adventure which, in today's terms, amounted to little more than state sponsored organised crime. In short, they began exporting the Indian poppy harvest to China in order to get the Chinese hooked on opium, and thereby open the door to more lucrative trade in other commodities. The Chinese, needless to say, did not take kindly to these drug pushers hanging around outside their primary schools – with the result that Peking went to war with London over it. Now, certain mandarins at the Chinese court seemed to be quite confident of success because they knew that Peking was in possession of a secret weapon: rhubarb. Yes folks, rhubarb! The thing is that rhubarb had been one of the many valued goods that China had exported along the Silk Road to the West for centuries, and it was highly prized in Europe for its laxative qualities – just as opium was, inversely, renowned as a cure for diarrhoea. Apparently, entirely unaware that rhubarb had been being cultivated in Europe for some time prior to The Opium Wars (in fact, there was even a variety named after Queen Vic herself), the aforementioned court officials seem to have calculated that if they were to deprive the interlopers of said purgative, the Brits would become so excruciatingly constipated (as a result of their love of opiates) that they would surrender in agony! The upshot of it all was that

Peking lost, and Britain, along with various other European powers, and the Americans, got their cantons and trade concessions – rhubarb proving not to live up to its potential as the weapon of war the Chinese had been hoping for. It is, however, amusing to imagine that perhaps, when confronted by this threat, a meeting of moustachioed, Victorian, military coves might have met up in Whitehall to discuss the question of rhubarb as a biological weapon.

Perhaps though, the Silk Road lives on even today. As any semi-conscious economist knows, the most valuable commodity that your average capitalist can invest in is cheap human labour: preferably sourced from areas of large and impoverished populations – and there is currently no shortage of that in the Far East - so, where has our journey taken us? From Jade Road to Silk Road to today's Sweat Road?

But, to return to Turpan. Although the burgeoning of this Silk Road culture was ultimately based on enhancing personal and national self-interest through the pursuit of patronage from local rulers, willingly or otherwise, it did breed a tolerance and acceptance of the new and exotic amongst the peoples that it touched, not least the Turkic groups of East, West and Central Asia - Turpan being a microcosm of this melting pot. To take but one example, the depression and surrounding area accommodated religious worshippers hailing from such aforementioned diverse backgrounds as Buddhism, Zoroastrianism, Manichaeism, Nestorian Christianity, Judaism and the Mongol cult of Tengri, often existing side by side at various stages during Yarkhoto's heyday; at least they did so until this permissive regime was bludgeoned into submission by the sword of Islam courtesy of the last prince of the Mongol Djaghatai Khanate. This intolerant, stifling and repressive policy of Khizr Khodja towards religious beliefs would be unlikely to have received the blessing of Genghis, had he been around at the time. Nor indeed was it a reflection of some of the more tolerant attitudes amongst followers of Mohammed in parts of the Middle East: such as the Baghdad Caliphate and in Moorish

Spain. Even during the era of the Crusades, Muslims (who had always been tolerant of both Jews and Christians in Palestine) continued to accommodate the invaders despite the treatment that was being meted out to them by these head-bangers who had 'taken the cross'. Who would you rather have been ruled by Saladin or Richard? I know what my answer would be. **("Before we become enmeshed in a diatribe about the Crusades, could we possibly get back to Yarkhoto? Ed)**

The city of Yarkhoto itself was not the only significant habitation in the Turpan depression. The Han Dynasty had also built a citadel known as Gao Chang (Kara Khodja, as it was called by the Turkics of the Tang era) some distance to the west of Yarkhoto. But what made 'The Place Where Two Rivers Meet' special was both its location and the way in which it was constructed, clearly with an emphasis on the need for defence. Unlike other cities of the day, Yarkhoto, for the most part, did not need to depend on walls to keep invaders out; it utilised the natural defences afforded by the fact that it was perched on a promontory that had sheer cliffs dropping away on three sides down to the valley below. Moreover, there were only two gateways, and with a civilian population of six and a half thousand, there was also a militia of some eight hundred and seventy odd soldiers. However, what made the city the exceptional place that it became (and still is in an architectural and archaeological sense) was the technique used in its construction. It was not built by building up but by digging down into the earth from the surface. Today, it remains the largest and best preserved earthen city in the world, with very little in the way of materials such as wood employed. Just to round things off, the defensive thinking also prevailed where the juxtaposition of residences and public buildings was concerned: access to which was not possible from the main public thoroughfares. Clearly, this was a place worth protecting. During the 13th Century Turpan City grew in importance, and Yarkhoto, along with its two thousand years of history, was finally abandoned at the beginning of the 14th Century. Despite the fact that today it lies in ruins, its preservation has benefited from the complete absence of rainfall, and the fact that it is largely sheltered from the desert winds; which means that what would otherwise, given its construction, be very vulnerable to considerable erosion, remains reasonably intact.

EPISODE TWENTY-FIVE
Reach for the Sky

It was truly a biblical looking landscape that lay before them. They had arrived! From outside, the ruins looked like a hodgepodge of the Monument Valley Buttes in miniature. However, despite its labyrinthine appearance, and notwithstanding the lack of any attempts at archaeological preservation, the surviving fabric of the city painted a sufficiently impressionistic picture for our friends to imagine what it might have been like before the site was abandoned over six hundred years previously. Nature had been kind. They split up into a couple of groups and meandered through Yarkhoto's nooks and crannies.

Quite serendipitously they later rendezvoused at a point overlooking the valley where the city's western cliff defence dropped vertically down to the river, acrophobics beware. It was approaching midday and the temperature was nearing meltdown, then........

"*Ecoute!*".......d' Vol-au-Vent.
"*What?*" ....Lemony Stirrup.
"*Iz zat a Merlin zat ah ear?*".......d'Vol-au-Vent.
"*Thought there was only the one.*"........Arbuthnot-Arbuthnot.
"*No, twenty-two thousand, excluding the Lancs and Mosquitoes et cetera.*"........d'Ath.

"What on earth are you boys on about now?"........Ricardo-Coutts.

"Yes of course, it's a Spitfire!"........Cholmondeley.

The lone Supermarine stormed overhead waving its wand through the air with an immaculate barrel-roll only a matter of a few feet above them before looping heavenwards through a solitary cloud. The backdraught kicked up vortices of sand across the Old Testament landscape.

"Sacre bleu! Ici! Pourquois?" exclaimed a bewildered de Vol-au-Vent,

"Your guess is as good as mine matey, but I do love the sound of that Rolls Royce engine: somewhere between a cello and a double bass, don't you think?" said de Ath.

"Per Ardua Ad Astra!" whooped an enthralled wing commander looking up with outstretched arms.

"Steady on Reg!" said Lister-Jag in an attempt to curb the wing commander's exuberance as he strayed backwards perilously close to the edge of the cliff.

It was at that moment that Callista spotted something leaf-like flailing around turbulently before finally making up its mind to float earthwards.

"Good heavens, it's a leaflet drop!" shouted an amazed Ricardo-Coutts.

"Bloody marketing campaign gone off course, I expect." quipped a flippant de Ath.

"Either that or they are warning us that the bombers are on their way." fretted Stirrup.

Fortunately, the object eventually made the sensible decision and touched down nearby, narrowly avoiding an excursion over the precipice. Our intrepid gang walked tentatively over to where it had settled. What they retrieved was a large manila envelope with **'For Claude: Marquis de Vol-au-Vent'** and signed **'V. Duc d'Vol-au-Vent'**.

"Incroyable!" said de Vol-au-Vent as he cautiously extracted a quadrangular sheet of parchment covered in bizarre symbols contained within geometric patterns.

At first, they were unsure as to which way was up, but it was only when de Vol-au-Vent spied the unmistakable signature of Dr John Dee along one side of the document that its bizarre hieroglyphic mist began to clear, if only partially. It was a message written in Dee's 'Language of Angels'. Now, they had yet another cipher to deal with.

"*What are you looking at me for? I still haven't made any sense of the last one.*" complained Arbuthnot-Arbuthnot.

"*It's okay. I think I can understand it.*" Stirrup came to the rescue.

"*Moi aussi.*" de Vol-au-Vent joined in.

"*Give us a while to consult, and we'll see what we can come up with.*" said Stirrup.

Thenceforth, a decoding huddle formed between Claude and Sister Lemony. Only they seemed acquainted with Dee's meanderings; thus, the task was left to their expert offices. The good sister had become a covert student of the occult at her Sikkim convent, not only to alleviate the tedium (doubtless it had been a kind of sex substitute), but also to get one over on the mother superior: "*I'll teach her who's superior!*" she muttered as she cast her spells through the night in the shadow of Katchenjunga. This then is how Lemony achieved proficiency in Dee's mystical script. De Vol-au-Vent couldn't remember how he had learned it. Either he was being cagey or his conversation with the Uzbek had affected more than just his thumb.

A short time later, the message had been revealed to them, and de Vol-au-Vent and Stirrup went into double-act mode.

"*So, who is this Dr John Dee character?*"........Callista.

"*Dr who?*"........Lister-Jag.

"*No, Dee. Ee vas Queen Elizabet ze First of Angleterre'z advisor on ze matters mystical.*"........Claude.

"*So, what revelations does he have for us?*"........Reg.

"*Not sure if you'll believe this.*"........Lemony.

"*Try us.*"........de Ath.

"*Very well then. He says 'Beware the Daleks of Amdo's Golden Dawn'.*"........Lemony.

"By ze vay, vat iz zis Dalek thing? You never explain zat to moi."……Claude.

"This Dalek 'thing' is the most colossally fearsome, destructive power ever to have graced the post-classical futurism of our very existence. They are merchants of chaos and devastation, wreaking havoc and death wherever their shadows are cast! The only creative act these recidivists from Hades have ever accomplished is to increase the population of zombies that wander the wastelands of our twilight zone. In short, they are the very emissaries of Satan." ……Lemony.

"So, ve'd better give zem a berse vyde zen?"…….Claude.

"Not quite as simple as that I'm afraid. It seems, according to the parchment, that the incinerated remains of a prosthetic Dalek brain were found preserved in a glass orb laced with Black Zircon containing traces of Osmium and Iridium. It resulted from the massive meteorite impact in Tunguska in 1908, and was discovered at the centre of the Siberian crater. Dee also points out that the immense heat undergone by the Dalek's grey matter has rendered it, in combination with equal quantities of the crystalline Black Zircon of the glass it is encased in, as the only known antidote to the malign concoctions and libations brewed at the Kum Bum Lamasery." ……Lemony.

"Poppycock!"…….Lister-Jag.

"My God! Titus! The elixir!"……..Callista.

"Precisely."……..Reg.

"All is not lost apparently. It seems that Dee has anticipated this, and provided instructions as to how we may acquire the aforementioned cure."……..Lemony.

"Tally Ho!"…….. the doc.

"Very vell zen. Our first port of call is zis Eavenly Lake, et once zere, ve must rendezvous with a gentleman oo goes by ze sobriquet of Yul Khan. Ve need not look for im, ee will find uz, according to ze mystic doctor."……..Claude.

"Apparently, said Yul Khan will provide us with a quantity of this remedy, and thence, we should take it post haste to Kum Bum."……..Lemony.

"Tosh! This is really becoming entirely too much."
……..Lister-Jag.

Needless to say, the return journey to Turpan was not entirely glitch-free. Well come on, what did you expect? Since time was obviously getting to be at something of a premium for our intrepid sextet, it was by then late afternoon, and they had had to divert their focus to Heavenly Lake; the unanimous decision, therefore, was that they would have to pass up on the possibility of taking in the nearby Bezeklik Caves. It wasn't that the caves wouldn't have provided yet more food for thought, it was simply that they felt duty bound to saving Titus from his misguided self, particularly as they now seemed to have discovered a potential antidote to the machinations of the management up at Kum Bum. Bezeklik was, after all, yet another Buddhist shrine, and they had already experienced quite enough fun at Dun Huang to last a lifetime, thank you very much.

EPISODE TWENTY-SIX
Yet Another Brief Historical Intermission

Construction on the Bezeklik Caves had begun around the sixth century AD, reaching completion some three hundred years later, and represented the period when the Uighurs and other Turkic tribes of the region had become converts to the Buddhism flowing into the Tarim Basin courtesy of the expanding influence of the Kushan and Gandharan Empire. It seems that Bezeklik was not graced by the massive statues of the type to be found in places like Bamiyan and Dun Huang; consequently, de Ath and Ricardo-Coutts supposed that the remains would doubtless be characterised by small shrines in which much of the artistry on the walls had been obscured by soot - as was the case with the numerous lesser caves at Bamiyan, and, to some extent at Dun Huang. De Ath had originally put this blackening down to the Philistine excesses of demented, fundamentalist Mohammedans during the initial flushes of Islam's expansion. There may have been a modicum of truth in this assumption given that so many Muslims seemed to regard the representation of the human form to be such a taboo; in fact, like the Iranians, who had produced many great paintings that included people in them, he had yet to find a passage in the Koran forbidding such depiction. The majority of blame for this vandalism, however, lay elsewhere.

During the upheaval of the 1917 Russian Revolution, the border between Russia and the Central Asian Turkic lands was porous to the point of virtual non-existence, with the consequence that the White Russians fleeing from Trotsky's Red Army utilised the ancient Buddhist shrines in Bamiyan as a staging post on their quest for sanctuary. Result: camp fires being lit in the caves. Whether or not the Bezeklik caves had been damaged by these fugitives, de Ath and Ricardo Coutts never did find out. What they were sure of, however, was that the caves had certainly been despoiled during the period of the Great Game (also referred to by the Russians as the 'Tournament of Shadows'. Don't ya jus love language sometimes? Ah yes: 'The Tournament of Shadows'), which endured throughout the nineteenth century. This was ostensibly a clandestine rivalry between Tsarist Russia and the UK for control over Central Asia; the British hoping to use the area as a buffer zone between their Indian interests and the Ruskies, who, in turn, wanted to establish a gateway to the subcontinent in order to take advantage of what the East India Company had already got its mitts on. Basically, it was open day for Europeans of a variety of hues to take advantage of the Turkic lands between Iran and China. The whole exercise was cloaked in that typical euphemism so common to espionage: surveying and map-making, with many of the individuals involved doubling up as archaeologists and ethnographers. This is not to suggest that the likes of Sir Aurel Stein, Major General Nikolai Przhevalsky, Pyotr Kuzmich Kozlov, Sven 'I have been in love many times, but Asia remained my bride' Hedin, Paul Pelliot and many others did not do sterling work; they were indeed pioneers in the exploration of Central Asia from the European standpoint: preserving many of its artefacts, and greatly increasing our understanding of the area's history. We know already of Aurel Stein's activities at Dun Huang, at Bezeklik however, the pillaging (sorry, meant 'collecting') was carried out by a German chap going by the name of Albert von le Coq (no joke, folks, it truly was his name). Von le Coq spent his time in Turpan by stealing Buddhist and Manichean icons, and hacking paintings from cave walls. These 'borrowings', as he modestly describes them, were done out of 'necessity'; seemingly to protect these priceless artefacts from the people who had largely ignored them for centuries. How thoughtful! Ultimately, this act of cultural vandalism led to the items being placed for 'safe keeping', as Von le Coq put it, in the Berlin Ethnographic Museum, where they were blown to smithereens during the Second World War. Funny old world. Oh, also noteworthy is the fact that Albert 'The Art Lover' was apparently obsessed with establishing the origins of the Aryan people, so doubtless he indulged in a spot of phrenology too prior to retiring to his tent for the evening to soothe his soul with a little Wagner after a hard day's work with his trusty chisel, callipers and plaster of Paris.

Twentieth century politics had affects on the Uighurs of Xin Jiang too. As previously mentioned, the Georgian thug, Stalin, had little time for pastoral nomads, nor did Lenin or Trotsky for that matter, and regarded their lands as possessing potential for the development of arable collectives. After all, wasn't nomadism simply a stepping stone on the journey to settled agriculture? This crass delusion is surprisingly common amongst many who hail from a settled background, even amongst venerable members of the academic community. The fact is that steppe nomadism is entirely in harmony with its surroundings, and the technology and culture of these peoples have developed accordingly: no more or less sophisticated than required. Generally speaking, nomads tend to settle only when they move into lands more suited to the pastoral tradition, and the steppes are just so. Presumably though, 'Uncle Joe' figured that he knew better, and was convinced that he would be doing these backward types a favour by accelerating their progress up the greasy evolutionary tree. Not to mention that there was very little historical good blood lost between Europeans (from regions such as Russia, the Ukraine, Poland and Georgia etc.) and the steppe nomads after the visitations of the Turko-Mongolian hordes. The result of this bonkers policy was that huge numbers of Kazakhs, in particular, fled the oppression and sought refuge with their kin across the border in Xin Jiang. Estimates of 300,000 fugitives are commonly quoted. This though was not such a serious impingement upon the settled Uighurs since the Kazakhs, like the Mongols, tended not to encroach on arable lands for their survival. What did give the Turkics of Xin Jiang serious pause for thought, however, came from a much more familiar quarter, far closer to home.

The Uighur-Turks appear to have started life as nomadic pastoralists in and around the Mongol Steppe at roughly the time of the Chinese Han Dynasty before eventually adopting a sedentary lifestyle further west some fifteen hundred odd years later. Some researchers have associated them with the Xiong Nu (Huns), but this remains unproven. What is beyond dispute, however, is the fact that they have been significant players at the roulette table of Central Asian political and cultural affairs for a very long time. Although since the late fourteenth century, they have been followers of the Mohammedan creed, they have also, as we know, embraced, Manichaeism, as well as acting as conduits for the dissemination of diverse religions amongst other cultures. At various stages in their history, they have established Turkic empires, and lost them; they have also run with the Mongol Hordes, and become victims of them. They have both helped the Chinese (the Tang Dynasty in particular), and suffered under them. The Chinese have, since time immemorial, had a tendency to regard all outsiders as either a threat or barbarians, and if you are of Muslim and Turkic origin, you have the distinction of qualifying in both categories.

During the first half of the twentieth century, China was in transitional disarray. Over two thousand years of monarchical rule in China came to an end with the collapse of the Manchu Qing Dynasty, and its replacement with the Republic. Upon the death of the popular Sun Yat Sen, Chiang Kai Shek took over the leadership of the ruling Kuo Min Tang Party with the result that China became riven with corruption and dominated by warlords - just like the good ole days. The Communist Party split with the Kuo Min Tang, and China eventually descended into even greater chaos - interrupted only by the Japanese invasion and the Second World War. **("Only? Only! What kind of joke is this? No comment on the mass medical experiments that the Yank High Command blessed?" Ed)** Mao and the Communist Party eventually prevailed at the conclusion of the civil war in 1949. It was during this period of conflict that a Kazakh leader by the name of Osman Batur declared Xin Jiang's independence from China, and the foundation of the new state of Eastern Turkestan. There had in fact been a succession of war lord types operating in the Xin Jiang area since the fall of the Qing Dynasty: Baron Roman von Ungern-Sternberg (a particularly nasty White Russian thug from Latvia), General Yang Zen Xin, and the rebel Ma Zhong Yin, to name but three who had designs on the area. None however, despite their belligerence, got as near to achieving a lasting independence as Osman seems to have with his slightly more diplomatic approach. Through negotiations with Chiang Kai Shek, Osman and the Turkic leadership accepted a promise of 'real' autonomy so long as Xin Jiang remained within the borders of China. This was a promise that Chiang could not keep, and doubtless never would have; it was certainly one that Mao had no intention of honouring. In 1949, a delegation of the separatist top brass died in a convenient plane crash on their way to negotiations with Mao, and in 1951, Osman himself was captured and beheaded in Urumqui – his surviving adherents eventually escaping to see out the rest of their days in Turkey. Much as Francisco Franco did in his subjugation of the Spanish Basques, Mao then embarked on a policy which amounted to little less than cultural genocide by suppressing all things Turkic and diluting the population with a flood of Han Chinese, who were induced by benefits unavailable to the Turkics, or other Han for that matter. The Han population in the province is today now on a par with what was once the largest group, the Uighurs, whose own population has plummeted to some 40% from around 90% of the area's pre People's Republic inhabitants. To compound all this, the Cultural Revolution brought executions, torture, imprisonment, political repression, and the destruction of mosques on an unprecedented scale.

It goes without saying that the Zhong Nan Hai leadership, always with an eye on the main chance, have naturally also taken full advantage of the carte blanche to persecute Muslims ever since the USA declared open season on mullahs. Oh, mustn't forget, the icing on the cake: since the sixties Xin Jiang has proudly hosted the testing ground for Peking's nukes, but we've covered that stuff already, haven't we? The Chinese leadership have such an exquisitely twisted sense of humour. As always, there's nothing really new under the sun, is there? One thing that is worryingly puzzling though: why is it that all those earnest campaigners for worldwide human rights are always banging on about those cuddly Tibetan types, yet seem blissfully ignorant of affairs concerning the Turkics in Xin Jiang, and almost entirely unaware that it is the very heartland of persecution in the People's Republic? Could there be a hint of Islamophobia here? Strange.

Above: The Turpan Big Band strikes up with some Turkic jazz standards.

Above: The walls of the furnace: Flaming Mountains in the Turpan Depression delineates the south side of this paradise of the Taklamakan.

Above: The East Gateway to Yarkhoto (Jiao He). Shambhalah? Yarkhoto, the world's largest surviving example of an earthen city. In its heyday it had a population of 6,500 and was guarded by some 870 troops; clearly there was something worth protecting.

Above: The 'Place where Two Rivers Meet'. Looking down from Yarkhoto's natural western defences. In the distance can be seen a section of Flaming mountains.

Above: Le Duc whips his machinery out. His Spitfire takes a well earned break between sorties over Burma.

Left: Local pharmacist, aka: 'The Purveyor of Dreams'.

Above: The approach of Mullah Nazrudin.

Above: Fatima arrives at the ICBM Centre to attend to the needs of our weary travellers.

Left: The other cult on offer in Turpan. Clearly somewhat past its 'sell by date' insofar as the Turks were concerned.

Above: A Buddha's eye view of the caravanserai at Bamiyan.

Right: An ageing Uighur weaves basket of mysteries.

EPISODE TWENTY-SEVEN
Musings with the Mullah

Hello again. Everything's back to normal, hope you didn't mind the rant. I will now be completing the adventure from this rather well-appointed prison cell. Needin' any new body parts? Okay, where were we? Ah yes.

They were approaching the outskirts of Turpan when Lister-Jag, who had decided to sit up front in order to be out of the way should de Ath embark on any more in-back-of-mini-bus physics experiments, noticed a red light flashing on the dash; all those years hanging around the pits were paying off again you see.
"Think you may be becoming a tad overheated, young man." she commented with a hint of urgency as she turned to the driver.
Said driver was duly shocked out of the hypno-mode that came over him whenever he sat behind a wheel. *"How did she know?"* he thought to himself whilst taking a quick glance down at his nether region.
"No, not that you dimwit! The engine!" Lister-Jag blurted out with a ribald laugh. Sure enough, no sooner had the words left her lips than the first hints of escaping steam began to billow from beneath the bonnet. The message having penetrated the driver's cranium, he pulled up and hot-footed it over to a neighbouring road house - returning with kettle in hand. He could only have been pouring for about five or so seconds when a most almighty crack resounded throughout the vehicle, and the engine promptly gave up the ghost.
"Holy Mother of God! I thought he was using hot water!" exclaimed Lister-Jag, *"What an undiluted buffoon! What a bloody comedy of errors!"* she rounded off.
They walked into town.

The walk had an agreeable effect: cleared the mind and got the stomach juices flowing. When they finally arrived in the main square then, they had worked up quite a healthy appetite. The tempting aroma of grilling kebabs that was wafting around in the early evening air decided for them.

"*Forget the hotel, let's just follow our noses.*" said the wing commander. His suggestion was not contested.

No-one cooks Kebabs quite like the Turks; they were truly delicious, as was the salad, bread, yoghurt, et cetera, et cetera. In fact, so good was it all that they felt unanimously obliged to go on a constitutional in order to recover from their gastronomic excesses. It didn't take long before they found themselves walking between flourishing cereal fields towards what appeared to bear a suspicious resemblance to a mosque built in the Afghan style on the eastern outskirts of the town.

"*Ah my friends, I was hoping to make your acquaintance.*" came the reassuringly pleasant tones.

They immediately looked around in the hope of providing some more material substance to the voice, and spotted a diminutive figure approaching on a donkey.

"*Welcome to our ICBM complex.*" the stranger continued.

"*Knew it was a missile silo soon as I clapped eyes on it. Just look at the shape of that bloody minaret!*" muttered the wing commander (donning his goggles) in an aside to de Ath.

"*ICBM?*" queried Ricardo-Coutts seeking clarification.

"*Yes Ma'am: the Institute of Caliph Berserker al-Mahdi, 'may the name of the Random One be praised'. It is the foremost centre in the land for the study, advocacy, and dissemination of Janbalani Sufism's divinely inspired Thirteenth Imam's teachings. Perhaps I may enjoy the pleasure of your company indoors awhile?*" said the mild mannered mullah look-alike.

"*We couldn't possibly impose.*" responded Ricardo-Coutts fully expecting to have to go through the traditional etiquette rigmarole.

"*Ah, my dear lady, your adherence to graceful formality is most gratifyingly commendable, and indeed, reveals your impeccable upbringing. However, whilst it is delightful to the recipient, such protocol may be dispensed with here. Come, allow me to entertain you. Oh, I almost forgot, how rude of me, I am Mullah Nasrudin the 'Diviner and Guardian of Histories'."* he said descending from his mount and extending a warm and welcoming arm in the direction of the mosque.

The mullah's endearing aura both captivated and intrigued the explorers, and they duly conformed with his invitation; it was an offer they felt they simply couldn't resist. His modest stature belied a disarming sense of mystery and mischief, nevertheless, he also emanated a control and confidence that they found had a quite tranquilisingly magnetic effect.

"So, now we are seven. Most propitious. A number that always augurs success." Mullah Nasrudin assured them as they sat shoeless on Mahan silk carpets around a Persian mangal. It should be pointed out that a mangal is a rather elegantly constructed bronze brazier (occasionally made of brass, or even silver, depending on how well appointed the abode one is residing in happens to be) utilised whenever friends are indulging in the steaming of opium.

"Mullah Nasrudin, perhaps if I may be so bold, I am curious to know how you, in your infinite wisdom, were so confident of our arrival. Why are we here?" enquired Lister-Jag.

"An excellent question, madam. Firstly, you are here because I am here, and secondly, I am here because you are here." he responded with a glint in his eye. *"In addition, I received a transmission on one of our secure channels some two or so days ago informing us that you would be attending these parts in the near future. The message came courtesy of one of our most eminent and devoted converts. It is my belief that you recently became acquainted, and spent a fruitful evening, with a distinguished erstwhile member of the Assassins whilst you sojourned in Dun Huang, is this not the case?"* said Nasrudin, who could have been mistaken for a cross-examining QC were it not for his impish visage.

"Yes, Hassan Babur." answered the wing commander.

"The very man." responded the cleric. *"Amongst other matters which we need not concern ourselves with at present, Babur pointed out that he had become aware of your having*

embarked on a quest for Shambhalah, 'may its name be eternally blessed'. Now, if you have no further questions, I would like to take you into our confidence. However, before doing so, I should point out that whatever you are apprised of in this room, and have already gleaned from the parchment in your possession - with the exception of the instruction to journey to the camp of Yul Khan at Heavenly Lake and thenceforth to Kum Bum - will be cleansed from your memories upon crossing the threshold when you depart. This you may deem to be something of an intrusion on your privacy, but, we have found through previous experience that what one does not know cannot hurt, and currently, you are aware of certain information which could have the most unfortunate consequences, not only for yourselves but for others should it fall into the wrong hands. If you are agreeable to this I will continue."

The stunned silence was broken by de Ath: "*Might as well go with the flow, I suppose.*"

"*How delightfully Daoist of you.*" said the mullah glancing in de Ath's direction. "*Very well then. May I be the first to congratulate you on the success of your quest, and welcome you to the Vale of Shambhalah; 'eternally blessed may be its name'. Your persistence has borne an abundance of fruitfulness. Furthermore, due to your consummate triumph, it gives me great pleasure to bestow upon you membership of the Third Degree Janbalani. Congratulations! Your receipt of the sacred parchment, your translation of it and your acceptance of my invitation completes the requisite trinity which confirms your initiation. As initiates on an assignment of such consequence, it is important, as I mentioned before, that you are not in possession of anything which may compromise either your mission or the cause. Therefore, I must request that you surrender the parchment. In substitution, I now give you this necklace. Upon arrival at Heavenly Lake, you will be approached by the great Yul Khan; His Eminence today masquerades as a Kazakh khan. I mean no disrespect by saying that he 'masquerades' as a Kazakh. The fact is that he is actually of Mongol descent but his family, through many generations, has acquired considerable prominence within Kazakh circles. In any case, when you reach Heavenly Lake, and in order to demonstrate your bona fides, you should give this necklace to him. In return, he will provide you with the antidote you seek. Without this, your mission is doomed to failure."*

Sister Lemony reached inside her shirt, extracted the parchment, and handed it over to Nasrudin in exchange for the necklace. Examining the object hanging from the gold chain, Stirrup asked: *"What's this?"*

"Looks like a Dervish double-headed axe to me." de Ath observed as he reflected on his time in Persia.

"Precisely, it is truly a pleasure to work with such well-informed initiates, you have no idea how retarded the usual fare we receive from foreign parts is. I daresay your SMOM heritage may not be unconnected with your knowledge in these matters." Nasrudin suggested to his by now bamboozled audience.

"I suppose that was just another little gem you picked up from Hassan." reasoned Ricardo-Coutts.

"Actually no. In fact, I occasionally take my summer breaks in Malta. I understand too that you yourself are descended from the family of the 'Saints of the Limitless and Unclouded Blue Sky', my Lady Callista. But more of that another time."

As Mullah Nasrudin picked up a long and decorative pair of tweezers lying beside the mangal, and delved into the ashes, Callista gave de Ath a sideways scowl as if to say: *"This is all your bloody fault, isn't it?"*

Having extracted a piece of incandescent charcoal with the implement, the mullah blew on it, and held it to the parchment. Once the parchment had been transformed, and become indistinguishable from the other ash in the mangal, Nasrudin said: *"Excellent, this concludes the formalities. Now we can relax and enjoy some of the more inspirational pleasures that it is our custom to indulge in here and wherever members of the Janbalani reside. Oh, before I forget, I should inform you that I have taken something of a liberty on the assumption that you would not object, and also because, in our experience, evenings of this type frequently become somewhat protracted. Earlier, the keeper of your current lodgings was asked to deliver your personal effects to the imaret here. I assure you nothing has been tampered with and everything was conducted with the utmost decorum and discretion. I believe you have met the gentleman in question; it goes without saying that he is one of us, and I apologise if I appear to have overreached myself, however, I feel sure you will find the imaret most commodious."*

Yet more confused looks before Ricardo-Coutts came to the rescue, *"Absolutely no problem at all. In fact, it is reassuring to know that we are in such capable hands."* she sighed with resignation, eyes rolling heavenwards.

"Thank you my noble lady, you are most diplomatic. Now I wonder if you are acquainted with these." said the master of ceremonies clapping his hands. Instantly, a young Turkic looking woman wearing Persian slippers and dressed from head to foot in a crimson silk salwar kameez with a matching dupatta draped over her head and shoulders entered the dimly lit room carrying a brass tray, and laid it at the mullah's side. *"Thank you Fatima. The imaret is prepared?"* The woman nodded. *"Very good, that will be all for this evening."* She closed the door silently behind her. *"Well?"* Nasrudin raised an inviting eyebrow in the direction of Ricardo-Coutts and de Ath.

"Yes of course, please excuse me, I became momentarily distracted. The thing is, aside from our sojourn with Babur, I haven't seen the Shah's cipher on a loole of opium in such a long while. And, if I may say so, that is the most exceptional collection of travelling pipes I have seen outside of Persia you have there." said a wide-eyed and drooling de Ath (fact is that he was rather taken by Fatima, if the truth be known).

"Ah, I feel we have much to talk about. Such a pity the musicians are entertaining down at The Oasis, otherwise we could also have indulged in some of the more exotic reels common to the Dervish tradition. I believe that the marquis is quite an exponent." said Nasrudin glancing in Claude's direction with a broad smile as he handed a pipe and a pair of zircon encrusted tweezers to each of them. Thenceforth, the

evening drifted from here to there and back again through passing clouds of narco-symbolism.

Nasrudin turned out to be a radiant font of information on religio-historical affairs: clearing up question marks over the relationship between the Templars, Sufism, the Turks, the Mongols and the Lame Uzbek - much to the doc's delight and Lady Callista's chagrin (Hell kneweth no satisfaction like de Ath's smugness). Apparently, so the story went, the good mullah confirmed that de Ath had been on the money in surmising that a troop of errant Knights had journeyed back to the relative sanctuary of the East in order to escape the treachery of the Franco-Papal conspiracy that had brought a rather hasty end to the Templars' Parisian residence permits. So what did the deserts of Syria and Palestine have to offer these chicly attired cavalry officers? Well, quite a lot actually. In fact, some forty-nine years prior to Philip IV's purge of the Templars, good relations were established between them and Hulegu: the Mongol Il-Khan of Persia as he eventually became. Although a follower of the Shamanist tradition himself, both his mother and his wife were Christians, and, as a result of his wife's successful intercession on behalf of the Christians during the 1258 sack of Baghdad (which brought an end to the Abbasid Caliphate), the Christians living in their city states along the Syrian and Palestinian coasts viewed Hulegu's insatiable thirst for Mohammedan blood as grounds for getting the bunting out in anticipation of his arrival. He duly obliged the following year and slaked his thirst yet again. This time on the Syrian Ayyabid Muslims. Not only that, but he had already enhanced his kudos with the Templars by 'sorting out' the order's old adversaries the Assassins in their Persian stronghold at Alamut. The foundation stone then for a diplomatic rapport between the Hordes of the East and the Templars had been laid. Prester John had arrived.

Soon thereafter, both Mongols and Templars suffered a series of calamities at the hands of the Egyptian Mamluks (expendable Central Asian, military slaves). Firstly, the Mongols were defeated at the battle of Ain Jalut during Hulegu's absence (he'd had to return to Karakorum for the election of a new Great Khan after Mönkhe's death, and foolishly taken a significant portion of his force with him). Then following quickly on the heels of this setback, Christian outposts began to tumble like dominoes: the last major action, as far as the Templars were concerned, being at Acre in 1291 - this too fell to the Mamluks. Whilst the death of the order's Grand Master Guillaume de Beaujeu during the siege is well documented, less publicised by Europeans is that not all the Templars who escaped the attentions of the Mamluks fled back to La Belle France. The embarrassing fact that France and Italy found so awkward to stomach was that a significant number of them made their way by ship to Anatolia and thence doubled back east to the sanctuary of the Mongol Il-Khanate in Persia. Although some recalcitrant Templar Castles had courageously stood out against the Mongols, the khan had been suitably impressed by their bravery. With their skills and background, it didn't take long before they established a reputation for honour and loyalty amongst the Mongol top brass, and in a short period of time, most of them rose to prominent positions within the Mongol Imperial Security Service: some eventually even becoming well-respected figures as far afield as the Yuan Royal Courts in Peking, Xanadu and Karakorum. In fact, there was nothing particularly unusual for these Frank Crusaders to form such alliances given that most of them had by that time come to regard the East as their homeland and pretty much gone native anyway. Indeed, there were even occasions when they had made pacts with local Muslim leaders in the Holy Land when it served mutual interests. So, by the time then that Philip gave the order in 1307 to lock up the Knights and raid the Templar bank vaults, a network of well-connected members of the order were well-placed enough to provide a leg up to the inner sanctums of the Mongol temples of power for their persecuted colleagues, stretching from Black Sea to the Yellow Sea. When, therefore, the Templar fleet slipped its moorings at La Rochelle on Philip's 'Night of the Long Knives', disappearing into the dark silence of European history, a welcoming party was there to receive them as anchors were dropped in the harbour of Mersin on the south-eastern Anatolian coast: the most easterly extreme of the Mongol sway. From here, a heavy escort of Mongol and Templar troops guaranteed safe passage to the Il-Khanate heartlands, stopping only to pay their respects to St Paul at nearby Tarsus, and to Hulegu at his grave on Kaboudi Island in Lake Urmia. Of particular interest was the cargo, containing not only much of the order's accumulated riches, but even more valuable were documents relating to matters of great sensitivity to the Catholic Church, as well as records of the order's financial dealings; all the better to eventually blackmail some of the treacherous members of the French nobility with (not to mention the fun they could have with the higher echelons of the church. If only they could be there to watch the cardinals squirm!).

In the generations that followed, it seemed that members of the order stayed in close contact with the seats of power throughout the empire. Indeed, although they remained very much in the background of political affairs, they nevertheless wielded considerable power. There was of course nothing unusual in this as the Mongols, once they had 'settled their differences with the locals', took a fairly cosmopolitan approach to their rulership of the various khanates (this practice owing itself to the principle of tolerance and meritocracy established in their legal code by Genghis himself). This is borne out by many of the appointments which were made by the khans. For example, Kublai appointed a Tibetan, Phags-pa, to devise a new script for the administration of the empire in order to deal with the ever increasing complexity created by ruling over so many diverse peoples with different linguistic backgrounds, and to avoid the accusation of favouritism by adopting a script hailing from a single source. Moreover, he assigned the task of constructing the royal palace in his new capital, today's Peking, to an Arab architect, Ikhtiyar al-Din. The Chinese suffered something of a fit of pique over this: *"Why should an Arab be heading up the planning and architectural design of a Chinese city?"* Naturally, they kept such thoughts very much to themselves. Another factor that doubtless incurred a touch of displeasure amongst the local Han mandarins was that Kublai also placed a fair number of Uighur Turks to positions of high rank within administrative circles. Foreign influence was not restricted only to matters civil though. During the campaign against the Song in southern China, when the 'cruise missile of the steppe', the horse-archer (with the composite reflex bow), proved unsuited to the terrain, Kublai appointed engineers from Persia to overhaul his artillery - with stunning results. So we see that Genghis' old tried and tested principles of promotion by merit, not by noble rank or nationality, was maintained by his grandson to great effect. This was an approach that not only irked the Han but the Mongol princes themselves, as we encountered earlier when discussing Kublai's perceived neglect of Mongolia in favour of his Chinese adventure.

Such open-mindedness also extended to religious matters; we already know the Mongols were extremely tolerant when it came to questions of freedom of worship. Khans set the example by not only marrying Buddhists, Christians and Muslims et cetera, but they themselves even converted; in particular the latter khans of Persia and Central Asia became followers of Islam. So too, such luminaries as the great Rashid ad-Din, chronicler of Mongol history, converted from Judaism to become a follower of the prophet Mohammed. Nor were the Templars immune to such a laissez faire approach to spiritual belief. Whilst numerous members of the order found themselves drawn into the Nestorian congregation, a number of Templars also gravitated to the traditions of Janbalani Sufism, and it was this which led them to the corridors of power in Amir Timur's reign over the Islamic world. Although Timur is better known for his later adherence to the ways of the Nusayris, he was brought up as a Jalanbani by his father; something that remained with him throughout his life. It was through this connection then that these Temlpar Sufis rose to become members of Timur's inner circle; amongst the posts that they filled, they were variously members of Timur's personal bodyguard, advisors on military strategy, Lord Keepers of the Treasury and confidants on matters of religion.

"Thus it may have been then, Mr Claude, that you came to see that singular piece of jewellery on the hand of the spectre. He, so the story goes, was initiated into Templar tradition and practices (the Templars themselves always maintained the unity and ways of the order despite their other more public religious affiliations), with the result that the 'Iron Son-in-Law of the Great Universal Ruler' became a Grand Master of the Knights Templar, albeit in a rather honorary ceremonial capacity. I hope then that all this answers some of the questions that have plagued your imaginations on this subject of the ring. I must remind you though, that, as initiates, you will no longer be privy to this history upon crossing the threshold of this room when you depart. I should also point out to you, however, that there is another caveat. Research into this aspect of Templar history is somewhat fraught due to the fact that most members of the order adopted aliases, usually of Persian origin, once they had embarked upon their new lifestyles in this part of the world, and thus, reliable confirmation of their activities is always open to question."

"No problem, I still think it's a load of deluded piffle anyway." whispered Dame Emily to Ricardo-Coutts and Stirrup.

"What are the odds that the next thing he says is: 'Today their descendents are all living up at some mountain retreat in Tannu Tuva as world champion throat-singers'!" Callista added with a wry smirk.

"Zis iz fantastique. May ah ask you, Mullah Nasrudin, av you ever met ze spectre of ze 'Iron Son-in-Law'?" enquired Claude.

"Indeed, I have had that honour." replied Nasrudin.

"And, if ah might be zo bold, vat did ee say to you?" Claude ventured further.

"Ah, yes, most memorable. 'Get out of my way, mullah!' is what he said." Nasrudin smiled as he glazed over with dreamy reflection.

EPISODE TWENTY-EIGHT
The Torn Fiver

"Nevertheless, I must inform you that this story of your knights is but a minor side-show, I believe you call it, when compared with what I am about to give you." enticed the mullah. *"The issue of the 'Iron-Son-in-Law' has more to do with the emptiness and inadequacy that Timur felt at not having been born into the fold of the Imperial Family of Genghis, but having had to marry into the royal blood as an outsider. Impotence, diminution of the gonads, absence of soul and all that. Allah! Blessed be his name. Hoda! Blessed be the Spirit of Mystery. How we have suffered under the 'Conjunction of the Eternal Nightmare': or, as he is remembered in our popular culture: 'The Ill-Considered Spirit of the Shrivelled Scrotum'."*

The room was lined in every direction with quite sumptuous Mahan silk carpets, finely carved teak furniture and utterly gorgeous decorative bronze fittings that reflected the quintessence of Persian and Turkic workmanship. Mullah Nasrudin rose and walked over to a dresser adorned with some of the most ornately carved geometric patterns de Ath had seen since he had strolled through the gardens of the Al Hambra in the company of the High Vizier of Granada. The good mullah didn't open any of the drawers or doors that may have seemed the more obvious choices, but reached down to the base and pulled open what, to all present had been theretofore concealed: a long narrow cradle, from which he withdrew what looked to all intents and purposes like the kind of baton that might have rested sceptresque over the forearm of a Roman emperor. He wrapped his palm around the bronze lion rampant handle, and returned the drawer to its invisibility.

Upon resuming his position at the mangal, amidst the steaming opium pipes, he held the object out horizontally in front of himself in both hands and said: *"My dear friends, distract yourselves not with tales of frivolity. Whilst your knights*

Templar may entertain the wish fulfilment of the gullible, what I am about to relate carries such weight that empires may be reduced to dust in the blink of an eye, no less than a spark from a twig may devastate the universe! In our discourses this evening, it has become clear to me that we have not met merely by chance. In 'The Secret History', chapter 69: 'Tales from the Tent of Clustered Fumes', it is written that an embassy of three men and three women from the 'Empire of the Bronze Binnacle' - sometimes also referred to as the 'Land of the Immortal Memory', and variously as the 'Islands of the Red Herrings', the 'Place over which the Banner of the Cluttered Crosses Flies', or, more popularly, the 'Pink Bits on the Map' - shall visit Shambhalah. It is my duty, therefore, to ask, is there any amongst you who is blessed by the name of a regal household pertaining to this heritage?" turning with raised eyebrow towards the wing commander as he said so.

"Now, look here old chap, no need to get carried away. Templar stuff, pretty rum business, don't you know. What with that bounder Philip et cetera." spluttered Arbuthnot-Arbuthnot.

"Listen Reg, just come clean!" Lister-Jag curtailed the issue.

"Okay. Fact is Naz. If I may call you that. Never entirely lived up to family expectations. Predecessors tried the odd coup and suchlike but didn't quite manage to pull it off." continued Arbuthnot-Arbuthnot.

His better half (on the verge of incontinent expectancy) again cut him short in order to hear what the mullah had to say: *"Look, just spill the beans, tell him your damned name for Christ's sake, blessed be the prophet's name of course!"*

Reg promptly snapped back from his opiated excursion, stood to attention, stiff as a board, and announced: *"Wing Commander Reginald Plantagenet Arbuthnot-Arbuthnot, Ex-Red Arrows, at your service. Sir!"* his arm descending from its salute like a karate chop.

"Well received, my good friend." said Nasrudin. *"Assuredly then, now that the trinity has been satisfied and you have joined the fold of the Jalanbani, it is my pleasure, nae, privilege, to offer you the opportunity to carry this sacred baton into the*

shade of Bogda Feng: the 'Mountain of God'. So called due to its association with the Revelation of John, in the last book of your Gospels. Under no circumstances should you even dream of attempting to open it prior to receipt of converse instructions from the appropriate authority. Indeed, you will find it impossible to do so without the total destruction of that which it contains. It is my understanding that in your tradition it is customary to tear apart a monetary bill, and, when the matching halves are placed aside each other an accommodation may be reached. Regard then this baton as your portion of the contract. Protect it with your lives. I am confident that you will be the very souls of discretion. All will become clear in due course."

Once the party had indulged itself to an appropriate degree, Nasrudin was attentive to the fact that they all left the 'Dome of Dreams' in unison. He couldn't, after all, be putting up with amnesiacs on the far side of the door and opiated initiates on the near side of the threshold conversing with each other. Given the cargo, it was sufficient only that they knew where they were bound and what they had to deliver. Yul Khan would be taking care of matters once they had emerged from the depression.

"Oh." said the mullah as he accompanied the team to the imaret: "I almost forgot. Do be attentive to avoid stepping on the threshold of the khan's ger. It is considered to be rather bad form amongst the nomads. May I wish you pleasant dreams."

EPISODE TWENTY-NINE
U Lu Mu Qui

When Fatima had bade farewell to her charges at the station, Nasrudin being otherwise engaged at the time, our band of explorers had only one focus on their minds: Heavenly Lake and the Mountain of God. Urumqui was far from inspirational. A kind of 'Post-Hiroshima Baroque' seemed all pervasive. Pity really. How retarded the Chinese imagination had become scunnered beneath Mao's suffocating wet blanket. One might think that if the empire was going to re-establish itself over the lands it had only managed to encompass under the domination of the Mongols, the imported new blood would, at least, have planted a flag representing some sort of cultural sophistication. Unfortunately, not. Too feart? No cash? Who knew? Was this just yet another mundane matter of: 'We rule, you do not, so fuck off!'? Hey, ho, apparently so.

Transport to their objective was conveniently on hand so they dutifully climbed aboard. Let's face it, there was a task to perform. But what did they know anyway? Seemingly, some khan called Yul awaited them at Heavenly Lake to hand over the antidote, and although they knew not why, they appeared to be in possession of a rather imperially Romanesque baton, which, however, since passing through the cranial-amnesia-interloop after ending their session with Nasrudin, they were puzzled by. Nevertheless, they felt certain that it had something to do with something. Dealing with the bizarre and unexplained was becoming the norm.

However, more of Urumqui anon. Plus the odd scorpion, of course.

("Feel sure we're going to get sued for something over this stuff." Ed)

EPISODE THIRTY
Ger away with It

Right now, you are probably thinking: *"This guy has totally lost the bloody plot!"* and who could blame you? After all, we've had saturated Frogs, incinerated Austrians and an Assassin who had had to take a few years out. Not to mention quite ludicrous nonsense relating Templars to the Mongols and Timur emanating from some mystic joker of a mullah brandishing a weird baton that apparently contains what? Who the Hell (excuse me Archangel Malik, blessed be the name) knows, cares or otherwise? Well, the way I see it, Larry, is that sometimes you just have to keep on readin. So, why not give it a whirl. Let's face it, the worst that could happen is that you'll only have wasted a mere microsecond within this beguilingly nebulous universe. If you have worked out that you can actually make a difference to it in human form, close the book now, and have a nice day. See you in an altered state sometime! Meanwhile, what the hell, let's have some fun! But first, we interrupt our tale to bring you ....

("This bugger's definitely on drugs!" Ed)

A Brief Technical Intermission

Now that we are on our way to encounter Yul Khan, I am reminded that despite the fact that we have covered background dealing with Mongol military organisation to some degree, due to Genghis establishing a meritocracy and breaking down the barriers between the feuding clans by appointing regimental leadership to officers hailing from clans other than the one making up the majority of a given regiment, we have, however, neglected one of the key features in the arsenal of the 'Devil's Horsemen' and their effectiveness on the field of battle, the AK of the steppe: the ubiquitous short, composite, recurve (reflex) bow.

This weapon served the apparently ignorant woolly-back thugs from the grasslands through Scythians, Huns (although the Hun version was usually longer and asymmetrical) and a slew of Turkic peoples, to the Mongols. Not to mention those thorns in the side of the Roman Empire, and who eventually contributed so much to bringing about its fragmentation and downfall: the Parthians and their successors, the Sassanians, of Iran. The composite recurve bow was much shorter than the longbow, and therefore, more versatile and easily accommodated by the cavalry (as the Romans found out at the Battle of Harran, when they were on the receiving end of the 'Parthian Shot'; the Parthians deceived Crassus' legions into thinking that they were in retreat and promptly turned and fired backwards at the pursuing Romans, completely routing the interlopers from Italy).

The weapon comprised three basic elements, which provided: form, tension and compression. A central wooden core provided its form, the outer surface (what the enemy saw) was composed of sinew, which took care of the elastic tension, the inner surface was made up of horn or bone, giving resistant compression, and the whole lot was bonded together with glue derived from boiled down fish stew or tendons. Finally, the weapon was sealed and weatherproofed: often by being bound with some kind of cord. This composite structure more than adequately made up for the power lost through the bow's lack of length; the technology employed made it just as powerful, if not more so, when compared with the non-composite wooden longbow. In 1794, the Secretary to the Turkish Ambassador to London was persuaded to take up a challenge to prove that the composite bow was the equal of 'the torment of the French': the great English longbow. Much to the chagrin of his British challengers, the well-built secretary proved with ease that the composite bow had a greater range than the old mainstay of the English army by some distance (the norm for the English Long Bow is around 350 yards, the ambassador's secretary managed an average of 448 yards). Oh dear. One of the great conundrums of military history is why it was that European armies, both BC and AD, seemed to pay such scant attention to the efficacy of this weapon. Hubris perchance? After all, how could nomad bowyers possibly produce a superior weapon to that made by more 'civilised' and sophisticated settled peoples? Indeed, making such a weapon was no mean feat; the entire production process involved some considerable skill and it took up to a year or more to manufacture a top of the range reflex bow. Not until the advent of the musket did anything come close to the power of the composite bow, and even then, it was some time before the gun could be reloaded and fired at speeds comparable to that of the bow. Strange.

Colour Supplement: Lifestyle Section

Having raised the issue of Mongol technology, this may also be an opportune moment to glance sideways at their everyday lifestyle. We know already of the marital arrangements and the distribution of power and labour within your average Mongol household, but little of their traditions with respect to their brand of pastoral nomadism, their food, clothing, and gers.

In terms of the annual movements of steppe nomad clans, they tended, and still tend, to inhabit the low-lying plains during the winter months and the highlands in the summer. Call it holiday-homing. Reasons for this include a combination of allowing pasture an opportunity to refresh itself in time for the following year's return, keeping cool during the summer by camping higher up, and this in turn also allowed them to avoid the infestation of insects that was so prevalent lower down during the warmer months. Clearly, to facilitate such a mobile tradition, the ger (home) required to be both easy to assemble (this could normally be achieved within an hour) and disassemble, as well as being easy to transport. Its structure comprised three basic elements; a vertical wooden lattice-work frame formed the circular wall of the home (taking care that the doorway always faced south), on top of this was placed a number of wooden rods, which at one end were connected to metal ring, whilst the other end rested on top of the circular wooden lattice wall. Looking down from above then, these roof beams would have resembled the radiating spokes of a bicycle wheel; the side on view, however, would reveal a conical rake to the structure which allowed rain to run off once the roof was covered. The whole frame was then enveloped in felt to protect the inhabitants from the elements. Finally, the hearth was positioned centrally to permit fumes to escape via the aperture provided by a hole in the felt around the metal ring above.

In terms of cuisine and clothing (including the covering for the gers), everything centred on the herds that the clans maintained. Food appears to have fallen into two brackets: white food and red food - both protein based. White food encompassed anything derived from dairy products: cheese, yoghurt and chigee (fermented, and lightly alcoholic, mare's milk: kumis, as it was known by the Russians). As previously mentioned elsewhere, the Mongols did enjoy the odd tipple too, and this was normally in the form of Chinese rice wine, or even grape wine from the Middle East and Central Asia (though Genghis apparently disapproved of its effects - quite why is a mystery): the concentration of alcohol in chigee, however, could hardly have satisfied the requirements at a clan booze up. Meat, of course, fell into the category known as red food, and in the main, it was cooked in stew form with root vegetables and onions, etc, or as kebabs. There was very little in the way of waste when it came to consuming their livestock; the blood, for example, was used to make black pudding from the slaughtered animals, and furthermore, whilst on the move, a spike and pot were always at the ready to tap into the blood vessels of the herd to provide nourishment for the travelling family, or regiment. Generally speaking, white food was predominant in Mongol fare during the summer months, and red food tended to grace tables through the winter; if animals gave up the ghost in summer, their meat was often dried and preserved for consumption later in the year. The carbohydrates, starch and etc, in the Mongol diet seems mainly to have been derived from noodles: grain for which was obtained through trade with the surrounding Turkic and other peoples; such trade also supplied the Mongols with chickpeas and spices amongst other culinary goodies. Of the livestock that the Mongols reared: horses, cattle and camels were utilised in the main as draught animals, and though their milk, blood and flesh also found their way onto the menu, this role normally fell to the sheep and goat herds. All of the above was supplemented by the product of the hunt: rodents, gazelle, wild boar, rabbits, fish and the like.

Their domestic livestock served a dual role in that they not only supplied the Mongols with food, but also with their clothing in the form of leather, fur, and woollen garments. The basic mode of attire, for both sexes, would have been leather boots, trousers, and a caftan secured around the waist firstly with a leather belt, which in turn was overlaid with a cummerbund; married women were apparently identifiable by their lack of belt and cummerbund. Status in the hierarchy of clan or nation was denoted by both the colours and materials employed in the garb: silk, satin, cotton, fine fur, and the like, for those of higher rank at special social events, etc. Seemingly, despite the fact that the Mongols were not overly keen on bathing, or washing their clothes, they did maintain a very rigorous protocol when it came to wearing the appropriate dress for given occasions: a kind of 'Sunday Best' culture if you like. As suggested above, everyday clothes tended to be worn until they fell apart, and the reason for the lack of washing machines and shower gels in the Mongolia of the day apparently had its roots in religion. Some historians have said that under Shamanist tradition the dirty water resultant from bathing etc would contaminate the sacred Mongolian land. One is, therefore, tempted to ponder the possibility that if the Mongols were encouraged to view themselves in such a low light (ie: as little better than the scum line on a bath), perhaps they may have suffered from some deep-seated inferiority complex which might in turn have produced in them a burning desire to prove something to themselves and the world at large. There again, I don't suppose improved personal hygiene practices have necessarily encouraged modern humanity to think twice before indulging in a bit of murder and mayhem, so that's probably a non-starter.

Aside from the absence of bathrooms and laundries, clearly this was not a lifestyle that had much of a role for the art galleries and opera houses more commonly associated with settled communities either; however, that is not to say that the Mongols took no interest in the developments - whether artistic or scientific - of the city dwellers. Indeed, during the period of empire, they positively revelled in such matters.

Anyhow, enough of this mini excursion into the manuals of military technology and DIY for the nomad anorak: normal service has now been resumed.

EPISODE THIRTY-ONE
Alps beyond the Muesli

Only to de Ath and Ricardo-Coutts did the territory seem familiar, due to their Afghan travels, as they surveyed the distant prospect of Ferghana before wheeling 180° from magnetic north to starboard and beyond. The Dzungarian Gates, Lake Balkhash, Bukhara, Samarkand, Tashkent, another day perhaps.

Strangely, they'd backed round on themselves having cleared Urumqui in the direction of Uzbekistan, and seemed to be heading back where they'd come from, but on quite a different tack. They saw it from afar: a virtually sheer natural cliff face leading up to their destination - the lake itself. Up and up, zig and zag, they got down close and personal with it, at least the gasping engine did. And finally, the view. Ah yes, the view. Incomparable! In front lay a Dambuster's paradise. They'd seen something almost identical at Bandar Amir in central

Afghanistan many years previously, but that was on a much more diminutive scale: a natural dam flanked by mountain peaks on either side, this was infinitely greater. Hoover? A mere midget by comparison. This was seriously high and seriously wide. Arbuthnot-Arbuthnot came over all misty, he could almost hear Gibson over the radio to the others in 617 squadron right now as the Lancaster barrelled in at 60 feet: *"Okay chaps, let's give Fritz something to think about. Line them up n' skim 'em in. Ought to keep that Krupp blackguard doing overtime for a while! 'Après Moi Le Deluge'!"* Pity it was all such a miserable failure.

Truly, it was a wonder of nature. At one end there was the immense natural wall, then, buttressing both sides, stretching back along its entire length to the foot of the snow-capped Bogda Feng (the Mountain of God), were the Alpine peaks that contained the lake. It was hardly any surprise that the place was held in such awe by the nomads who pastured there in the summer's months. Bogda was kind to them. In fact, the mountain had no necessity to be cruel. Situated amid the Tien Shan range, and permanently snowbound, its beneficence had served not only the nomads who journeyed to its foothill pastures, but had also fed the gardens of Shambhalah to the south in Turpan and elsewhere for millennia. Both nomadic pastoralist and settled agrarian understood how the clock of nature ticked. Bogda even allowed a team of Japanese mountaineers to surmount its 17,864 feet back in 1981 and get away with it - but what did they learn? The nomads and people of Turpan, quite unafflicted by such egotistical cravings (in fact they had no time at all for them), they are happy to simply benefit from the abundance that the Mountain of God has provided for generations. Such matters are not questioned.

So, this Alps beyond the Alps was then the summer pasture of the Kazakhs at the time our valiant travellers caught their first vista of the heavenly mirror. Beyond the dam to the north lay the winter pasture of the steppe, parched by the scorching summer heat, whilst here in the mountains, the nomads bathed their herds with the grassy lushness of The Tien Shan Range.

EPISODE THIRTY-TWO
The Pony Express

"*Welcome to the Mountain of God.*" came the greeting. The horseman had remarkably piercing sapphire blue eyes - most unusual for a Kazakh - but nobody was about to ask why. "*My khan informs me that you are emissaries from the 'Islands of the Red Herrings'. Is this so?*" he enquired.

"*Quite so, my man.*" responded de Ath, unsure of where the conversation may go next.

"*Trafalgar!*" exclaimed the Kazakh.

"*The Immortal Memory!*" rejoined de Ath. They were clearly singing from the same hymn sheet.

It is fair to say that de Ath, not least the others, were somewhat consternated at this exchange, and this was not helped when the horseman descended from his mount, and unsheathed his sabre; their concerns immediately lapsed into something akin to panic. To most, this may have seemed a reasonable reaction, to de Ath however, the adrenaline began to drain away. It seemed to him that anyone who was willing to dismount and get confrontational surely wanted to indulge in something a tad more social than your simple decapitation. After all, he could have done that on horseback with far more ease and efficacy, couldn't he?

"*Sir, I would appreciate it if you would accept this sabre as a token of our bona fides. Its provenance dates back to Bukhara at the time of Genghis Khan.*" The Kazakh knelt and presented the blade.

"*Thank buggery!*" thought all present.

De Ath accepted the weapon with due decorum and in accordance with nomad protocol adding "*You do us great honour, however, we come hither to your realm to perform a task that even we know little of. Suffice to say that we are most gratified to have your support and guidance.*" And with that, he handed the sabre back into the hands of the horseman. The Kazakh smiled appreciatively and shook de Ath's hand.

"Formalities now concluded, allow me then, ladies and gentlemen," our Kazakh charge said in the most immaculate Oxbridge English, *"to escort you to your abodes for the duration of your residence with us. Please forgive us if it is not what you may be accustomed to, but we hope that they will meet with your exacting standards. Should you require any assistance at any time, we will be close by, and more than happy to oblige. One simply has to blow on this goat's horn and you will need want for nothing. I assure you that in these parts are amongst the best appointed gers to be found in Central Asia. Not to mention our tiger friends. I should also point out though that tomorrow is a Muslim festival day, the consequences can often be, how should I put it?"* he pondered for a moment, *"Unpredictable. Many Uighurs congregate here to picnic. So, my recommendation is to maintain your distance, since matters can occasionally become a trifle entertaining. This is not a matter that you ought to unduly concern yourselves with since His Magnificence Yul Khan will be in attendance along with myself and another five members of our clan. We generally find that our presence has a remarkably subduing effect upon events. In the meantime, we have prepared these three gers for your pleasure. After tomorrow, Yul Khan will invite you to his own ger to discuss the past, the present and the future. And, on that very subject, I understand that there is a Plantagenet in your midst."* Arbuthnot-Arbuthnot owned up immediately. *"Excellent,"* continued the Kazakh, *"I am led to believe that you are in possession of a sacred baton which you received from a certain Mullah Nazrudin, am I correct?"*

"You are indeed, sir." responded the wing commander.

"His Magnificence the Khan has instructed me to collect it from you and deliver it to him. This is simply a precaution. Due to tomorrow's 'festivities', he feels that it may be unwise to run the risk of its falling into the wrong hands. He also instructed me to inform you that it will remain sealed until you are in his presence." Arbuthnot-Arbuthnot obliged and handed over the baton, which the Kazakh inserted inside his black silk blouse. *"Until we meet again then, my friends."*

"Wait a moment please, sir. I simply must ask you, where did you acquire such an immaculate command of our language?" asked Stirrup.

"Ah yes, you are not the first to enquire. Many moons ago, our khan's great-grand father - currently residing with Tengri - oh, I should point out that he was of Mongol stock, as of course is our current khan, despite the fact that our clan is Kazakh; the fact that our Kazakh clan should be led by a Mongol khan may raise an eyebrow or two amongst you, however, the story is long and complex, and may be discussed in more detail at a later stage in the presence of Yul Khan himself. Nevertheless, to return to the point. Our khan's great-grand father commissioned me to journey to your 'Islands of the Red Herrings' in order to discover what I could concerning this sport that goes by the name of cricket. The thing was that we had found that our traditional game of buzkashi: a raiders game dating back to the time of Genghis and before, was incurring far too many fatalities amongst our men-folk, and the khan felt that perhaps something more sedate would be appropriate. So, initially, prior to my departure, I took instruction in your tongue from an Assassin gentleman going by the name of Hassan Babur, who had recently returned from London and was renowned for his linguistic talents. In fact, I believe you may have made his acquaintance. Thenceforth, I enrolled at your renowned sporting academy at Loughborough University, nearby to your famous motor racing circuit of Donnington, to study this activity called cricket. Since then, the toll upon our young Turks has reduced greatly. Unfortunately though, many of our bowlers have yet to master the art of the Googly and the Chinaman. I hope that answers your question. Until tomorrow then." And with that, sabre aloft, our Kazakh friend galloped off up towards Bogda Feng.

EPISODE THIRTY-THREE
The Magnificent Seven

Our Kazakh chum had left our friends far from prepared for what was to follow. Without question the ger, whatever you call it, exceeded all the bounds of luxury. Adorned with Isfahani silk carpets, brass samovars, bronze mangals (with enough Afghan opium to induce an entire regiment into a coma), and a veritable abundance of the best Glenburn Estate Darjeeling tea supplied by Taylor's of Harrogate, it's hard to assess where to start with Michelin Stars when it comes to gers but these nomads really had it taped.

Morning then dawned. Callista always said that it was the best part of the day. Others differed. Well, at least the male contingent did. Maybe they were just hankering after the womb or something as the sun rose. Anyhow, there was no way they were getting out of the warmth of their opiated residue. The opposite sex, by contrast, were all up for a brisk stroll along the shoreline, and off they went. In their absence, the wing commander, always alert to the sound of unfamiliar engine notes, managed to prise open an eyelid. *"Sounds like we've got company chaps."*

Claude and the doc crumbled into life. Eventually, our French fried friend managed to articulate *"Ver zi phuque ar ve?"*

"Ve are ere. In case you hadn't realised, you demented blobby Flog." Plantagenet had still to kick his pismonunciation into gear, but at least he now had both ears and eyes functioning.

"Reckon the Uighurs have just started to encamp." he said, peeking out from behind the flap of the ger. *"Now listen here chaps, just do your ablutions and look casual. By the way, what happened to that goat's horn thing?"*

"Mais, A zot zer vas zom stuff ozer iz appen between ze Kazakhs an ze Wegurs before we meet im, non?" queried Claude; his memory banks were clearly, if haphazardly, sparking into life.

"Yes, I think perhaps that that was what Reg was concerned about." de Ath chipped in as he joined the wing commander in his birthday suit at the entrance to the ger.

"Bugger me!" exclaimed Reg surveying the scene.

"Listen, matey, keep the Her Majesty's Navy out of this!" protested de Ath.

"Looks like it's going to be some kind of party!" said the wing co.

"Don't think those are bottles of water they're unpacking!" the doc concluded.

"Yes, probably one of the few places they can escape the gaze of the mullahs if you ask me." added Reg. *"Haven't seen too many of Yul's clan about either. Where on earth is that bloody goat's horn thing?"*

"Let's just remember what the chap said: we'll see how the day goes and take it from there. Okay? I'm sure he's got an eye on the situation. In any case, it's just a bunch of picnickers." de Ath attempted to placate.

"Bunch! More like a bloody horde!" said Reg, eyes popping out. *"What did you do with that Mauser I saw you with?"* he added.

"Gave it to Hassan, ole bean. Thought it was the best policy at the time." responded the naked de Ath.

"Bugger!" came the reply.

"Listen, told you already to keep the navy out of this!" responded the irate father of a submariner.

"My, hasn't this place become popular in our absence." glowed Lister-Jag as she approached the cowering trio behind the flap. *"We should go for strolls more often. And for God's sake, doc, do put some clothes on why don't you! You're not in a bloody submarine now!"*

"Why don't we go down and become better acquainted." added Lemony.

"Bit early for a party, don't you think?" quivered Reg.

"Never too early for a party!" said Callista settling the matter with some enthusiasm.

"*Okay dokey.*" de Ath conformed, reaching for his pants. It also passed through his mind that this might be one occasion that his Mauser could have provided a certain kind of reassurance. Anyway, too late for that now.

What the previous day had been emerald green grazing pasture had now become a picnicker's paradise. As far as the eye could see, Uighur families had staked their claims stretching from one side of the lake's northern barrier to the other. And who could blame them, it was a place of exceptional beauty, but why the congregation? Surely such magnificence might be better appreciated, contemplated, absorbed, whatever, far from the claustrophobia of the lumpen masses. Was it some inherent sense of insecurity? Was nature so threatening that it could only be entertained enmass? Why was grass so much more intimidating than concrete? Was this a sign that perhaps the Uighurs had managed to bury their nomadic past? The place had changed in a matter of moments from Granchester to a kaleidoscopic litterbin like some Benidorm beach. The bulls, however, were not perturbed at all by such question marks.

On the previous evening, it had become apparent to our travelling sextet that gelding was not part of the Kazakh tradition; bullock was simply not in the local vocab. It wasn't that the male of the species was overwhelmed by aggressive testosterone, in actual fact, they were remarkably placid creatures on the whole; much like male tigers, idle buggers given half a chance. Callista had discovered this on a personal level when the gang had gone for a stroll the night prior. As one might imagine, fences are few and far between in nomad lands, in short, they are quite non-existent. So, when our troupe had decided to embark on the evening's post Mongol hot-pot constitutional, Callista found herself inadvertently isolated mid-meadow in the company of a pair of cannonball sized testes. When said bovine commenced to establish its territory by overturning the odd divot or two with its hoof, the good lady's pupils dilated in the direction of her chums.

"*Walk, nice and casually in our direction. Whatever you do, don't run!*" came the instruction from de Ath.

Sure enough, panic-stricken, Callista, bicycle-clips full to bursting point, made it, and they all mingled their way through the forest back to their gers. The bull meanwhile munched his way across the meadow cute as you like.

But, back to the festivities. The thing was that the Uighur picnickers and the Kazakh bulls didn't see exactly eye to eye when it came to caring and sharing. Casual socialising did not come naturally. The herds that had journeyed up for their summer hols from the sweltering heat of the plains below had come to regard the territory as personal. So, the sudden arrival of hundreds of picnic baskets appeared like some kind of manna from heaven. Naturally then, they consorted with the visitors. Before long, the interlopers began to find the creatures somewhat tiresome and attempted to usher said beasts away in no mean fashion. Little beknownst to the visitors from Urumqui (frankly, they should have known better), the Kazakhs were well on top of the situation, goat's horn or not. The moment that trouble broke out between the Uighurs and the Kazakh herd, all hell broke loose. Initially, there was a simple mêlée down at the camp site between the humans and the bovines, however, those (namely our crew) who were initiated into the ways of the nomad, knew when to take cover. Having said that of course, they kept the flaps open to guarantee a grandstand view. Let's face it, how often do you get a chance to see a Mongol khan lead a Kazakh charge? It should also be pointed out that there were a couple of Chinese coppers present, but they too knew when to make themselves scarce, in fact, they managed to become quite remarkably invisible until things had settled down.

Ultimately, the whole thing went off in a remarkable dignified fashion. Not surprising really. At first, a clutch of seven horsemen fired along the shoreline, and their bantam Mongolian steeds reared to an abrupt halt just in front of, and within feet of, our friends' accommodation. The riders were all attired in the same armour, under which they wore raw black silk - except one, their leader: Yul Khan, for it was **He**. He wore the same armour but his silk was a regal, golden hue of yellow. The Uighurs, and there were hundreds of them, stood in awe. If only one of them had had a flash camera, they could have disabled him, but none did. He reached into his saddlebag with a robotic motion and withdrew his mobile phone. He said nothing. He didn't need to. He simply dialled in the number '666' and hit send! Instantaneously, every hillside as far as the eye could see was adorned with horse-archers. Sometimes you just know when you are beat. The Uighurs really should have been a bit more accommodating with the bulls. The up-shot was that the Uighurs high-tailed it back down to Urumqui leaving picnic baskets et al to the grazing cattle. Yul: one, Uighurs: nil. Once the Chinese coppers had emerged from their bunker, they chained a couple of the poor Uighur bastards to a tree, and on an hourly basis throughout the night electrocuted them with cattle-prods. Just to make sure they were still alive, you understand. After all, human organs were fetching fairly good prices down in Shanghai at the time.

EPISODE THIRTY-FOUR
Spinning a Yarn

Yul was a thoroughgoingly jolly nice chap, once he'd got his armour off, not to mention put his mobile back on to recharge in his saddlebag. The morning after the riotous exchange with the Uighurs, the 'Magnificent Seven' trotted down to greet our friends with an invite up to the highlands. After a brief chat with the Chinese cops; resulting in the release of the wayward Uighur duet, Yul returned with transport for all. He even persuaded the cops to be on hand to assist in aiding those less familiar with horse travel to mount their steeds. Our pony express companion pointed out that the khan was unfamiliar with tongues other than Mongol, Kazakh, Uighur and Assyrian, and therefore, all communication would have to be directed through his good self. Firstly, Yul insisted upon taking everyone on an excursion around the neighbourhood, clearly he was something of a romantic.

Finally, they reached his corral. It wasn't hard to see how he'd been able to monitor the goings on down in the valley. He had prime position. Excellent grazing, direct route to the lake, and a view of Bogda Feng second to none. This was the kind of thing people pay good money for! And it was free, as far as the eye could see!

Once they had all dismounted and corralled their horses, they followed Yul to his ger. Careful not to step upon the threshold, as Nazrudin had warned. They entered the khan's abode. Yul accommodated himself opposite the entrance on an immaculate silk carpet in the ubiquitous Turcoman style, at the same time spreading out his arms with a regal nonchalance to invite the others to join him around the mangal. Our pony express rider, whom the group had encountered the previous day, positioned himself aside the khan. Yul instructed one of his minions to provide him with a decorative bronze container, which was duly laid at his feet. Upon opening it, he withdrew two batons, one of which he gave to Arbuthnot-Arbuthnot (the wing co knew it well) and the other he held to himself.

"Xx, xxxx, xxxxxxx." said Yul, as an aside to his translator.

"The khan would now appreciate it if you would open the baton that Nazrudin gave you, and withdraw its contents, Mr Plantagenet." said the pony express rider.

At the same moment, Yul Khan opened his own baton and withdrew a parchment, which he laid in front of the wing commander. Eventually, the wing co managed to extract another parchment from his own baton and laid it beside Yul's, both facing our favourite adventurers. It took some time for it to sink in. But sink in it did.

"Golly! This has to be some kind of joke, surely?" exclaimed Callista. Being a mathematician, she was pretty quick on the uptake, and was the first to realise the significance of it all.

"This is beyond a joke, it's bloody ludicrous!" joined in Lister-Jag.
"Vat ar u talking ov?" Claude was still feeling a tad saddlesore.
"Holy Moses! It all links up!" contributed de Ath, completely flabbergasted.
"I'm utterly lost." Stirrup.
"Quite." the wing commander.
"Look! Follow the lines. It's perfectly obvious!" said Callista. And, sitting bolt upright, that is precisely what they did.

EPISODE THIRTY-FIVE
Shagger Khan

Elizabeth II and Phil 'The Greek'. It couldn't possibly be true, could it? Okay, let's work it back along the line. The glaringly irrefutable algebra of the blood-line soon began to dawn upon all.

To be honest, it's a hell of a long story, and involves a considerable quantity of biblical he and she 'knew each other' and begat this and that without an insurance policy. But in the interests of brevity, to cut a long story short, let's take a glance over the last few hundred years.

As is well documented, Genghis sought the secret of eternal life, so much so that he required a decrepit Daoist eminence to endure a three year round trip to meet with him in Afghanistan during one of his package tours in order that he might be privy to such enlightenment. When the two finally met up, the khan, you understand, was a far from easy man to locate at that particular juncture (despite the trail of devastation he usually left behind him), didn't hear precisely what he had been hoping for.

The Daoist monk suggested, in the most polite and respectful of terms of course, that perhaps the khan should abstain from his notorious proclivities in the booze and sex departments. Quite why Genghis granted tax free status to the Daoist priesthood upon receipt of this advice remains something of a mystery. Suffice to say, he paid not a blind bit of attention to it, and proceeded booze away to his heart's content, and give every noble woman that took his fancy in Central Asia, the Middle East and Russia a bloody good servicing. Whilst, as we already know, your average Mongol cavalryman was expected to turn up for duty with at least five horses, condoms, you see, were not part of their survival rations kit. Result: The Star Cluster. Now to you and I this might approximate something to do with astronomy, but talk to a geneticist, and you could find yourself involved in quite a different discussion altogether.

Although more renowned for his brutality, Genghis was also reputed for his sexual prowess and generosity. Not for him any of those Hitlerian hang-ups when it came to bedroom antics. In fact, it was common practice, once he had experimented to his satisfaction, to pass on his 'conquests' to his favourite generals. So, what are we talking of here? A man who had shagged his way around a massive swathe of Asia and Eastern Europe with considerable abandon: no market for Viagra here. Is it any surprise then that, given the generational time frame involved, and the areas covered, our 'Casanova of the Steppe' might have left one or two genes around? No joke, folks. Current opinion amongst the genetics community has it that today there could be upwards of billions chromosomes originating from the same source floating around the planet, all dating back to around the time the man himself embarked on his excursions. For those doubters amongst you, it may be instructive to consult Oxford University's Department of Biochemistry. So then, back to the parchments. **("Definitely, we are heading for the courts!" Ed)**

Allow me firstly to offer my most sincere apologies for not designing a cute little family tree, and for taking one or two shortcuts, frankly, I'm not much of a computer buff, and I just figured that straight prose lines seem to make more sense, albeit travelling in reverse gear. We start then with Elizabeth II, for it is **We**. Thenceforth, cutting a few corners, George I (Hanover), afterwhich to Sophia, married to Ernst-August (Duke of Brunswick). Sophia, being the daughter of Elizabeth Stewart, legitimises the Hanoverian line to the British throne. Oh, almost forgot, Liz (Stuart, that is) was hitched up with some chap called Fred V of Bohemia (Like the sound of that: Bohemia, don't you?). Then, what do you know, there's another Fred: this time it's the IV of Wittlesbach (God, these names are so much damned fun). Then, we come to something pronounceable: William 'The Silent' of Orange (since when were oranges ever vocal?). Anyhow, he had something going down with this cutie going by the moniker of Charlotte Bourbon. Now then, if you can be bothered to do a bit of tracery, we rapidly carve our way through the houses of Stolberg and Silesia until we arrive in front of Elizabeth (funny how the name keeps recurring) Basarab of Wallachia. Now, Liz was begat by a gent going by the name of Nick who, in turn was the product of no less than Ivan 'The Great' of Wallachia (don't you just love the name? Ah yes, 'Ivan the Great': brother of Marija of The Blue Horde). Now, here's where things begin to get really interesting, not to say a touch confusing. On the one hand, you can follow one route, whilst on the other, you may choose to follow another. Whichever you follow, the destination is the same. You know what these royals are like. Route one: Ivan, you remember him, don't you? Well, he was connected to the Byzantine Imperial Family, and descended from that great Mongol tradition of religious inadequacy and the search for eternal life (you know, the belief that Tengri's drum simply didn't beat loud enough). So, what happened? Previously, Tochtu Khan had left his mark on Ivan's family by marrying Maria Palaiogos of Byzantium. Now, to cut to the chase, Tochtu was the son of Mönkhe Timur Khan who, in turn, was the grandson of Batu 'The Splendid' ('The Splendid', marvellous!) of the Golden Horde (ah yes, The Golden Horde), and, wait for it, yes, Batu was the son of Jochi Khan. And who in the name of all that is sacred may you ask was Jochi? No, not some stray lying prostrate on Sauchiehall

Street after hours, but no less than the eldest son of Genghis Khan! If only Franklin, Crick and Watson had been around at the time, many a dispute within the Borjigin family as to Jochi's parentage could have been resolved. Route two takes you to the same destination: via one of Genghis' daughters. Result: identical. (**"No kidding!" Ed**)

So much for Brenda. Want to hear about Phil? Oh, what the hell, why not? (**"Oh, who…….." Ed**)

Consort of Liz, aka: Phil the Greek. Descended from Prince Andrew of Greece and Denmark (why in God's name Greece had any connection with Denmark, Christ, blessed be the prophet's name, only knows?). Oh, sorry forgot the missus: Alice Von Battenberg. Family had to change the name during the First World War: tad inconvenient being related to the British royal family and having your name associated with a Kraut sponge cake at time of the Somme. Anyhow, down to business; the Greek royals had a number going down with the Russian Romanovs, not to mention the Prussians. Apparently, Peter III couldn't get it up, so exactly where Phil actually descended from is open to question; certainly the female side of the family had no problems between the sheets. And so the story goes on, from Catherine the 'Great' to Peter, the incomparably 'Great'. Thenceforth, we wend our way through a variety of Romanovs until we arrive at Ivan. Yes, another Ivan, but this time the IV (otherwise known as 'The Terrible': demented bugger went and murdered his own son. Can you believe it?). Again, to cut long and somewhat entangled stories of regal incest short, we wend our way on to Theodora 'Grand Duchess of Vladomir', thenceforth to yet another, yes, you've guessed it, another Theodora. But this time: Queen of The Blue Horde. Now we are really talking business! She was no less than the great granddaughter of Jochi Khan. And, who was he precisely? Well stone me! What do you know? So, what's good for the goose etc, don't ya dink?

Once they'd all taken in the significance of it, all, except the marquis that is, looked like they'd just received a jolt from 'Old Sparky'.

"*Gordon bloody Bennet!*" exclaimed Lister-Jag. "*If I may be so bold as to ask, why does the khan wish to disclose this knowledge to us?*" she ventured. There then followed a lengthy exchange between the pony express rider and the khan. Claude, by this time, had become somewhat the worse for wear and keeled over onto Stirrup's shoulder lapsing into deep snoozedom.

"*Zzzzzzz!*" he snored.

"*XXXXXXX!*" exclaimed the khan in highly miffed tones. At which point the errant Frog found himself pinned to the floor by the surrounding Kazakhs and force fed a mixture of chigee (fermented mare's milk) and fresh warm horse blood. Within seconds he sprang back to life and demanded know who had pilfered his reflex bow.

"*X-ho ho! Blah di blah.*" laughed the khan.

"*Our khan is amused to see that you have now become one of us, Mr Claude. He also says that any time you wish to utilise his mobile phone, you are more than welcome. I might add that this is regarded as a great privilege.*" translated the pony-man. "*But, to return to the original enquiry. Some time ago our khan's great grandfather conversed with the supreme Shaman god, Tengri, atop Burkhan Khaldun, also known as Khan Khenti: the most holy of places in Mongol tradition. During this encounter, Tengri explained that the Secret History of Temujin's descendents must never be lost. Tengri duly revealed the map of the Great One's genealogy. The Eternal Blue Mountain God also intimated that one day the khan's great, et cetera, grandson would receive a visitation of six voyagers from the 'Islands of the Red Herrings' bearing a baton. Our khan's ancestor was then instructed to depart with the two batons we now see in front of us; one of which, detailing the Asian half of Genghis' family tree, he was to maintain in his possession and pass on to his descendents. The other, detailing the European half of the tree, he was to hand over, for safe-keeping, to the Mullah of the sacred mosque at Shambhalah, a certain Nazrudin. Finally, Tengri pointed out that whenever the two batons should come together under the same roof in the presence of the aforementioned six Janbalani from your islands, all obligations would be rescinded and passed on to you: the 'Voyagers from the Land of the Immortal Memory'. At the time, Tengri was not entirely clear on why exactly this should take place, however, we have since consulted our shaman on the subject, and according to his divinations, he informs us that, when in one of his trances, Tengri made clear that as a result of the conjunction of the two lines in November 1947, the time had now come for the Borjigin family name to finally take its rightful place of supremacy in the Almanach de Gotha. Please do excuse my split infinitive. In fact, events of global import may result should these instructions not be carried out. Indeed, the very survival of the world as we know it may be at stake. Our shaman also added that you should take these parchments back to the curator of the Mongolian collection at the British Museum, an individual who, aside from being a fellow Janbalani, is an expert in the mysteries of Central Asian Steppe Nomad breeding traditions. Apparently, she is one of only three people on the continent of Europe capable of verifying the secrets contained within the khan's genealogical map. Thus then, you must now don the mantle of 'The Guardians of the Great Universal Ruler's Immortality'. In short: become 'The Bearers of Genghis Khan's Burden'."* explained the pony express man.

"Ta muchly." sighed Lister-Jag, *"Just what we were hoping for."* Turning to Lady Callista, she muttered, out of Yul's earshot: *"What in God's name this 'one-size-fits-all Lothario' has got to do with us, I utterly fail to comprehend."*

"Lothario! What? Jack the bloody Ripper!" corrected Stirrup.

Callista simply looked daggers at the doc, as if to say: *"Damned clot! What kind of jiggery-pokery have you got me involved in now!"*

"In any case, shouldn't all this codswallop be down to the Y chromosome?" Lister-Jag continued.

"Don't think this is the most appropriate moment to start querying the parchments, darling." said Reg in an attempt to avert a crisis.

"X-uuup?" the khan intervened, followed by yet more interchange between his eminence and the Wells Fargo man.

"Our khan was simply enquiring as to your reaction to the proceedings thus far. He also expressed interest in your necklace, ma'am."

"Of course. It was given to me by Mullah Nazrudin himself." responded Stirrup, unfastening it and handing it over to the khan.

"X-blah." The khan said to his right-hand man.

"Our khan says that the antidote to the venom of Amdo's Dalek will be delivered this evening." translated the right-hand man whilst Yul admired the Dervish axe as if mesmerised.

"Listen, we aren't going to suffer from some kind of amnesiac condition when we depart from the ger as happened down at the ICBM, are we?" enquired de Ath.

"No, not at all. Don't concern yourselves with such matters. Nazrudin has his own amusing little peculiarities. Our practices are much more direct. Just make sure that you don't tread on the threshold upon your departure." the translator replied, fingering the pommel of his sabre.

"Well then, I trust the formalities are over. If so........" the doctor said, reaching into his trusty photographic equipment case and withdrawing a crystal decanter of 1928 Sandeman port, "perhaps I could interest Yul Khan in a glass or two of this excellent vintage?"

"X-ah!" articulated Yul Khan with pleasure.

"Indeed, please do pass the port." responded the khan's ADC, clearly well up to speed concerning the etiquette involved.

De Ath then poured a glass for the khan, who was situated to his right, and passed the vessel to Stirrup ensconced on his left, who, neglecting tradition, filled her own glass.

"X-humph?" exclaimed Yul, staring directly at the good sister.

"Our khan was curious to know, Sister Lemony, whether you were acquainted with the Bishop of Norwich." explained the translator.

"Well, actually, I did meet the........" Stirrup began to respond, but was abruptly cut short by Ricardo-Coutts.

"I think, Lemony, he is suggesting that perhaps you should have filled the doc's glass, and passed it to myself to perform the honours for you, and so on around the circle." Lady Callista pointed out in a brief lesson concerning the correct protocol when dealing with port wine in polite military society. Stirrup, exhibiting an appropriately ruby blush, muttered something under her breath about the shortcomings in convent education and the quality of communion wine before swapping glasses with de Ath and passing the decanter on to Callista, apologetically.

"X-blah." chortled Yul.

"Yul Khan is delighted to see that standards of etiquette are not slipping in The Islands of the Red Herrings."

After several toasts accompanied by some ritual sheep's milk, cheesy nibbles, Yul and the other six stood in unison. Our intrepid travellers took this as a cue and corresponded. They all duly returned to the corral and mounted their horses.

"X, doobldey-do." said Yul Khan in a soothingly melodious tone.

"Our khan would like to express his pleasure at having made your acquaintance, and wishes you an eventless and pleasurable journey back down to the lake. Don't forget that we will rendezvous later tonight in order to supply you with the antidote that your friend in Amdo requires." our man from Loughborough rounded off.

("This bloke is completely off his bloody cloncker! Ed)

Above: Ya beauty! The north end of Heavenly Lake.

Left: Bogda Feng. Summer pasture land for the nomadic Kazakhs. At the south end of Heavenly Lake lies The Mountain of God, whilst at the north end the lake is contained by its immense natural dam (the top of which is situated on the left and in the foreground of the above illustration).

Above: Kazakh cricket (aka: Buzkashi).

Above: Yul's pad; in the heartland of Kazakh summer pastureland. The Mountain of God lies beyond the ridge on the right, and Heavenly Lake is down at the foot of the valley.

Yul Khan dials 666 into his mobile!

Actually, according to the latest parchments, it should have been 616. But, who's quibbling over a number? Fact is, it did the trick.

Left: Yul's mum spins a yarn. And what a yarn indeed!

Below: Some of Yul's neighbours gather for a family portrait. The great man's yurt lies on the right, animal skins curing on a trestle out front.

Above: Fly this in China at your peril: the flag of Eastern Turkestan.

Right: The melon men of Hami. Note raw nostrils from overly snorting their product.

Above: A rare and darkly dangerous species lurks at the Bogda Feng end of Heavenly Lake.

Above: Bandar Amir, in the central Hindu Kush; last known whereabouts of K-141.

EPISODE THIRTY-SIX
Monster in the Moonlight ('The game's afoot, Watson!')

"*Red lighting. Come to periscope depth.*"……..Captain to X.O.
"*Red lighting! Come to periscope depth!*"…….X.O. to captain and crew.
"*Up periscope.*"…….Captain to X.O.
"*Up periscope!*"…….X.O. to captain and crew. Moments later, the top window broke water.
"*At periscope depth, Ma'am.*"……..X.O. to captain.
"*Thank you, Alexei.*"…….Captain to X.O.

A sinister eye surveyed the moonlit scene.

"*Very good. Surface.*"……. Captain to X.O.
"*Surface! Full ahead together, blow all main ballast, foreplanes hard to rise!*"…….X.O. to captain and crew.

Oscar II Class, K-141: double-hulled, equipped with nuclear tipped, sea-skimming missiles, capable of taking out any battle group within hundreds of miles, emerged surrounded in a froth of heavenly water at the far end of the lake. The Yankquis quaked at the mere thought of it. Truly, a 'God-Almighty-Mallet-of-a-Beast' as it lurked at the foot of Bogda Feng!

"*Prepare to flood number one tube.*"…….Commander Duscha Duncanova.
"*Prepare to flood number one tube!*" The instruction echoed beneath the fin.
Commander Duncanova turned to Crabbe: "*Listen Buster, I'm giving you 40 minutes, tops. Good luck.*"
"**Long Live The Revolution, Ma'am!**"…….Commander Crabbe to Duncanova.
Crabbe was escorted by the X.O. to the starting line up at the sharp end of the boat, and the rear door was shut behind him.

"Flood number one tube!"…….X.O. to crew.

Crabbe swam out under his own steam, still much befuddled by life. A few minutes later, he had reached the shore of the lake.
"Yul Khan, I have a delivery."…….Crabbe.
Yul climbed down from his steed whilst Crabbe pulled out his Zippo and fired up a Turkish. Only then could Crabbe begin to know that he was dealing with Mongol bona fides. He took a long drag and handed it over to the khan. The khan accepted, glancing, somewhat askance towards Crabbe as he did so, then, took a toke.
"Delightful. Do you happen to have any more where these came from, old bean?" responded the khan.
"Only when the pink elephant lands." conjoined Crabbe.
"That would be of the Indian variety, of course."……. Yul Khan.
"Naturally, old fruit!"……. Crabbe.
They understood each other. Realising immediately that they were on the same wavelength, Crabbe handed over the silver-plated canister, and, as a gesture of comradeship, left behind his trusty Zippo and the remainder of his pack of Sullivan's. Yul Khan turned to his compatriots and said: *"If This Crabbe ever returns, give him the keys to my ger. Now gentlemen, we must deliver some of this antidote to our friends."*

Once tube one had been drained down, and Crabbe was inboard, normality prevailed. God! Life could be so bloody boring sometimes!

"Slow ahead."…….Duncanova.

K-141 submerged. Ten days later, it arrived at the Bandar Amir lakes in mid Afghanistan. Never to emerge again.

EPISDODE THIRTY-SEVEN
The Incontrovertible Invisibility of the Silent Reflection

("Help!" Ed)

EPISODE THIRTY-EIGHT
The Brown Paper Package

Lady Callista Ricardo-Coutts had been finding sleep hard to come by. Duly, she dragged herself from the slumbering Dr de Ath and opened the flaps of their ger around midnight. She emerged, and immediately found herself encircled by six mounted Kazakhs and a casual Mongol khan. Realising immediately that such circumstances required a certain amount of cordial diplomacy, she hesitated to gather her thoughts before crossing the Rubicon. Yul Khan dismounted, a Turkish burning in his left hand, advanced towards her in his usual robotic manner, and saved the day (night or whatever, you know what I mean).

Dressed in black silk camouflage from head to foot, he bowed his shaven head before Callista *"Ma'am. I believe that this is what you were looking for."* as he proffered a sealed locket in the direction of Callista.

'The Magnificent Seven' had previously worked through the night, under the supervision of the local shaman, mixing Crabbe's delivery of charred prosthetic Dalek brain and Black

Zircon, laced with traces of Osmium and Iridium, together with the required catalysts of dried Hami melon and preserved Yak's fat into a paste before stoking up the locket.

"*You must wear this until next you see Titus, at Kum Bum. Never open it or take it from your neck before you meet him!*" said Yul solemnly.

"*How can I thank you enough, Yul Khan?*" replied the good lady.

"*I'm sure I will think of something.*" responded the khan with a leery glint in his eye.

Callista pondered momentarily why it was that the khan had suddenly become something of a polyglot, but eventually put it down to the effects of the full moon. She saw the Kazakhs off and dashed back under the flap of the ger.

"*Look!*" she whispered urgently whilst attempting to revive the dormant doc from a delightfully exquisite relationship he had been having with Catherine de Medici. "*I've got it! Kum Bum! Come on.*" she exclaimed.

"*Oh, not now darling, Ta Er....... feel sure I've a headache coming on!*" groaned de Ath.

"*No, not that you bloody pervert! Yul has just given me the antidote!*" she explained.

Next stop then: Urumqui.

EPISODE THIRTY-NINE
Nothing Much Had Changed

One or two more contusions on the high street, but, let's face it, one really should have more sense than to argue with Kazakh cattle and their herders. Otherwise, everything looked fairly similar to the last time they had passed through. The first stop for the team was to book themselves on to the earliest train they could get for the following morning. Arbuthnot-Arbuthnot was keen to know what kind of loco would be hauling them. The ticket official looked rather taken aback, but obliged nevertheless, and shambled his way to the backroom.

"How in the name of Mao did this shower ever obtain permits to get into Xin Jiang in the first place?" he muttered silently to himself.

Shortly thereafter, he returned with the news that it would be a QJ. 2-10-2: a monster of the first water! Both de Ath and the wing commander were positively drooling! The poor minion was quite unprepared for the next intervention.

"We were just wondering if it might be at all possible, in the name of the Revolution naturally, for the good doctor and myself to ride on the footplate for a while during the course of the journey. Do you think that this could be arranged?" enquired Reg.

"One momen prease." replied the, by now almost suicidally comatose, ticket salesman as he disappeared off beyond the horizon of the office into the distance again behind the magic door. Upon returning, he stated, somewhat curtly, *"The dliva infolm me tha you wi do so at yaw own lisk, and have to sign the applopliate self-confession doclumen to that effec plior to depalture. Do you aglee to this"?*

"Confession to what, precisely?" queried the wing commander, with some concern.

"Anything that may justify anything." came the silent response.

"Just sign on the dotted line!" de Ath nudged Reg.

"Without question." Reg conformed automatically. De Ath sensed a sudden need to make an excursion to the loo almost beginning to overwhelm him.

And so to the inn.

De Ath, having experienced the perils of foreign parts upon previous occasions, Egypt in particular, was attentive to the dangers of the nocturnal arachnid community. Duly, he gathered together four Heinz beans cans from the local refectory, and filled them with water. He then inserted the legs of the bed into said water-filled cans. Peace of mind folks, peace of mind. Having only just accomplished his precautions, he heard a scream from the ensuite shower.

"There's a bloody scorpion in here!" exclaimed Callista.

The doc responded as fast as he could. Fact was that he had only just taken a swig of laudanum from his hipflask. He never travelled without it (having acquiring it from some poet chap during a highly intoxicated constitutional in the Lake District a few years prior), it had excellent provenance.

"Kublai-bloody-Khan! Just when you think that you have the pleasure dome all worked out, it goes haywire. Life can be such an infernal pain sometimes. What a bloody farrago! Confounded scorpions! All you want to do is relax with Morphia for a while, and what happens? A damned pointy-tail turns up!" the doc complained to himself.

"Okay, I'm coming, darling. Just get out of the shower for a sec or two." he related to his better half.

De Ath dragged himself away from his dreams, replaced the cork in his treasured hipflask, and stumbled his way into the shower to be confronted by his favourite member of the arachnid community. (*"First snakes, now this. Where did I go wrong?"* de Ath muttered). Opium has an inordinate facility for focussing the mind with a calmness that renders even the most challenging of situations to nothing more than a daily chore, quite unlike alcohol by contrast; although de Ath's favourite tipple did contain a certain quantity of spirit, it was far from being the active ingredient. De Ath stretched out and picked up the offending article by its tail, marched over to the balcony, and defenestrated the poor bugger over the edge. Unfortunately, he had been incognisant of the pre-slumber social gathering of hotel workers taking place beneath. No sooner had this temporarily aerial member of the animal community crash-landed upon the nearest mattress than panic ensued! Smoking cigarettes flew every-which-way, sandals stamped like some Spanish gypsy dance, this way and that, and Chinese wails of *"Help!"* cried out in every direction! De Ath was far too other worldly to take it all in, not to mention which, he couldn't really care less. Callista, meanwhile, had by then returned, secure in the knowledge that she could bask in the soothing, glittering warmth of the shower without any unwanted intruders, to her ablutions.

EPISODE FORTY
Chuff Chuff

("Please, please, make it easy on me." Ed)

The boys climbed aboard. The wing commander and the doc could hardly contain themselves. They were behaving like a couple of lads who'd just visited Hamley's for the first time. They sniffed here, they ogled there. They couldn't believe their luck. The aroma of burning engine oil and coal combined with the effluent from the steaming boiler had almost reduced sex to mere side-show **("Think we've been here before." Ed)**. The driver seemed overwhelmed by a vast array of knobs, and, all of them were scarlet! The interior of the cab was decorated in a regal golden yellow, as found on temples and palaces throughout the Middle Kingdom.

De Ath soon became aware that it was not advisable to meander around the cab inspecting the knobs and dials when he, taking a step forward, found the floor give way beneath him and the furnace doors suddenly flew open. The driver and fireman were reduced to stitches; it took some time before they were eventually able to contain their hilarity. De Ath took much longer to regain his composure. Off they went then. The Panhandle revisited. Fact was, it was an elegant but clever device, utilised by the fireman when stoking the furnace: stuff the shovel into the awaiting coal, turn, step, floor pedal opens furnace doors then tip said coal into the fires of locomotion. Simplicity itself really.

No particular causes for concern; no snakes, scorpions, etc. Only, almost forgot, there was the odd melon or two. The QJ thundered its way downhill to Hami. By the time they had reached the Mecca of the Chinese melon, the wing commander and de Ath had finally worked out how to manipulate 2,980 horses with a light twist of one or two scarlet valve taps. Magic. One simply cannot pass through Hami, and not pick up the odd melon. De Ath bought a cartload! The guys flogging them would gladly have donated the donkeys along with them, but recognised that the tourists had few difficulties with horsepower. So, melons it was.

The thing is that, being a privileged and well salaried wog, the doc couldn't go back to the Party Secretary, residing in one of the more shrivelled portions of the Middle Kingdom, and say that he hadn't checked out a Hami melon given that he had not only the dosh, but also the opportunity, far exceeding the official's wildest dreams, to actually visit the place (whether or not Hami looked like one of those places that God had utterly forgotten about in his grand design). So, there we are then. A bunch of fruitcakes with far more melons and money than they knew what to do with on a train destined to who knew what.

EPISODE FORTY-ONE
After-Eights Perchance?

The Han Chinese, it should be said, are a polite, discretely arrogant, hospitable, imaginative, inventive and a justly proud people. Not only that, but they are bloody good cooks. No idea at all what they are like in the bedroom (actually, on second thoughts, probably fairly hot given the size of the population), but, when it comes to the kitchen, you just can't beat the buggers. Well, perhaps I should correct myself. If one happens to be French, Turkish or Indian, then we might have a bit of a competition on our hands. However, frankly, I reckon that the Frogs would likely stumble at the first hurdle.

Take the Trans-Siberian Express for instance. No, I haven't lost the plot, yet. We are still maintaining a largely culinary thread here, promise. (**"Oh yes?" Ed**). Forgetting for the moment the engineering master-class upon reaching the Mongolian border: where the entire train is lifted, carriage by carriage no less, from standard gauge bogies to the more unconventional Brunel broad gauge bogies preferred by the Ruskies and the great man himself, the cuisine change is truly educational. But, since we've brought up the subject of bogies (**"I thought we were supposed to be forgetting the engineering master-class?" Ed**), it should be pointed out, in the passing, that having traversed one or two thousand miles of almost impenetrable forest through the good old USSR, the carriages are thenceforth transferred back on to standard gauge. Funny old world. But, when your middle name is Kingdom, I guess anything goes - and boy, did he try to live up to his moniker, or what! Invented broad gauge, became chief engineer of Plymouth, Bristol and Cardiff docks, created the Great Western Railway, designed and built bridges, steam locomotives, vacuum driven locomotives, tunnels and massive ships. Piece of cake really! (**"What a relief!" Ed**)

But, back to gourmet-land. From Peking to the Mongol border one is graced, truly graced, by something which your average British institutional cooks would be quite unable to recognise as anything approximating the word 'food', largely because they can't actually spell the word in the first place. Oh dear, what a snob! Thenceforth, one confronts the cavalry, in its most decorative form of course; hey folks, we're talking tourism here after all. In actual fact, the Mongol fare is pretty bloody tasty, so long as you are partial to lamb, mutton and variants thereof. Only when one enters the land that came up with such superlative inventions as Beef Stroganov, and other goodies such as: Borsch, Chicken Kiev, Koulich, mushroom dishes too numerous to count, and pickles enough to keep Horatio preserved for another couple of millennia, does one really begin to comprehend the expression 'The Greasy Spoon'! It's the slide-factor folks, that's what it is! In China, when one grabs hold of the dining car door handle, it opens with ease. The grip is secure, reassuring - always a good sign. In Mongolia, similarly so. Oh, should have pointed out that along with the change of bogies, so do the engines and dining cars. Only when one enters Russia, does one have to beware. The less said the better. However, forewarned is forearmed as they say: make sure that you have packed enough sustenance to survive the trip. And, if you really must traverse the dining car, do wear gloves! Otherwise, one's hand is more than likely to slip off the handle, and who knows where one may end up!

Anyhow, back to China, and the journey down the Panhandle. Civilisation. So infuriatingly bloody polite those damned Chinese! Fact was that the gang had overly indulged on just about everything going, including of course the liquid refreshments, and still they had to confront several pounds of melon. What to do? *"Get to know the natives better."* thought de Ath with logical elegance. And that is precisely what he did. Well-versed in local etiquette, he completely outwitted the table of back-up engine crew, ticket inspectors, guards and DJs, etc. *"Listen folks, imagine that I've offered you the dessert course three times already. So, what I am really trying to get across here is that if you don't take these bloody things off my hands straight away, I'm going to pull the communication cord. And, if I hear the merest hint of good manners from anyone, I'll plant these buggers on your craniums!"* he put to the gathered assembly in the most diplomatic way he could muster at the time.

It had quite the most remarkable effect. Suddenly, pound upon pound of melon flew off in the direction of engine cab, guard's van and DJ studio. The direct touch always works quite wonderfully well, don't ya dink?

EPISODE FORTY-TWO
Lanzhou

Lanzhou was much the same really. No offence to the locals you understand, but Christ folks, nice pagoda n'aw that, however, you've really got to do something about the air down there!

("So, where the eff are we going now?" Ed)

EPISODE FORTY-THREE
The Long Goodbye (aka: The Seeds of Armageddon, The Garden of Clustered Fragrances, The Plot Thickens. Oh Bugger, Who the Hell Cares Anyway)

("Christe! Chririst! How the hell do you spell that stuff anyway?!" Ed)

And so to Kum Bum.

How to end then? Such are the deep and searching questions that haunt us from here to there, and from now and then until the treasure is buried. Who knows where, when, how and why the answers lie? But, lets it a give a try.

EPISODE FORTY-FOUR
Ah, The Sandlewood Tree

"A drop of blood fell from Tsongkhapa's umbilical cord when it was cut after his birth. From this drop grew a wondrous white sandalwood tree. It had a very broad trunk and 100,000 leaves, in total." Or so they say. In 1379 a stupa was erected around the tree by Tsongkhapa's mother. Thus was born Kum Bum. Funny how this business of blood clots at birth keeps cropping up: Genghis, Timur, etc. Funny also how close the Mongols were to the Tibetan Buddhist tradition. There has always existed something of a conflict between the Han and the Tibetans when it comes to the control of the Hexi Corridor (Gansu Panhandle to you, me and the Chinese, or an extension of Amdo to the Tibetans). The thing is that both have claimed it over the

centuries as theirs to dominate. Who's right? Who's wrong? You choose. The Tibetans ain't so damned cute as many in the earnest right-on-politically-correct-Western-community seem to consider them to be, by the way. The bottom line is that they can be just as vicious as any other members of the human species.

As you well know, the author has been conducting something of a charm offensive on behalf of the steppe nomads, and, frankly, with some just cause in his humble opinion. Let's face it, it's a hard life. You spend your existence herding your flock from summer to winter pasture and back again all your life, hoping to get your mitts on the best plot; then some bunch of bloody headbangers comes along to deprive you of it. Hardly surprising then that someone like Genghis should eventually emerge from the woodwork to try and sort matters out, is it?

Neither have the Tibetans had the life of Reilly in their long and tortuous history. It's equally awkward, if not even more so, up there in them there mountains. In fact, Tibet has surely got to be one of the most oppressive environments that a human being could choose to settle in - and if you are a Tibetan, you don't exactly have a hell of a lot of choice. Nevertheless, the Tibetans are as opportunist as any, and historically, they have formed alliances with their enemies' enemies for political reasons, just as the best of us have done: more often than not in their case with our Mongol sweethearts, and bugger, did they know how to solve a problem! But, when push comes to shove: *"Power grows out of the barrel of a gun."*, and if you don't know that by now, it's about time that you grew up! The Tibetans have done numbers on the Chinese just as the Chinese have returned the compliment. However, it so happens that the Han have the upper hand at the current stage in the proceedings. And don't for one moment delude yourselves into thinking that the Dalai Lamas used to treat their own folks so kindly; they weren't necessarily as cuddly as many may wish to believe (the term Dalai Lama, by the way, was introduced by the Mongol Altan Khan when the Mongols adopted Buddhism as their national religion). Don't also get me wrong, I'm not one of Mao's apologists. After all, was it not he who showed Stalin how to conduct a party purge?

Not, as is commonly assumed, the other way round. As a guerrilla he was probably one of the most talented of them all, if not the most talented, but, as a statesman? Well, the less said the better. In fact, I believe that one of his generals once said of Mao something along the lines of: *"Had he died in the 50s, he would have been regarded as a God. Had he died in the 60s, he would have been regarded as a very great man. Unfortunately, he died in the 70s. Alas, what can one say?"* Hey ho.

Let us also not forget that the current Tibet issue stems from the groundwork laid down by the Yuan (Mongol) dynasty. China's modern day borders are based entirely upon the adventures of their horse archers some eight hundred years ago, who were enticed to go on their grand tour, in the politest possible fashion you understand (but, I feel sure I've covered that stuff already too). (**"Oh, you remember!" Ed**) Interestingly, the only way that the Han seem able to accommodate the uncomfortable fact that this bunch of 'unruly thugs' have left them with such an enormous territorial legacy is to claim that the Mongols, and the Tibetans too, are actually 'Chinese'. Tell that to a Mongol, a Turk, or a Tibetan, and see how far you get!

Anyhow, enough of such heretical suggestions and back to our story.

Above: Sunset over Amdo (Qing Hai).

Above: Tibetan supplicant.

Left: Tibetan (the ruled) and Han Chinese (the rulers) at Hui (the middle men) corner shop.

Below: Temple Central.

Right: Kumbum (Ta Er) from above.

Below: See, it's clockwise. Even the kids know that: *"Wheeeee!"* Dad introduces his youngest to the funfair of Buddhism, whilst his eldest seems to have cottoned on to it all.

Above: Ommmmmmmmmmmmmmmmmmmmmmmmmmmmmmmmmmmmm.

Left: Brother Wolfred has his doubts.

Below: The Celtic head coach inspects the pitch prior to the big match.

Right: Crowley as he is today.

Below: So, that's it then. Encased in rancid butter for evermore. Thus it is said.

EPISODE FORTY-FIVE
Tantrantisimo: The Battle of Kum Bum

Kum Bum, Ta Er, call it as you wish; the land where the air is rare, is a bit of a climb, but a short hop from Lanzhuo. Certainly made a change from Lanzhuo, where the air's as thick as a pig's fart! It's a funny old place Ta Er. The Han rule the roost, the Muslims run all the businesses, and the Tibetans come to dream of a better life. And the monks? Bunch of complete nutters! All that rancid butter and stuff. Hey, keep yer hands offa me! Seriously folks, this celibacy thing is bad news. No sooner had Callista, Lister-Jag and Lemony set foot inside the confines of the lamasery than every prayer-wheel in the neighbourhood stood to attention. They were enveloped by a veritable horde of deprived testosterone: it was worse than a Roman scooter club! Hands here, hands there, hands every-bloody-where! Surely there has to be a less frustrating way of getting closer to God. The gents meanwhile were desperately looking for an escape route to remedy the situation.

"*How about a brisk stroll?*" ventured the puzzled wing commander.

"*Jolly good notion, old chap.*" responded de Ath at a complete loss as to how to cope.

"*Vat iz un stroll?*" said a bemused de Vol-au-Vent.

"*Don't worry, old bean, you'll soon catch on.*" responded Arbuthnot-Arbuthnot.

"*Brisk stroll catch old bean?*" de Vol-au-Vent scratched his head with his deviant thumb.

At this point, the males of the species intervened. Arbuthnot-Arbuthnot took matters in hand. "*Scuse me gents, but thought the good ladies and ourselves might venture out to inspect the hinterland awhile, if that wouldn't be too much of an inconvenience.*"

Those British military types, don't you just love them? Such a way with words. Leaves you utterly speechless! The depraved monks looked on agog holding their (well, we won't talk about that) as the visitors from the 'Islands of the Red Herrings' disappeared into the distance.

They had, however (life seems so full of 'howevers', don't you think?), made one fatal error. Never go anti-clockwise round a Tibetan lamasery, ever! The thing is that, should one avail oneself of a Tibetan prayer-wheel, and learn something of the script, one will soon become aware that dreams only go to heaven in a clockwise fashion. This, you must know! They did not. And, nor did the various monks of the local persuasion inform them of their misdemeanour as they wandered off on their wayward journey. The fact was that they were contravening the religious protocol. It soon dawned on the clerics that they had something of a challenge on their hands.

"I'm sure I saw one of them with hooves when he took his shoes off!" the rumour rebounded around the temples.

"What are we going to do with the Rattle Snake?" worried a huddle of monks.

"Just kick him in with the rest!" came the response from the bald-headed figure residing in the darkness. Ah yes, the darkness.

"How about a game of footie?" came the distant call from Temple Central.

(**"So. Is this it then? You can't actually resolve it, so, you're going to have a bloody football match!" Ed**)

Once Brother Wolfred had given the pitch a detailed inspection, our team assembled across the flagstones in a traditional four, four, two formation, and awaited the arrival of the opposition. (**"Listen. Even though I have managed to struggle through it thus far, it doesn't mean that I've forgotten how to count. Yet." Ed**) Soon afterwards, they heard the unmistakable sound of studs on flagstones emanating from the tunnel. Imagine their horror when out from said tunnel emerged a full Tibetan eleven kitted out in immaculate Glasgow Celtic-like strips! The newcomers immediately huddled together not dissimilar to the Kiwis preparing for the Haka.

"Don't worry chaps. Probably just some kind of charitable donation from Parkhead." soothed Arbuthnot-Arbuthnot.
Burgermeister didn't look quite with it. In fact, he looked a touch bamboozled by events. He stumbled forth from the Temple, as if rejected, and joined up with the rest of the big noses. One could have been forgiven for thinking that he had embarked on some kind of bad acid trip; the poor man appeared so deranged. What had they done to him? FBI? LSD? A mere shadow of his former self. And Babur? What of him? The Mauser? The spirit of the assassin? What was happening here? Was all lost? Callista delved beneath her shirt and desperately tried to force-feed Titus with the potion from Heavenly Lake, but, to no effect. Perhaps it took time to act?

"Done about as much good as listening to canned whale music!" Lister-Jag summed up the potion's efficacy.
Something very strange indeed seemed to be taking place. Things were not looking too good. They didn't get any better.

The doors to the Celestial Temple creaked open to reveal a brace of monks built like Olympic weight-lifters bearing a tall wooden podium which they transported, accompanied by appropriate ceremonious chanting, to the centre spot, and deposited it in position.

"I'm not kicking that damned thing around for ninety minutes!" exclaimed d'Ath.

The two monks marched back to the temple entrance, up the steps, and positioned themselves at either side of the doorway, in a fashion reminiscent of the guards outside Lenin's tomb. Soon thereafter, in vocal unison, the guardians of the doorway announced, as if heralding the arrival of guests at a dinner party:
"Brother Wolfred!"

A cloud of rancid butter fumes wafted from the void beyond. When it had cleared there stood the hooded and bowed, but unmistakable form of a Jesuit monk. Due to the shadow cast by his head-dress, it was virtually impossible to discern his facial features, however, what appeared to be visible looked not to have a whole lot of flesh upon its bones!

"My brethren." he pronounced with much gravitas, *"We have prepared some amusement for you!"* (**"Oh, dear! Here we go again." Ed**) It had begun to dawn on our friends that this was to be no ordinary game of footie! Then came the announcement that struck fear into their very souls! *"The Lord High Priest and Magus of the Trouser Leg!"* Brother Wolfred withdrew to one side, and thus was revealed a tall but rotund figure dressed in a dinner-jacket overlaid with an unmistakable white surplice emblazoned with a vibrant scarlet cross.

"Sacre bleu!" exclaimed d' Vol-au-Vent, *"Ah knew it all along. Iz vrai. Zis place really vas built on ze ruins of a Templar preceptory!"*

"Jesus Christ man, it's Aleister bloody Crowley! What kind of damnable skulduggery is this?" bellowed de Ath.

Sure enough, there were those penetrating eyes topped by that trademark Telly Savalas-like copula with third eye protruding from the centrefold of his forehead! Crowley didn't so much as walk, but floated, his feet at least six inches from the paving. When he reached the centre of the quad, he levitated, Dalek-like, to its summit.

"You didn't happen to pack your little, black number, did you?" said Callista to de Ath in desperation.

Quick as a flash of crusader steel, the doc flipped the catches on his photographic equipment case, whipped out a freshly pressed Hospitaller surplice and threw it on.

"I say doc, that does look rather dashing! Better than that canned whale music stuff we got from Yul!"…….Lister-Jag.

Somehow, in the course of donning this last word in mediaeval sartorial elegance, de Ath now appeared resplendent in full chain mail beneath his black surplice, with the white Maltese cross of the sovereign order advertised fore and aft, whilst securing his helmet under his left arm, and holding the ancestral broadsword, point down, in his right hand. His dramatic change of attire had the most magical effect on the other members of the team too. No sooner had the words left Lister-Jag's lips than she herself was to be found sporting green, Team Lotus pit mechanic's overalls, her face and hands smudged with gearbox grease. Clenching a torque wrench, she eyed up Crowley's Dalek substructure calculating where to begin. Nor did the wing co escape the spell: kitted out, as he was, in the g-suit and helmet of a fast jet pilot; he studied the flight plan in detail then gave his RN Fleet Air Arm Sea Harrier the 'walk around'. Callista and de Vol-au-Vent, however, preferred the garb of quite another dimension: the Napoleonic to be precise. Callista appeared in a sumptuous, deluxe, silk taffeta ball gown with a dazzlingly rich purple sheen, and despite the somewhat revealing nature of the gown's low cut, she shielded her face coquettishly with a fan bearing the Sinclair family crest. As for the marquis, he had gone in for the uniform of a flamboyant captain of the French 10th Regiment of Hussars: in 'Attila' jacket, pelisse with sable trim slung over his shoulder, armed with a pair of pistols and a sabre, and topped off with the regimental busby - the very image of the foul-mouthed, hard-drinking, womanising swashbuckler of hussar repute. In fact, de Vol-au-Vent's own commander, beau sabreur General Lasalle, had once said of his men, in a variation on a theme by Bonaparte himself: *"If any of them are still alive by their thirtieth year, they are blackguards!"* De Vol-au-Vent was twenty-nine. And then there was Stirrup. Despite her attempts to put some distance between herself and the Vatican, Stirrup looked altogether rather fetching in the vestment of the Sister Adorers of the Most Precious Blood. The fact is that she'd always regretted not taking her vows in that particular order, as they definitely had one of the swankier designs to have emanated from the couturiers of The House of Saint Peter: a gold heart dangling from a gold chain and, wait for it, a bright crimson sash tied around the waist, its ends hanging down framed against the black habit. To die for! Even Titus was not exempt from the costume department's wand: his muscles distorting the lines of a top of the range nineteen-twenties three piece suit much in the same way that his overly tight bowtie was making his facial expression look like that of a participant in a Cumbrian gurning contest. The whole outfit was capped by a dapper little FBI boater. Hoover really had the most peculiar taste when it came to uniforms. Give me an SS officer any time! Directly behind our favourite special agent, however, a curiously ethereal mist enveloped the goal mouth, and as it slowly cleared, the most bizarre sight of all was revealed.

Any connoisseur of fine port wine would have been familiar with the figure immediately. For there stood the Don: draped in the black cloak of a Coimbra university student, and sporting the wide brimmed hat of the Caballeros - in such a manner that it obscured his facial features. He differed from the icon of Scotsman George Sandeman's company in that his silhouette was reminiscent of Orson Welles in the autumn of his career, and, in place of the glass of vintage ruby, he held in his palm what appeared to be a cannonball with a fuse wire dangling for it. Apart from the fact that he looked for all the world like a parody of a late nineteenth century anarchist on a mission, he seemed to be babbling in an obscure Austrian dialect about having left his insulin on an express train whilst traversing the Taklamakan. Yes folks, you've guessed it, for it was none other than the spectre of Schultz himself. He had, rather abruptly, had to cut short an altercation he'd been having with the Archangel Malik on the subject of fire-raising in order to help his erstwhile comrades out in their hour of need. This was clearly not going to be one of those low budget 'made for television' affairs that Hollywood churns out for daytime viewers. They were ready for the big time!

"*What's all this hocus pocus about? Where's the ball?*"....... Lister-Jag.

"*What does it matter? If he's the ref, we're stuffed!*" ....Ricardo-Coutts.

"*Don't worry chaps, we're going to give them a ruddy good pranging!*".......Arbuthnot-Arbuthnot.

"*Don't like the look of that Wolfred character.*" ....Stirrup. Both de Ath and d'V prepared to mount their chargers.

"*Good Lord, I think I've cracked it!*".......Arbuthnot-Arbuthnot

"*Cracked what?*".......de Ath

"The code!"……..Arbutnot-Arbuthnot
"And?"……..de Ath
"It's the picture …………"
Thence it came. **Crowley addressed the visitors.**

"ABRACAMUMBO,
DALEKPOCUS,
JUMBOSANCTISSIMUM!"

At first, it felt like an almost imperceptible breeze, but, it gradually ascended the Beaufort scale as it circulated around our team. They immediately sensed the impending danger. Everything happened at once. The wing commander scaled the cockpit ladder in double quick time, threw himself on to the ejector seat, closed the jump jet's canopy, strapped himself in, fired up the Pegasus, and started the vertical take off sequence (though, under the circumstances, the revolutionary Rolls Royce engine turned out to be a bit redundant); Lister-Jag, with a glint in her eye, cranked up her torque wrench to the highest setting and whispered to herself *"Just you wait till I get a purchase on your nuts you sham wizard, you!"*; needless to say Burgermeister reached inside his jacket for his shoulder holster; Stirrup began incanting little known verses form the Apocrypha; both de Ath and de Vol-au-Vent leapt onto their mounts (well, leapt is probably overstating it a bit in de Ath's case). The Hospitaller raised his blade in the direction of the opposition and was about to say something rousing, but was beaten to it by the Marquis. De Vol-au-Vent whipped out a bottle of Dom Pérignon from his saddlebag, and applied the physics of sabrage with a flourish to its neck: *"Champagne! In victory one deserves it, in defeat one needs it!"* Callista, doused in Champagne spume, and quite taken by the antics of the hussar, began to fan herself energetically. No-one was entirely sure what effect this would have on the enemy, but de Vol-au-vent clearly had something in mind, since he immediately hoisted the good lady aloft, and positioned her side-saddle style behind him (*"Bloody hussars!"* thought de Ath: *"Outrageous! Grounds for a duel when all this is over! Must get myself one of those pistol thingies."*). No sooner had Callista made herself comfortable than there came the most deafening roar as the Rolls Royce Pegasus of Reg's machine blasted the flagstones beneath with a haze of incandescent fuel, and rose gently skywards. In doing so, however, it inadvertently ignited the end of Rolf's taper!

It was then that Crowley raised his plughole–plunger and exterminator-arm requesting our friends to levitate just as he himself had done. They were quite unacquainted with the technique required to accomplish such a performance, and so it came as something of a hair-raiser when, in unison, their feet began to depart from the temple quadrangle! The higher they rose, the more the draught increased in intensity. Another curiosity was that the paving beneath had begun to turn a vibrant hue of chrome yellow. By now though there spiralled a full-blown tornado with the visitors atop; it was at that moment that the temple horns blew and the Celtic look-alikes struck with the speed of aerial hobgoblins! De Ath cut here and thrust there at anything that screeched by in green and white hooped shirts. It should be said that he felt some discomfort in doing so since, although he wasn't a fanatical football fan by any means, he had been brought up only a stone's throw from the Parkhead ground in the 'Workhouse of Empire'; he nevertheless consoled himself with the knowledge that he was dealing with impostors anyway. De Vol-au Vent, however, felt no such compunction, and managed to despatch one of their forwards with a resounding thwack on the conk from his bottle of Dom Pérignon! *"Vat a vaste ov Champagne!"* he cried. Behind our favourite buckler of swash though, Callista had truly come into her own. She'd established a rather novel double act with Sister Ruth. The thing was that every time one of the green fiends flew close enough, she would raise her skirt and dazzle them with her well-proportioned ankles. This had the effect of rendering the enemy temporarily paralysed, and therefore, made them easy meat for the Sister Adorer of the Most Precious Blood to deliver the coup de grâce; she by then had moved on to casting spells from some of the more apocalyptic passages from the Revelation of John.

This had a dramatic, but quite painless, consequence for the victims as they sank from part-time paralysis into terminal catatonia. The pair of them must have taken out at least three of the demons thus within the first few seconds of play! Meanwhile, Burgermeister, as was his wont, was blasting away in all directions with his automatic, with the result that he'd managed to annihilate several spectators and a grand total of none of the opposing monks. Directly above the team, however, the wing co was having a battle royal all of his own in trying to control the Sea Harrier. He found it simply impossible to counter the vortex that they were all caught up in no matter what he did; the only upside seemed to be that the plane was circulating at the same breakneck rate as the other players. Eventually, he decided that enough was enough. Calculating the delays as best he could under the circumstances, he primed the sidewinders and let fly with everything he had. It was his lucky day! 30mm shells scorched the atmosphere winging a couple of the 'Hornets from Hell', and the last of the missiles scored a direct hit in the opposition goalmouth: vaporising it, the keeper and one of the defenders in a most comprehensive fashion! Rolf though had been somewhat distracted by all the amateur dramatics and hadn't noticed the glowing fuse disappear within the bomb he was holding. In fact, it wasn't until he had begun to feel an unusually warm sensation emanating from the orb that he realised his moment had come. He straightaway adopted the stance of a WWI grenadier and tossed the offending object into the event horizon of the tornado. It went off immediately, producing the most devastating result: a totally silent void!

The whirlwind ceased to be, with such intensity that one could have heard a pin drop! There was no pin. Nor was there any sign of our intrepid adventurers! They were gone! Forever? Who knows? And what of the lamasery team? Well, they had obviously suffered a defeat that would take years to recover from, if ever. A couple had been atomised by the wing co, others lay lifeless littering the flagstone pitch, and the remainder floated in comatose states some fifty feet up in the air: no one had the remotest idea how to retrieve them. Some short time later, one of the monks devised an ingenious system whereby these zombie floaters could be fed by tube at night, and left detached by day, thus providing the lamasery with a healthy revenue from the many New Age Travellers who had journeyed from afar to witness the extraordinary phenomenon. Mystical stories were concocted as to how it had all come about - none of which ever touched on the facts. After all, who in their right mind was ever going to swallow a tale explaining that they had been rendered into such a state due to being stricken by glimpsing the alluring ankles of a racy, redheaded aristess, who was being carried on horseback by a French hussar?

Whilst none of the remaining spectators in the quad, who had been unaffected by Burgermeister's attentions, seemed to be at all ruffled: not a hair out of place (largely because they didn't have any), the only indications that anything untoward had happened was that the prayer wheels appeared to move in the wrong direction, and the High Priest, with prosthetic attachments conjoined above his head, stigmata in full view, seemed to be in some considerable discomfort. He had gained an extra body part, you see: a torque wrench attached to one of his more vital organs! Lister-Jag too had been busy during the fray.

So, the moral of the story is then: when in Tibet, never play football with the monks at Kum Bum. Ever! Unless of course, you have a top of the range spanner to hand!

("Bugger! That's me telt then." Ed)

EPISODE FORTY-SIX
Stupafaction

To this day, at the entrance to the Kum Bum Lamasery, there stands a row of eight stupas, as if guarding the gateway. Should you ever visit the site, you might care to glance at their bases, in doing so you may observe the names, inscribed in Aramaic of the Mongol variety, of our friends. It is said that within each stupa apparently lies the remains of our travellers, preserved for all time in rancid butter. The locals maintain that any who dare to disturb the seals thereof will reawaken the spirit of the Great Universal Blacksmith: a chimera that even the amir himself would bow before! And we certainly don't want to do that now, do we folks? Hee, hee!

EPISODE FORTY-SEVEN
Certificate X

As the camera panned beyond the last in the line of stupas, the command came: *"Okay, cut. That's a wrap!"*

    Stanley Kubrick stood up and ambled towards his Roller. The chauffeur, bearing a peculiar resemblance to Boris Karloff, closed the door gently behind the director, and drove off at the regulation 30 mph in the direction of Shambhalah. The breast pocket of the chauffeur's blazer, decorated with Heavy Brigade insignia, contained a solid silver cigarette case, the lid of which was engraved with the Bingham family crest. Within was the cipher that Arbuthnot-Arbuthnot had eventually cracked.

Beneath his Passing Clouds lay a priceless scrap of papyrus alongside a mysterious photograph taken in a Peking park. Arbuthnot-Arbuthnot had overcome the first of the hurdles, the chauffeur was one of the very few who possessed the means to decode its true meaning. But he was invisible anyway.

The more observant of the Ta Er community, outwith the walls of the monastic community, would have noticed that the boot lid was open, just a crack, but nevertheless, sufficient for the snout of a Mauser to project, albeit with discrete modesty. Fortunately for Babur, neither the Muslim shopkeepers, nor their customers were into observance at that particular moment in time and space. In fact, they were rather more taken by the winged 'Spirit of Ecstasy' that adorned the car's radiator than anything else as the quintessence of white man's magic pulled away.

"Will they ever get it? And, if they do, is it the end? Even when ultimately they manage to reach their destination, will they believe it?" Mr Kubrick mused out loud.

"I doubt it, sir. I doubt it very much indeed." came the sinister response from the driver's seat. *"By the way, sir. I was just wondering why this is called Episode Forty-seven?"* the chauffeur queried.

"Ah now, therein lies a question indeed." Kubrick replied mysteriously.

"Some theremin music perhaps, sir?" the chauffeur suggested.

"Excellent notion, Richard." responded the director with a mischievous smile.

Oh, almost forgot. You've probably clicked that there are eight stupas guarding the entrance to Kum Bum. If you happen to have a stethoscope on hand, and listen really carefully to number eight, you might just find that you can detect the muffled and distant echoes of Radio Loyola.

Some hours later, after Brother Wolfred had concluded his incantations at the post-prandial gathering of monks, the establishment descended into pandemonium. The thing was that all present had come to the realisation that The Lord High Priest and Magus of the Trouser Leg was not actually slumped in the front row deep in a coma of meditative delusion, but in fact had become quite other-worldly. It was Brother Wolfred who was the first to notice that all was not well. He had just concluded his evening's philosophical challenge to the monks ('how to get round the off-side rule') when he observed that the front of Crowley's habit had become stained an unusual, luminescent hue of turquoise over its traditional rust colour. It was never wise to interrupt such an eminence when they were entranced, but the abbot was concerned. As he approached, he was immediately aware that the bizarre colour of Crowley's habit was resultant from what seemed to be a gloopy radioactive fluid dripping from the mystic's head. He tilted the man's cranium back, with no reaction at all from 'The Dalek of the Golden Dawn' (the moniker by which he, Crowley, was known to those of the inner sanctum of the 'Hell Fire Society'). There it was then, for all to see: where once projected the stalk of his third eye was a neatly sculpted 9mm hole, plum centre in the middle of his forehead.

The job was done, and no one knew how. The Roller followed the sunset, and the boot lid closed silently to the strains of an eerie sounding electronic instrumental, two batons lying aside the Assassin.

Hope you enjoyed it all, and do have a jolly good day. See you another time, in another place. Perhaps. 'Acta est fabula'.

Frivolity, folks, is far stranger than fiction.

("Did I Get that punctuation stuff right, Boss?")
("Errr, not too sure about all those commas, can we take that shot again?" Ed)
("Okay, here goes guv…….)

LE FIN.

THAT'S IT FOLKS. THE END. GEDD'IT? HAD ENOUGH. THANK YOU AND GOOD NIGHT.

EPISODES X, Y AND Z.

A rare portrait of Rt. Hon. Quincey Riddle Esq. as a youthful boy scout.

Above: A recent shot of de Ath, taken in Shan Dong Province, China. He contemplates how life might have been had he not saddled himself with a canary.

Above: PLA search party hunting for the cast on top of a secret Chinese mountain.

ART FOR ART'S SAKE N'AW THAT.

("Is that really it then?" Ed)

Well, actually, I was just thinking……………………………………
………………………………………………………………………………
……………..

The wing co's last vision. What do you make of it? It also puzzled him as to why this was called 'The Great ***Dessert*** Raid'. Well, don't ask me, I'm only the author! But, to pass a totally gratuitous comment, I kind of like the way that grand-dad and grand-child are heading off over the horizon unnoticed, don't you?

WHERE IS THE REVOLUTION, ANYWAY?

"None of this would have been possible without my mother, my father and blah di blah di blah……..":

M.F: Congenital Lunacy.
B.F: The Young Turk.
M.B: Lyrical Language and Testosterone.
D.R: Religious Conspiracies.
A.L: Geographical Abnormalities.
R.W: Surreal Music.
J.F: Mother Earth.
J.R: Convent Bells.
S.K: Peter Sellers.
D.T: Quills dipped in laudanum.
P.N: Keeping this bloody turkey of a computer running till I finished!
J.A: Random jiggery-pokery.

In volume two discover how:

De Vol-au-Vent had actually been working undercover for his distant Albanian cousin Enver Hodja all along.
Stirrup became Jiang Qing's wet nurse.
Cholmondeley achieved world renown as a baroque harpsichordist.
Arbuthnot-Arbuthnot invented a planeless pilot.
Ricardo-Coutts was exiled to Bermuda for insider trading on behalf of the Chancellor of the Exchequer.
De Ath was appointed Hannibal Barca's Veterinary Surgeon in Chief.
Burgermeister joined the Red Army Faction.
Schultz proved his Unified Field Theory to God.

Acknowledgements:

The author would like to express his gratitude to the following individuals and organisations for their generosity in permitting the publication of their material in this text:

Marquis Claude de Vol-au-Vent www.theflaneur.co.uk for the illustration of le Duc Victor de Vol-au-Vent. Copyright © La Société des Flâneurs Sans Frontières (Liverpool Chapter).
Marquis Claude de Vol-au-Vent www.theflaneur.co.uk for the shot of his father's spitfire in Assam. Copyright © La Société des Flâneurs Sans Frontières (Liverpool Chapter).
The Corps of the Royal Electrical and Mechanical Engineers Museum of Technology www.rememuseum.org.uk for granting permission to publish the photograph of the 9mm Model, 1916 version of their Mauser Pistol. Special thanks is due to the curator, Julie Booth, in particular. Copyright © The Corps of the Royal Electrical and Mechanical Engineers Museum of Technology.
The Imperial War Museum www.iwm.org.uk for the photograph of a Royal Navy diver. Copyright © The Imperial War Museum.
The British Museum www.thebritishmuseum.org.uk for the image of Hulegu Khan. Copyright © The Trustees of The British Museum.
The Chicago History Museum www.chicagohs.org for the mugshots of Al Capone. Additionally, the author would like to thank the gentleman in the **Office of Public Affairs at FBI Headquarters, Washington DC www.fbi.gov** for his good humour and advice concerning the publication of said portraits of Alphonse Capone. Copyright © The Chicago History Museum and The Federal Bureau of Investigation.
The National Palace Museum www.npm.gov.tw for the portrait of Ogedei Khan masquerading as Rt. Hon. Quincey Riddle Esq. Copyright © The National Palace Museum.

Wikipedia www.en.wikipedia.org for the Mongolian transcription of both Genghis Khan's name and that of Mongolia.
Wikipedia www.en.wikipedia.org for the illustration of the flag of Eastern Turkestan (Xin Jiang).
Adrian Fletcher www.domparadox.com for the illustration of the Gerasimov bust of Amir Timur (albeit somewhat modified by Glasgow's most pre-eminent experts in the field of Central Asian criminology: **Chief Superintendent Fortescue-Carruthers** and **Sergeant D. Tracey**.
Bernard Cloutier www.berclo.net for his photograph of Flaming Mountains, Turpan.

The vast majority of the remaining photographic material included in **The Great Dessert Raid of 1882** is owned under the copyright of the authorship of: Copyright © **Rt. Hon. Quincey Riddle Esq** and Copyright © **Wing-Commander Reginald Plantagenet Arbuthnot-Arbuthnot**. Special recognition is also due to James William Crofton Abell III www.croftongraphics.co.uk for his deft touch in image manipulation.

NB:

Every effort has been made to locate the copyright owners of unaccredited material contained in this work. Any omissions brought to the attention of the publisher are deeply regretted, and will be duly acknowledged in further publications.

The author also extends a warm and most sincere handshake to the good folk of **The People's Republic of China**, without whom, he could never have accomplished any of the above. All you have to lose are your chains folks. And, by the way, never underestimate your imagination.

Oh, nearly forgot, the author accepts complete responsibility for the entire written text: Copyright © **Rt. Hon. Quincey Riddle Esq.** Moreover, he would like to express his heartfelt gratitude to **'Bristolian'** for his tutorials on the argot of the submariner.

Finally, last, and far from least, the author would like to pay his deepest respects to the officers and crew of Oscar II Class K-141, their families, relatives and friends.

Random Bibliography:

Having carefully raked away at the sediments of information that have deposited themselves within his memory banks over the years, it occurs to the author that he owes a considerable debt to the following writers for their contribution to his haphazard knowledge of matters historical pertaining to 'The Great Dessert Raid of 1882':

'**Between Oxus and Jumna**' by Arnold Toynbee (Oxford University Press, 1961).
'**The Secret History of the Mongols – And Other Pieces**' by A. Walley (George Allen and Unwin Ltd, 1963).
'**The Royal Hordes – Nomad Peoples of the Steppes**' by E. Phillips (Thames and Hudson, 1965).
'**The Exploits of the Incomparable Mullah Nasrudin**' by I. Shah (Jonathan Cape Ltd, 1968).
'**Foreign Devils on the Silk Road**' by P. Hopkirk (University of Massachusetts Press, 1984).
'**Genghis Khan – His Life and Legacy**' by P. Ratchnevski (Blackwell Publishers Ltd 1991).
'**The Genius of China**' by R. Temple (Prion Press 1991).
'**The Great Game**' by P. Hopkirk (Kodansha Globe, 1994).
'**The Silk Road**' by Frances Wood (The Folio Society Ltd, 2002).
'**1421 – The Year China Discovered the world**' by G. Menzies (Bantam Press, 2002).
'**Tamerlane**' by J. Marozzi (Harper Collins, 2004).
'**Kublai Khan**' by J. Man (Transworld Publishers, 2006).
'**Barbarians**' by T. Jones and A. Ereira (BBC Books, 2006).